Alan Watson is a serial expatriate, having lived all over the Mid-East and in many European countries for the past 40 years.

For the last 30 years, he has worked as an International Financial Advisor, serving clients ranging from senior oil industry executives to entrepreneurs and wealthy expatriates who wanted to change countries and 'live the dream'.

Now based in France, close to the Alps for the last 20 years, his broad knowledge of the money business, and the bizarre situations that people fall into, does create some spectacular thriller plots.

Alan Watson

THE LAWYER'S LAST WORDS

AUSTIN MACAULEY PUBLISHERS™

LONDON · CAMBRIDGE · NEW YORK · SHARJAH

A CIP catalogue record for this title is available from the British Library.

ISBN 9781398400405 (Paperback)
ISBN 9781398400962 (Hardback)
ISBN 9781398400986 (ePub e-book)
ISBN 9781398418141 (Audiobook)

www.austinmacauley.com

First Published 2023
Austin Macauley Publishers Ltd®
1 Canada Square
Canary Wharf
London
E14 5AA

To my incredible wife, Chanel, who has witnessed a writer navigate the highs and lows of putting a book together.

And my two great sons, Mike & Chris, who have always believed in me and in the quality of the book. They are convinced that one day we will meet the actors when the book is adapted into a film.

Chapter 1

Marseille, the southern French port city, and one of the largest in France, has a colourful and complex reputation. Known by some as a gateway to Europe, an entry to the Mediterranean, or the darker side, simply a bad place where low-life's breed and somehow survive.

Marlon Crappy formed a condescending smile as he enjoyed a short intake of breath; he raised his eyebrows, stiffened his back, looked from left to right, and then bowed his head slowly. He appeared almost tame for the moment. Prison officer Mando stood two meters behind the man's massive shoulders. The orange prison uniform did not sit well. Two other guards displayed severe unease whilst balancing from heel to toe either side of the prisoner; they clearly wanted this guy released and their duty over in the shortest time possible.

Baumettes prison in Marseille has never enjoyed a tolerable or even remotely correct reputation for the job it's supposed to do. Now over eighty years old it has become absorbed into the city, 1,380 cells house around 1,700 prisoners. An unsanitary and crowded place, certainly one of the worst detention centres in France, and the man who was being released today allowed even the most hardened guard to consider that tomorrow could bring a small change for the better.

Crappy knew this familiar ritual would take time; it always did. A rap sheet like his required several signatures before a discharge. So many years of his life had been served in claustrophobic and cramped prison cells where the beds were too small for his large frame and time became irrelevant, his mood swings ensured fellow prisoners gave him space outside of the cell. The regular promises of lawyers 'reviewing his case', which never materialized, and the weaker guards who offered him favours, but declined when he shook his scarred head in doubt. Crappy simply preferred violence to the verbal option, hence the constant irritation of the daily showdown. Some made the grave error of challenging him, most made the intelligent decision to show him respect. Just how many inmates had suffered from his infamous nose chop was impossible to calculate, but it never failed, a lightening quick right fist, the shocking spurt of blood across the left side of the victim's face gave him instant satisfaction, nobody had ever dared to fight on after his party piece.

The prison administrators delivered quick updates through the walky-talky in Mando's right hand; the yellow receiver was old and soiled, every word was distorted, but it seemed the paperwork was almost ready. Crappy was getting itchy feet, he began to feel cocky, so exercised his hands simply to piss the guards off. After ten long years could he really be close to freedom? Mando took two paces to the left and shot a quick glance towards him, it lasted a few seconds. Crappy was doing exactly what Mando had seen so many times over the years, smiling, clenching his teeth, eye's wide blinking rapidly and staring towards the ground, his breathing irregular. Two possibilities could result from this pose, another inmate was about to be attacked, or Crappy was satisfied with something; Mando hoped for the latter.

Their history was long. The first encounter was in Paris at *La Santé* prison, in the *14th Arrondissement,* the heart of Paris. A prison with one of the worst suicide rates in the world. A fellow prisoner, Carlos, the Jackal, was for many a much sought after encounter, but Crappy never managed to meet him, even though on one occasion he smashed three guards and four inmates, the nose chop dropping six men on that morning, resulting in three months solitary. He had hoped that this display would encourage Carlos to show interest in such a warrior, but his hopes were dashed. Carlos had more important things to consider, he already knew many of the world's most disgusting thugs, and meeting one more had little value for such a well-connected terrorist.

The brief exchanges carried on between Mando and the administration office. After two more minutes, the small party was invited to move forward through a large rusty metal fire door, followed by a short walk of fifty meters. They passed a depressing line of locked cells with rusty bars covered in spit stains probably aimed at a passing enemy. The walls had not seen paint for at least forty years. A powerful smell of sweat and cigarettes filled the hanging walk way. The cold stares of prisoners who knew their release day was long off followed the party; one, an older man with a straggly grey beard and bloodshot eyes pressed his face hard against the bars and greeted his departing neighbour, "over and out, badass." Meters further they stopped on a faded red line with Mando tapping on a stained grey door, the plastic sign announced,

Mando pushed the door open with his right palm, it squeaked in resistance as if it wanted to remain closed.

Thick green bars separated the room in half with a small opening one meter above the ground, a flat working top around one meter square was the only form of surface in the room where documents could be placed. On the other side of the bars, a small frail looking man with unusually long fingers, who could only be a prison administrator, looked sad in a poorly pressed business shirt which his shoulders poked through like tiny metal rods. He was seated at the makeshift desk, his head bobbing slowly from side to side reading a white paper. Crappy looked down and stared at the head as if he was also reading a document; he jutted his enormous chin directly at the frail man. Mando slid his hand onto his cosh, just in case. The room remained silent for at least one minute.

Suddenly in a stern voice for such a feeble looking man, the administrator spoke, "You are aware, Mr Marlon Charles Crappy, that you are now entering your final hour in *Baumettes* prison."

"At least I certainly hope so," said the balding head in a whisper under his breath still focused on the documents.

"But as seems the custom in your case, once you leave the prison gates you are to proceed to a meeting with a lawyer, Maître Perroquet, one of our more… well talked about criminal lawyers," his voice drifting off. He then raised his uncleaned glasses towards Crappy.

"This is of the utmost importance; it seems he has some family related papers that you must collect."

Crappy gave a faint disinterested nod of his head avoiding eye contact. All of the guards stared suspiciously at the expressionless gaze thinking the same thought; why would a well-known Marseille lawyer with a quirky client list request a meeting with such a loner, a dumb career criminal, immediately upon his release.

A stiff brown envelope was cautiously retrieved from the side of the administrators chair and wedged through the small opening towards the orange suited giant.

"Your personal belongings, you will find everything inside that you gave upon arrival."

Another small nod followed as Crappy stretched his right hand towards the envelope. His massive hand was sweaty and surely unwashed for at least a couple of days. The prison tats showed as his sleeve came back. Now all of the guards flexed their shoulders and felt for the safety of their cosh.

"You must sign this three-page document at the place marked X, a copy will be given to you before you leave today, this will confirm you are a free man in case one of our more inquisitive police officers demands you prove your identity." The administrator offered a sour grin towards Crappy's bowed head which instantly fell away when Crappy patted his left hand on his chest. As the large man shook his head, the massive upper body jumped up and down with it, a bizarre mix of fat and muscle took the attention of all in the room. He would have dearly loved to carry out his party piece on the bug in front of him, but his pending freedom controlled his instinct, fortunately this day.

Crappy signed where he was told, looked bored and hoped the process was now completed. He tucked the envelope under his right arm. Officer Mando gestured towards the door with a jerk of his head, one guard was already in the corridor, Mando and his colleague following close behind Crappy's hulk like back. The room next door was already prepared, the largest clothing sizes the guards had ever witnessed were hanging on cheap metal hooks, a dark grey Puma jacket, denim shirt, jeans with a plastic belt, fake Nike trainers were neatly placed on a wooden bench. Crappy turned towards his guards as if asking for privacy, but he knew this was in vain; privacy would begin on the outside, not in this hell hole.

He dressed quickly with seriousness in his eyes as if the lawyer meeting suddenly became more important, throwing the orange prison uniform under the bench, then sat down and opened the brown envelope. His Casio watch had stopped years ago, his wallet remained empty but for the old yellow and grey pictures of his parents. His Nokia mobile looked ridiculously useless; how could anybody use such a small screen? And the French identity card was crumpled. His gold chain still slid through his fingers as before, this was one of the best feelings for a long time, a twenty first birthday present, given during a prison visit by his brother Gerard, a brother he suddenly missed so much.

As he stared aimlessly towards the ground, the guards took a pace back, a short moment of respect was observed. This gave Crappy ample chance to reflect, being so close to freedom he could now cast his mind back to those long miserable days that never ended. The many times older inmates gibed him over the death of his brother.

"A well-off Swiss player, a billionaire, big friend of a bunch of wealthy chateau owners, they sorted out that pissy little accountant brother of yours, he was a fucking crook, a limp thief faking at being an accountant, they all took him down in Saint-Tropez, he fell off his yacht, that jet-ski did it, he was the opposite to you, bags of money, and you're skint."

Crappy was about as full of revenge as any man could be, he just lacked the means and contacts to arrange a pay back.

It was customary for the released prisoners of *Baumettes* to be offered a short taxi ride, not far, just enough to take them well away from the prison walls. Where they were taken gave little concern for the prison director, as long as he did not see them walking into the distance from his third-floor office.

The Algerian driver was now on his third prison pick up. He kept the Citroens engine running, it was a cold February morning. He was borderline polite, but clearly had never seen a brute like this before, a man of almost two meters firmly planted in the centre of his back seat, the rear-view mirror became useless, he could feel Crappy's left knee in the middle of his back, it was obvious that this man had enormous power, but a man with so much aggression in his eyes should be treated with ease, no requests to move over. A once white Stetson took Crappys attention on the shelf behind the seat.

The driver understood his single sentence, "Take me to 750 *Rue Montgrand* now." He shoved the stick into first gear, and then began tapping his wheel nervously. Faint Arabic music played, but Crappy was oblivious.

No other conversation came about during the journey. Crappy stared out of the window with a childlike gaze as if he had never seen the sea before, and the driver reflected on the football match that evening, *Olympique Marseille V Paris Saint Germain*.

Nearing the old port, the bony Algerian became agitated, his head darted left and right swearing at the scooters which buzzed around the car like flies. He appeared almost excited that the address was so close; he pointed enthusiastically to the brass plate next to the faded oak doors announcing the office of,

Pierre Perroquet
Avocat

Even though the taxi ride was a parting gift from the director, the driver turned in expectation towards Crappy, smiling an awful smile of brown and yellow teeth, at least four of the upper line were broken and jagged. But Crappy was already out, he slammed the car door and turned, stretching to press the door buzzer, the door clicked open automatically and Crappy shouldered the heavy old wooden door hard against the brick wall, he was only interested in knowing why this well-known criminal lawyer wanted to meet up literally moments after his release. Once inside the building he had doubts about trusting lawyers and considered, why am I doing this?

The secretary's door on the first floor was half open so Crappy tapped three times and pushed gently with his thumb. His breathing was still heavy from the twelve stairs. Typically pile upon pile of bulging legal files crowded her desk, dull in colour, mostly black and grey, if she had been small she could have hidden behind the paperwork mountain, only her long bronzed legs gave away the fact that somebody was working.

Crappy edged a little further into the office whilst coldly staring at the girl, he could not resist, she was shockingly beautiful with shining hair and a confident twinkle in her eye, the olive skin of a person whose family probably originated from North Africa gave her a healthy appearance for a cold February day. As she lifted her left hand to offer entry Crappy noticed the many gold bracelets sliding back down her arm, this girl had style, a pose he had not been able to enjoy for so many years. Instinctively, shyly he turned away towards the only other door in the room, it was closed, but he could hear a faint telephone conversation going on behind, this was obviously the room where all would be revealed.

The secretary spoke, clearly with little interest, and a glint of worry in her eyes.

"I believe you must be Mr Marlon Crappy?"

Crappy detested his Christian name; his mother's affection for the famous actor caused this embarrassment. So many men had paid the price for laughing, but this sweet charming lady with the most hypnotic eyes he had ever seen could be excused.

"That's me, is he in there?"

"Maître Perroquet is on the telephone, would you mind waiting a moment?"

"I suppose I have the time."

The secretary twitched with discomfort, she saw the light go off on her office main line, so decided there's no need to offer Mr Crappy the waiting room. But the new arrival in her office had serious body odour problems; she tried to hold her breath, wishing her boss would open his door immediately.

Crappy bowed his head, simply because he had no idea what to say next to such a lady. Her perfume reached his nostrils, he breathed in gently, swallowed hard and raised his eyebrows, this was a pleasure he had been denied for so long, his mind froze as he blinked, he snatched a quick glance sideways, she was perfect, but she quickly bowed her head concentrating on a thick black dossier. He tried to gain more of the wonderful sensation that Coco Chanel was so famous for. As he fought back a weak smile the door of Maître Perroquet opened behind him and the lawyer stretched out a pale right hand.

"Yes, Mr Crappy, welcome to my office, please come in. Hati, could you bring coffee."

The hand shake was quick, but the ex-prisoners sweaty hand-shake caused the lawyer to brush his palm against his trouser leg.

Crappy followed in silence still enjoying the pleasure of Chanel.

Perroquet gestured with both hands at a worn dark green leather couch pushed against one of the confined office walls, but his guest was edging around the marble table towards the double doors which led onto a tiled terrace. Now he could smell the sea air, a pleasure he sometimes enjoyed from *Baumettes*, but the ozone was never this powerful.

The lawyer said nothing and still attempted to cleanse his right hand as Crappy eased the doors open and walked outside, the tiles grated under his weight. The harbour appeared so close, he wished his brother could cruise in and take him far away.

"I would guess you are a man who enjoys the sea air-the tang of the salt, and that's important."

The ex con quickly considered the lawyers comment irrelevant; thinking, *he has no clue what I enjoy.*

Hati entered the room confidently on very high heels, winked at Perroquet and placed the two small Arabic coffees on the marble desk, shook her head arrogantly in the direction of the terrace and left.

Crappy focused on her undulating bottom.

"I think you like this; I know Arabic coffee is a regular pleasure in *Baumettes*."

Crappy stepped back inside whilst surveying the marble desk. The preparation was perfect, small traditional cups, a few centilitres of coffee covering the bottom of the cup, the steam showed it was served at the correct temperature.

The lawyer's double breasted Italian suit took the large man's attention for a second, *why do they all dress like this,* he thought.

"Nice view, nice coffee, and I like the smell here, so what do you have for me?"

"Please sit down; I will try to keep this clear and as the English like to say, to the point."

Crappy displayed a look of anger.

"Don't mention the English, or any other damn foreigners, we are French, and in France, let's keep it clear!"

"Very well, I will try my best, but please understand what I will explain today will probably change your life −forever."

Crappy looked vague, with a couldn't care less expression and showed his empty cup to Perroquet who nodded and touched Hati's buzzer.

"As you are aware your brother Gerard died last year along the coast from here in the bay of Saint-Tropez, his death…"

"I know he's dead, I read the newspapers, heard all the stories in *Baumettes*, I was not allowed to go to his funeral, for *security* reasons, but he was murdered, why don't you tell the truth."

"Sorry Mr Crappy, I understand this is emotional for you, I am only doing my job, that's to make sure you receive what is rightfully yours."

Hati slid two more cups of perfectly poured Arabic coffee between the men. Crappy again enjoyed another waft of Chanel.

"Are you saying you have something for me from my brother?"

"Exactly that, but it's complicated, you see your brother left a simple will, my job is to see that his wishes are carried out correctly in our legal system, now that you are a free man."

"Our legal system stinks; I'm not a fan, so this is some trick to screw up my life again, what are they paying you?"

The lawyer became visibly uncomfortable fingering his tie with both hands. He was well aware of Crappy's reputation, especially his violent mood swings. But this meeting had to proceed; somehow the massive man had to understand his new position in life.

"Look Mr Crappy, I cannot change anything; your brother did some things in his life which were complicated, I have no interest in those things, only his final wishes, my job is to make sure you benefit from those wishes, no more no less, please let me explain."

"Ok, carry on, but no dirty lawyer shit, my whole life is one fuck up, I don't even know where I'm sleeping tonight and you won't change that, will you Mr Lawyer?"

"Maybe, I only ask you to hear what I have to say."

The desktop phone flashed, Perroquet began to stretch out his arm, Crappy shook his head from side to side, he mouthed NO, and the call was ignored.

With hands placed either side of an open dossier, Maître Perroquet began to speak in a calm determined manner.

"I understand you are a man who has no time for legal correctness, so I will simply tell you the exact situation, no more, no less."

"Your brother Gerard Frederique Crappy wrote this will on August the twentieth, two thousand and fourteen, one week before his death. This is not a complex will; however, the contents are genuinely serious and will certainly change your life from this day on. You are the sole beneficiary.

It appears your brother was very busy in the days before his demise. He transferred large amounts of money from one bank to another; he closed his accounts in Switzerland. Strangely he did not have a normal home address, the only way mail could reach him was via his bank in Antibes or the Marina of Sainte-Maxime, why, I have no idea, maybe you will find this out, it has little relevance for this meeting."

Crappy held his filthy hands tight together across his chest with no idea that the next few minutes in this lawyer's office would change everything from at least bad to genuinely different.

"If I can put this into a simple sentence Mr Crappy, you have become a very wealthy man."

Crappy showed little emotion except for the raising of his upper lip and the narrowing of his eyes.

"I have no idea how this has been arranged but you appear to be one of the co-signatories for two very significant bank accounts; one holding the largest deposit in Dubai, and a slightly less significant one in Oman, as your brother is no longer alive, this means you are the controller-owner of the accounts. The total value of the deposits is very close to eight million Euros."

Now Crappy stroked his upper lip whilst breathing quickly through his nose.

"Naturally I will provide all of the contact details, account numbers, everything I received in a complete dossier."

"And that's by no means the end, you have also become the owner of a Sunseeker yacht, a Predator 68; it's very impressive, the craft is currently in the marina here. It was rescued last year drifting 30 kilometres off the coast by the marine police, they quickly identified that the owner, your brother, had drowned so they impounded the craft. As you are now the rightful owner. A mooring fee will be payable to the harbour administration for the safe keeping of this magnificent craft.

This will no doubt be a large fee but not a painful one for you due to your brother's last wish."

Maître Perroquet cautiously slid a silver metal box across the table towards Crappy, offering a small key with his thumb and index finger.

The shiny box was large enough to accommodate a small pair of shoes, no more. Crappy stared at it, as always suspicious, thinking what sort of trick this could be. The lawyers promise of a dossier to confirm all, where was this? Could it be the simple safekeeping place for his brother's personal documents, the keys to the yacht? Maybe the lawyer's large bill.

"I do think you should open it now." Perroquet stroked his thick black hair behind his ears and turned his gaze towards the family dossier on his desk, offering a brief degree of comfort for Crappy's doubtful posture. Both men could hear the secretary welcoming a courier with loud phony laughter.

Crappy placed his left hand on the box and slid the key in, two left turns and the key stopped. With his right thumb he pushed the lid open, it fell loudly on the marble top, Perroquet was determined to show disinterest in this moment.

"Umm, how much?"

The lawyer exhaled deeply, almost like an actor preparing for the vital line, "I counted it at least four times; five hundred and sixty-four thousand Euro's, that's what it came to every time."

Marlon Crappy was experiencing a strange emotion, one which caused his body to shake slightly.

"Would you like to be alone for a moment Mr Crappy?"

"Yeah, I would."

Perroquet stood silently smoothing down his double-breasted jacket and left his office closing the door as if a small child was sleeping inside, he raised his index finger across his lips towards Hati, and she reacted perfectly.

Marlon Crappy felt too warm, uncomfortable; almost questioning why was this happening to him. He became aware of the sensation of water in his eyes, he rubbed it away quickly, no person should see this weakness. Unknown emotions came and went, small shocks flowed through his large body. Two hours ago, he was an irrelevant convict with an empty wallet, now he could upgrade his old Casio watch for any make in the world, a Sunseeker yacht was awaiting him in the harbour, maybe those models with large red lips that he loved to look over in his cell would be interested in him now. Maybe Perroquet's secretary was available.

So much tension flowed through his shivering body, questions were popping up, could he trust a lawyer? Was all this now his? He was hit by a sudden negativity, no way could his miserable life change so much. But the doubt gradually turned into belief when he imagined a mental picture of his brother, Gerard would never do this to him, he loved him more than any other person. He recalled one of the many special moments protecting his tiny brother, who was cornered in the school playground, three low life kids from a well-known and vicious street gang tried to steal Gerard's lunch, laughing as they kicked his apple away, but their control ceased immediately when big brother arrived. The largest gang member tried to face Marlon down with insults. But he misjudged his role that day.

"What a big fat pig, did you bring your lunch for me dumb fuck?" A large sweaty hand immediately covered his face and crashed it into the school fence, a second member tried to run, but Marlon's other hand was already deep in his collar, as the kid recoiled back his nose cracked and broke against the head of his larger friend, blood covered both of their heads, now they looked scared. The third member was hiding behind the spectators. Marlon could not stop, rage took over, the two blooded gang members could see very little as they cowered on hands and knees, Marlon kicked and kicked, into ribs, neck, stomach, his fists were clenched in case they managed to stand, anything to show that they had made a very wrong decision to pick on Gerard Crappy.

The freezing cold water shocked the raging bull. Three large sport teachers pushed Marlon against the fence, the water had the desired effect, stop, shake the head and refocus.

Crappy was unaware that his hand had been deep in the metal box flicking through the notes, experiencing the pleasure of stroking so many fifty Euro bills. The smell of ozone caused him to relax. He was again in the office of Maître Perroquet.

The door was pushed open slowly, "Mr Crappy, I trust everything is okay, you look a little warm can I offer you some water; maybe take some air on the terrace?" This was said with a clear disdainful look and hollow eyes.

Crappy stood cautiously, closed and locked the metal box and brushed the sweat from his brow with his shirt sleeve.

"I only want to leave, give me everything you promised, I don't like being here."

"Well, there is not much more for you, here is the full dossier, inside are pictures of I believe the people your brother lived close to, his old home, couple of beautiful women, maybe girlfriends, your brothers' personal documents, identity card etc, contact details for his neighbours at the Chateau."

Crappy narrowed his eyes and shook his head recalling the last words of the older prison inmates.

"I see you have the box under your arm, as I said the harbour administration will help with the yacht, that's about all I can do at this stage, however I do need you to sign a few papers for me, we must keep things legally correct."

The neatly prepared documents were pushed slowly towards the ex-con; the lawyer offered a heavy gold pen towards the massive right hand. The open shirted thug scoffed, snatched the pen and signed at every point the lawyer indicated with his index finger. His signature was simple and nervously quick, like a young child at the first attempt.

Easing back in his chair Perroquet suddenly reached under his desk, Crappy gave a nervous twitch, a hasty move like this in *Baumettes* could often result in a knife being brought out of its hiding place.

"This may help."

Perroquet, with a superior look, held up an old brown leather lawyer's document case, dusty but perfect to house the thick dossier and valuable metal box. The inside was tawny and immaculately clean compared to the outside. Crappy rudely grabbed the case, pushed his new paperwork inside and clicked the locks, not even bothering to brush the dust away.

"I wish you the very best of luck Mr Crappy, again my condolences for the loss of your brother.

Who knows, maybe money does bring some people happiness?"

The lawyer's cold smile would have normally agitated Crappy, but this time he ignored the hand of courtesy, opened the office door, breathed in as he saw the surprised face of Hati, and enjoyed Chanel one more time as his face fell to the ground.

Maître Perroquet and Hati listened as Crappy thumped down the stairs, the office shook slightly. Hati looked relieved that this inheritance dossier could now be closed.

As Crappy marched down the stairs he pondered as to why the metal box was so clean, yet the lawyer's case was so dusty.

Rue Montgrand was busy in the early afternoon, shoppers, satisfied lunch guests, and badly parked delivery vans were crowding the street. It was about the time of the day when tension grows, and horns were vital for anything on wheels. Crappy retained a mental picture of the short walk to the old port. *Baumettes* was full of local expertise on the area, conversations often drifted towards the favourite bar, or the most ideal place to steal a motorbike or scooter, where the ladies' handbags were most easily snatched, or the men occupied over a business lunch, so much so that their jacket resting over the chair back became an open invitation to slide a hand in and ease the wallet away. These thoughts made Crappy tighten his grip on the old brown case.

As he turned, looking across the busy street a Harley V Rod Muscle stopped next to him, the rider shouted, "*Salut Nicky,*" a girl with the tightest white jeans Crappy had ever seen smiled a broad perfect smile and pursed her lips towards the rider. The beat of the massive engine caused the pavement to shudder; Crappy was mesmerised by the machine; something drew his attention towards a small metal plate on the rear mudguard.

Harvey Davidson Massilia Marseille
158 Cours Lieutaud.

If Marlon Crappy had gained one benefit from living in prison for so long, it was a reasonable short-term memory.

He reached out and touched the rider's right shoulder.

"Where can I buy a beast like…?"

The rider's reaction was at first a cautious smile, he checked out the massive hand, followed by a glance back to the girl, he hoped this freak was talking about his bike.

"Best bike shop in Marseille, back there, couple of blocks from here, you can't miss it."

Crappy turned whilst giving a heavy slap on the riders back and decided to ignore the tight white jeans.

The Harley Davidson showroom was typical of the modern biker world, the latest models showcased behind glass on the first floor, automatic sliding doors and a polished floor that appeared out of place for a bike shop. Once inside the shine from the polished machines made Crappy wince, as a salesman noticed a man far too large to be ignored.

The brand-new Harley V-Rod Muscle in silver received one hundred percent of Crappy's attention; he could almost smell the warm air as he gunned it down the Auto route.

"*Oui Monsieur*, same for me, this is also my favourite, a real guy's bike!"

As was normal for Crappy, the salesman did not exist.

"We have a test model available if you fancy a try?"

The salesman found himself in two minds, be over the top polite, or call Jimmy the kick boxing mechanic to show support.

Still mesmerised by the bike Crappy growled, "I want this bike tomorrow morning, just as it is, I'll pick it up at ten maybe eleven. Do you have a jacket in my size?"

Now the salesman became confused, he stuttered, did he hear this right.

"Yes maybe…real um, really no problem, I will do my best for you, this maybe a little difficult."

For the first time, Crappy looked directly at him.

"How much is it, I can pay in cash, an extra five hundred for you, like I said tomorrow morning, now the jacket."

The salesman, Jimmy the mechanic, and two girls from the accessories shop watched Crappy leave in the direction of the old port. They never intended to sell the, *Harley Owner*, jacket, it was a promotion gift from a visiting US executive, the black leather XXXX-Large was intended to be draped across bikes in the showroom, or hung around several models posing on the cruisers. The new owner fitted well into his biker clothes.

February in Marseille, like all popular places along the southern French coast has good and bad days, but still a wonderful atmosphere to enjoy. The Cafés are more frequented by the local population. The occasional tourist stands out, the choice of a lighter shirt supported by over optimism about the Mediterranean sun causing even the most motivated traveller to head for the warmer corners of the bar, as opposed to the outside terrace.

Marlon Crappy flicked a visit card through his greasy fingers.

La Cavalier
39 Quai du Port

The card had been lying on the back seat of the taxi, as it gave an address in the old port, he took it.

Every single building looked individual and so much more inviting than his previous address. The Mediterranean colours, the design, even the conversation around him was light, people laughed regularly, he even heard the occasional, "*Pardon, Excusez-moi.*" These words did not exist in *Baumettes.*

Two ladies gazed out of a florist's window; they hoped that this man had no desire to buy flowers.

Hotel Belle Epoque appeared to be a part of the Cavalier, the bar terrace over the entrance, hotel rooms above to the fifth floor.

Crappy looked around him, he wanted this to be his kind of place, fade in, but he felt unease, almost every passing person checked him out, he heard mutterings, "That jacket…could fit my whole family in it."

"Must be a bodyguard, some shady boss will arrive in a black German car, wait and see."

The only things he craved for were a comfortable bed, a long hot shower, and a quiet corner where he could reflect, drink good wine, and examine the contents of the lawyer's dusty old case.

Within half an hour, he was booked into the hotel, a room on the fourth floor with the largest bed available, and overlooking the old port. A light mist descended on Marseille, but across the water he could clearly see the *Notre-Dame-De-La-Garde.*

His mind was in overdrive, so much had happened this day, within the last few hours he had travelled from the status of prison resident to multi-millionaire, owner of a yacht, and tomorrow a Harley V-Rod Muscle, he could not help considering what circumstance would follow to take it away as quickly as it had arrived. He kept having dirty thoughts about the lawyer's secretary.

Now mid-afternoon and the time had come to inspect the dossier, Crappy knew this would be hard, so decided to head for the bar on the first floor, alone in a room would be a repeat of the last seven years and his new found wealth needed to be experienced.

The bar was cosy, filled with old wooden furniture, the cushions in bright colours well-padded and comfortable, bright paintings of old yachts and the coastline on every wall, soft lounge-jazz music played and the smell was a mix of fresh flowers and something meaty emanating from the kitchen door. Now he saw posters, some new, some faded promoting Samba and Reggae bands, but all seemed so sharp and colourful compared to the walls of his last home, where inmates placed old photos of girlfriends, wives and children, most of whom had long moved onto another relationship or parent.

The barman was demonstrating the art of cocktail making to an enthusiastic trainee, the shaker made that irritating rattle sound; both lost their concentration when the massive Crappy edged along the bar.

"Good afternoon Sir, can we offer you something?" Said Claude, the senior barman.

Crappy knew nothing about cocktails, but felt the urge to be polite, someone just called him Sir! This had never happened before.

"Yes…please…could you give me a glass of good red wine?"

"Certainly sir, inside or maybe the terrace, the view will surely add to the taste of the wine."

Crappy struggled to handle such polite banter, "Fuck you-screw you" was the standard reply for his recent human contact.

"I would like to sit inside, over there; I have some papers to look over." He remembered the lawyers often said exactly that.

Pointing towards a large wooden corner table where the last guest had left the, *Nice Matin*, spread open as if the reader left in a rush. It looked like the best place to go over his brothers' effects.

As he eased his massive legs under the table keeping the lawyer's case tight to his right side, the barman kindly pulled the table back, he smiled at Crappy in a way that made him uncomfortable, surprisingly not aggressive but a little prickly, did this man really want him to sit comfortably, or was he planning to join him?

Crappy surveyed the room, two ladies were sipping their Pina Colada's and making, 'hum' sounds with eyes closed, their chic shopping bags almost blocking the waiter's walkway. A couple of businessmen were drinking beer on the terrace and nervously checking their mails, and the trainee was again focused on making the perfect cocktail, the barman walked neatly towards his corner table with a glass of red Sancerre for the largest client he had ever served.

"Anything else you need sir, call me over, we have some fine bar snacks."

Crappy shook his head, now he wanted to look inside the case, discover his brother's photographs, and learn more about the last days of his dear relative.

His choice of seating was perfect, nobody could look over his shoulder, the large table protected him from passing snoopers and he placed the lawyer's case in the middle as an extra layer of privacy.

He took his first sip of red wine, it tasted better than anything he had drunk in years, so another and another sip followed; He opened the dossier, a plastic file was pushed full with photographs, he decided to look at these first.

All of the residents of Chateau Montjan had been photographed, although Eva Critin and Anna Tina Geisinger featured more often, several shots of Anna Tina seated at his brother's computer were taken from peculiar angles, as if the camera was hidden. Also photographs of two large northern European looking men, on the back of these photographs his brother had scribbled, *the bastards.*

Crappy randomly looked up towards the barman who had been staring at him for the last minute, he moved his thumb and forefinger making a small wobbling movement, the big man enthusiastically nodded in agreement.

More photographs showed a beautiful chateau, the vast grounds; it reminded Crappy of pictures he had seen years ago in exclusive property magazines, properties where he was attempting to steal valuables, jewellery, anything that would fit into his rucksack.

A couple of shots of teenage boys had, *the leverage,* penned above their heads; then laying out what he considered to be the most important photographs and forming them into a square; Unknown to Crappy he had formed the chateau team perfectly, Jack Rafter, Arno Van Bommel, Dan Lancaster, Eva Critin and Boris von Phren.

For a reason which he had no control over, he felt hatred for each and every person in front of him; certainly, they were responsible for taking his only trusted companion to a sudden and cruel death.

Then the bank statements which indeed confirmed he was worth several million Euros. The light blue statement for the Dubai account held his attention more than any other document; the number of zero's made him snigger. These papers were then shoved into the side of the case rapidly as if they should be hidden. He chose to ignore the shots of the Predator. Prison had taught him to hide any signs of advantage in life; there would always be a thief behind your back.

The barman held a bottle of red *Sancerre* in his spread hand by the side of the table, for the moment Crappy had not noticed, he was buried in the square of photographs trying to understand who was who and which individual could have been responsible for his brothers last moments.

Interest urged the barman to bend forward, he also could not resist taking in the beautiful ladies, and even more the handsome men, suddenly Crappy was aware of someone too close, and he shot out his left arm violently.

The bottle of Sancerre smashed open upon hitting the wooden floor, glass and quality red wine shot in every direction, the trainee screamed, "Claude get away," but that was not possible, the front of his shirt was badly ripped and he felt himself being pulled towards Crappy's left shoulder, he was truly powerless.

"Why are you looking at my private information?" Crappy's voice was so deep that small vibrations filled the corner.

Claude struggled breathing heavily but knew he had to speak; he unwillingly stared directly into Crappy's eyes, "I did not...no, I am sorry, only wanted to offer you this bottle sir, I just heard you are a hotel guest, a welcome that's all."

Crappy suddenly realised he was no longer in *Baumettes*, all faces in the bar stared at him, pure fear showing but nobody said a word. He concentrated hard as he opened his left hand and released Claude.

"I am sorry, you surprised me, this is my dead brother's personal things, I will, no, I have to buy you a new shirt, maybe two, what have I done?"

Claude brushed his chest as if he could repair the shirt and did his best to regain some composure as the two ladies rushed past behind him.

"Not a problem sir, I must apologise, I had no idea, please accept my excuses." Claude flicked his fingers towards the trainee;

"Bring another bottle over for our guest"; the guilty looking one shook his head doubtfully and dropped his gaze towards the photographs.

As he mentally repeated over and over again the bank account information, because he could not believe what he was looking at, and the location of Chateau

Montjan, the dimensions of the wooded terrain surrounding the monument and the names of the chateau residents, he looked up and realised that the early evening guests had begun to arrive. A collection of good-looking people, well dressed, at least two of the ladies caused Crappy to stare, their dresses were very tight. Although nobody dared to sit at his table at least thirty happy and loud men and ladies were starting their evening enjoyment, and Crappy started to feel uneasy.

"Claude, my bill please."

Walking slowly with a slight air of, *Free Man,* confidence towards the harbour the following morning, approaching the marine police administration building. Crappy knew he had to show some level of politeness, not exactly humble but at least appear like a normal person. Being in the company of such individuals, again, would be a challenge, but a challenge he had to go through, like it or not.

The marine police were a mix of administrators and regular gendarmes who spotted his lumbering presence at least fifty meters before he arrived at the glass door, the largest gendarme sized him up, but the whispering halted before he entered.

The office smelt of stale hamburgers and onions. The reception walls were full of posters for wanted villains, mostly names of North African origin. Charts of the harbour and local shipping lanes covered every possible surface towards the back of the room.

"*Bonjour monsieur.*" The youngest officer placed his hands on the counter and mustered his most confident pose, tilted his head to one side and locked a stare with Crappy.

"I um…have some papers, my…my brother passed away, I have become the owner of a Sunseeker yacht."

Every single person in the office now stared at the giant, silence took over, some showing pure surprise, one female officer in the back, clear disgust, and the young officer dropped his gaze down to Crappy's dusty case.

"Could I see your identity card Mr…"

"My name is Crappy, it's in my case, I also have a lawyer's letter to confirm I am the yacht's new owner, there's nothing wrong."

The young officer suddenly realised who this man was, his colleagues had swapped many stories about, "The *Beast of Baumettes.*"

The noise level in the office rose, it seemed everybody was whispering. Crappy could not make out the words, but for sure this was all about him, he felt a little flattered.

"Thank you, Mr Crappy, I am sure everything is in order." The young officer studied the identity card and lawyer's document doing his best to reason out the strange situation that he found himself in. Was he seriously about to give the keys of such a craft, a Sunseeker Predator to the *Beast of Baumettes* prison?

"I am afraid the mooring fee does need to be paid before you can take the craft Mr…" "I won't be taking it now," snapped Crappy, "I have some business to take care of, I'll pay what you want and maybe sail off in a month or so, I guess that's no problem?"

The officer nodded whilst at the same time remembering what made this man so famous in prison, screw the rules he thought, his party piece would ruin any chance of dating for a long time.

"No problem Sir, the craft is safe and available when you need."

Crappy wondered if he would remain a Sir for the rest of his days.

The winter sun was warm and comforting; Crappy's hand was stiff as he walked back towards his hotel, this case had been responsible for changing his miserable life so he eased his grip. Suddenly he became aware of another person walking very close by, much too close for his comfort zone.

"Mr Crappy, Sir, how are you today?"

Claude the barman from the *La Cavalier* beamed up at Crappy as if he had just found a long-lost friend.

"Good morning Claude, and again sorry for that problem yesterday, all my fault."

"Not a problem at all, I must say your generous tip was so much appreciated."

Crappy shot a quick glance at the crisp white shirt covered by a Red Bull body warmer; obviously that's where the tip went.

"I saw you walking away from the Marine Police office, no problem, I hope? Can I help in any way?"

This became a difficult moment for Marlon Crappy, instead of his normal instant reaction, "Fuck you man, get out of my face now!" He knew such attempts at polite assistance had to be treated in a different way to the most recent period of incarceration.

"Claude, I don't know you, in fact the only thing I do know is that you are the most polite person I have met in the last ten years."

Claude shook his head thinking where the hell could this man have been in the last ten years, but he coyly played along.

"Just a simple offer of help, I know this area well, but I'm a poorly paid barman, if you're looking for a boat/yacht maybe I can help? I have my powerboat certificate, took it in Antibes." The giant was not comfortable with optimists.

Crappy said nothing for the next fifty to sixty seconds, his mind was in overdrive considering a possible new friend, a valuable contact, could this be a person to trust? He clearly had no one on the outside world since the loss of his brother; could Claude be a reliable aid? Crappy felt one hundred percent sure that he was gay, but the gay guys in *Baumettes* were the most reliable, they formed their own club, protected one another and always delivered on promises, unlike the macho tough guy losers.

The whine of a passing scooter brought Crappy back to life, he stopped walking and stared down at Claude; who had the look of an innocent simple youth on his face.

"The last few years of my life have been hard, to trust someone is not easy for me, can I trust you, Claude?"

The innocent youth like face fell away quickly turning into a more mature confident gaze.

"Yes, I am a decent guy, more attracted to men than women, but I think you know that already."

The big head of Crappy wobbled from side to side.

"I don't care about that, over the last years I have seen things that some would not see in ten life times, I only need somebody to trust, help me with some matters, and I can pay well."

"Give me a try Mr Crappy, that's all I ask, test me." They moved on.

Again, thirty to forty meters passed without a reply from the big man.

"I don't need a yacht, I already own one, it's in the harbour here, could you look after it for me?"

Now Claude almost froze on the pavement lifting his arms out straight in a rigid pose, his head was slightly bowed. It reminded Crappy of a statue on a hill in Brazil.

"I'm good with boats, spent most of my life on and off them, cabin boy, cleaner, barman, even sail if you want? The owners always appreciated my technical skills, I seem to be real good with computers, mobile phones,

27

technology, some sort of gift, I can set up the latest systems, repair problems even…well do the things that some people call illegal, I'm just good, you know modern yachts are more computers than crew."

Claude desperately needed money but halted his flow abruptly, for the first time in their short relationship he saw a broad smile on Marlon Crappy's face.

"So, you can get around computers, phones Claude, well what the hell, I can see an interesting future for you."

Sitting back on the terrace of *La Cavalier* Crappy decided to offer Claude his first test.

He slid an envelope across the table but retained his massive hand on top.

"I bought a bike, a Harley Davidson V Rod Muscle. I want you to go to the *Massilia* showroom and pick it up for me. This is the cash for the bike plus two hundred for the salesman and some for fuel. I don't like complications; they piss me off, and if you rip me off! Can you bring the bike back here for me this morning?"

"Been riding big bikes all my life, no problem, shall I go now?"

"I also need a pre-paid phone, a nice one with a big screen, have to contact some people, but they cannot know it's me calling, can you fix that too?"

Claude promised everything would be faultless and left the terrace mentally repeating word for word of his new boss's instructions. He literally bounced down the street.

Marlon Crappy sat alone and sipped a glass of beer under a large red umbrella. The heat from the glowing red bars behind his head made him feel calm, and he started reflecting on the last twenty-four hours.

Now slipping back into his normal character, a sly grin came across his round face.

He could buy anything or person he needed.

Someone was happy to work for him, a simple soul to prey on, and being gay he knew, he would focus and go the extra distance if asked. And the people living in a peaceful chateau four hours to the north would soon be pushed into a nightmare so bad that even he found it difficult to comprehend. He put his thumb under his gold necklace chain, raised it to his lips and gave a gentle kiss, but totally ignored the faint vibration from the lawyer's case resting against his left leg.

Chapter 2

"This sounds so cool, I could listen all day," the hum from the 200 horses gave the young man a feeling of self-confidence, "Dad, I am so happy," An enthusiastic Nick Rafter wrapped his right arm around his dad's neck and gave him a serious peck on the cheek.

The dark blue Jeep Wrangler was an eighteenth birthday present from Jack and Carly Rafter to their oldest son, who was truly satisfied with his purring gift.

"One more quick blast, promise the last for today."

"Too much work on the desk and sorry these winter days are short ones, but tomorrow is another, look's better," said Jack with a serious glance.

"Guess you gotta do what you gotta do Dad." Nick was clearly not impressed.

Dan, Arno and Boris stood side by side in front of Chateau Montjan, smiling and sharing the pleasure of a young man getting the feel of his first car. They could not resist reflecting back to the same moment in their own lives. The ladies of the chateau were resting on the penthouse balcony rail also partaking in the emotion of this young man's day, one that would never be forgotten.

As the men of the chateau congratulated Nick with the usual guy jokes, "First girl passenger, cute blonde maybe? Automatic leaves one hand free!" A chilly February afternoon motivated the ladies to move inside. Carly, Stephanie, Annabel and Eva worked like an experienced catering team arranging the glasses, plates and cutlery for an eighteenth birthday party that would be impossible to forget. Nick's cake had been snuck in by Benoit the gardener who was still staring down at the Wrangler, and wondering why his sit on tractor sounded so much less sexy!

Jack eased himself back into his office chair whilst pushing his mouse back to life, he would have preferred cruising the mountain roads with Nick, but as was always the case, business first. Due to the recent interest rate rises , the Euro was gaining against the Pound, the US Dollar also looking pretty solid, and

Jack's European based clients benefitted from the currency movement in a big way; On top of this, his continued faith in active fund management had paid off well, one was up 18% over the last twelve months, another up a similar amount since the middle of last year, he was doing a very good job for his international client bank, and enjoyed the pleasure of regularly clicking on the company websites to assess the latest performance figures, the charts looked good. His Prudential clients were on Steroids considering the misery of 2022.

Arno could not hold back any longer, it was late afternoon, his throat was dry, and the urge to catch up with his good friend literally pushed him up the stairs, not forgetting his love of parties, and for the whole chateau.

"Hey Carly, is Jack in?"

"Usual place, his office, and as we both know if he's not here, it's probably the gym."

Arno patted Carly affectionately on the shoulder, frowned and eased towards the office door.

After knocking gently and around twenty seconds passing the door remained closed, so Arno got fed up and pushed the door enough to see Jack immersed on the phone. Arno's reflection in the window caused Jack to spin his chair, raise his head and nod towards the low leather couch; Arno sat gently shaking his head from side to side whilst watching Jack under full concentration.

"Plus, we have gained well from the US Dollar strength so I suggest we take some profit."

Arno continued shaking his head, "why oh why did he not take up Jack's suggestion of getting into these funds last year."

Jack replaced his desk phone then stared at Arno with a fair degree of seriousness.

"Nothing personal, but please support me with Nick, you have a racing background, you drove at Les Mans for Christ's sake, so no hot driver stuff, that car is bloody powerful, high centre of gravity etc and Carly keeps reminding me. Tell him to be sensible, I know he respects your driving experience."

"Already told him to garage it in the week, enjoy the weekends, but got the impression he chose to ignore that piece of older man advice." Arno looked a little lost.

Jack's iPhone played Apex as he grabbed it swearing;

"Same fucking blocked number at least twenty times today, and no message."

Arno gave a faintly concerned look, "Happens to me lately, probably SFR trying to sell you a new package."

"Dan also had this problem since yesterday, but he's with Orange!"

Both men stood simultaneously, clearly with better things on their mind to fill the day.

"Before tonight I need an hour in the gym, think Dan is already waiting for me, join us?"

Arno reflected back on the guy's pact, they vowed to stay in great shape, just in case, after the disastrous situation caused by Gerard Crappy, where they nearly lost everything they had built up.

"You bet, I'll bring the gloves, teach you guys some respect, a technique lesson."

Jack smiled confidently as he winked at Arno.

Nick and Simon greeted the guests at the apartment door. Dan shoved a box wrapped in pink paper into Nick's hands, flashed a perfect Hollywood smile and eased past, "Something to wear my young friend," Nick had doubt all over his face.

Boris Van Phren arrived minutes later with Anna-Tina Geisinger who for some reason had an attack of the giggles. He gave a perfectly packaged present about the size of a decent mobile phone, nodded towards Nick with a very confident "I'm a tech genious," pose, and took a deep breath.

"This is unbelievable, we have put something incredible together, enjoy my older…buddy."

Anna-Tina and Boris gave the boys a warm embrace.

Simon yanked his brother's arm in the direction of their rooms, "Shall we miss the dinner, and let them talk, drink and be happy, boxes to open my brother."

"I wish, but I'd like to keep the keys to the Wrangler, can you imagine how Dad will react if we are not the perfect sons tonight."

From the lounge area, Carly's raised voice demanded attention from the birthday guests asking if they had also been pestered by, "no ID calls lately."

The evening was a clear success. Nick diplomatically accepted all of the parental advice on safe driving, four by fours suffering from a higher weight trajectory-sensitivity, and Arno's insistence that with the right respect for this, this car is as safe as anything else on the road.

By eleven, most guests were flagging. Dan was still taking the odd party skiing, so excused himself, gave Nick and Simon an excessive man hug, which they gave back equally to his surprise. Boris and Anna-Tina offered to help clean up. As Boris had purchased the old apartment of Bernard and Sophie Mardan, he emphasised he could stay as long as needed; Arno constantly requested, "One more glass of champagne, for the long walk home." All other guests politely left at five-minute intervals thanking, Jack, Carly, Nick and Simon, for, "A night to always remember."

Within half an hour, the Rafter family had tumbled into bed; Even though all mobiles had the volume reduced, the vibration from a *no caller ID,* caused Nick to place his phone in the drawer.

Since the near financial meltdown of the Chateau Montjan owners, things had changed in the building. Boris Von Phren, the master of all things tech, who made no small contribution in saving a near disaster, had become close to Anna-Tina Geisinger. As he decided to purchase an empty apartment in the chateau, it became a cosy nest for the two. As they were both regarded at technology genius level, all other residents adored their presence, from the simplest request to help with a social media problem, to teaching Jack's boys ways around internet security, they were constantly in demand.

The ladies of the chateau were close, almost religious in their support for one another. And the three men who oversaw the demise of Gerard Crappy, Jack, Arno and Dan, had formed an alliance which would continue for the rest of their lives; each of the men had a background in martial arts, Jack being a third Dan at karate, Arno a Dutch heavy weight judo champion, and Dan, a former US Navy Seal.

A boxing ring had been added to the chateau gym, the three guys used it daily, the ladies preferred to train when the men had left, the violence and grunting was sometimes a little over the top. The level of training just seemed to increase the confidence; they hoped it would never be needed.

Fifteen of the tiniest security cameras had been cleverly inserted in walls, trees, and even on the parabolic dish which scanned three hundred and sixty degrees over the chateau grounds. Boris and Anna-Tina set up an instant surveillance access for the three men who requested this high level of security. The chance of unwanted intruders close to Chateau Montjan was these days akin to entering 10 Downing Street without an invitation.

The time was passing quickly, spring was around the corner, the snow cover was receding from the mountains close by, and a healthy tan was evident on the chateau skiers.

Dan, out of the blue, proposed a late February ski day, not the favourite period for his chateau neighbours, as the hordes from the European school holidays would fill all pistes, high and low. But the atmosphere in Chateau Montjan had returned to what was originally intended, hard work, followed by playing even harder. The terrible problems of last year had been put fairly firmly behind them. Annabel still showed the pain of losing poor Henry, which was shared by all; his special character would never be forgotten.

But with teenage boys rapidly turning into men, and the newest neighbours, Boris and Anna-Tina regularly living in the chateau this made the atmosphere close to perfect, a family of totally different backgrounds and interests, but one that events forged into a relationship for all time.

"Keep the body weight lower Arno." Dan could never forget his previous career of ski teacher.

"Yeah and concentrate straight ahead, bloody smartass yank." Whispered Arno.

Dan's suggested descent from Pointe des Mossettes at 2277 meters winding down to Avoriaz appealed to the group, the snow cover was still good for early afternoon, and the crowds were occupied taking lunch on the bursting terraces.

Jack was showing more than passing interest in two young British snowboarders who appeared to appreciate the rears of Carly and Stephanie, but his interest became more intense when he cruised close enough to hear their indiscrete conversation.

"Don't be a prick, these tarts on their own, experienced women, you know what that means!"

The smell of stale beer hit Jack's nostrils.

"I saw them get off the chair lift, its real mate, two horny tarts, look how they take the time, waiting for two dogs like us, this is a take-away."

Carly became aware of the sound of a scraping snowboard a couple of meters behind her skis, she turned to Stephanie who had no idea what could be about to happen. As she stretched out her left arm with the ski stick pointing towards Stephanie's shoulder the chest of the larger snowboarder pushed the stick back aggressively onto her own breast. His hands immediately fondled the bottoms of the surprised ladies; the second snowboarder slid close by the left side of Stephanie sliding his hand around her waist.

"So girls, my round, let's go and get pissed, it's the holidays."

Both snowboarders blocked any possible manoeuvre from the ladies, their weight advantage dragging the girlfriends towards a steeper piste. Both letting out a dirty laugh as they calmly groped the women.

"Yeah, you just met the snow dogs; we keep pulling day and night."

Jack's right fist arrived so hard into the guy's lower left back that his whole body twitched, locked up and turned left, then slumped across Jack's skis. For a few seconds, his happy groping mate was unaware of his buddy's immense pain.

Jack slid on for a few more meters bending and throwing the boarder off onto the piste. Dan arrived with a perfect parallel stop, and then slid one ski across the boys' chest, making sure he would not be standing until it was allowed.

The larger boarder had released the ladies pushing Carly so hard that she fell awkwardly losing a ski and sliding against a pile of packed snow on the edge of the piste.

"You fucking git, I'm gonna kick the shit out of you mate, you don't do that to us, those bitches belong to you?"

The larger snowboarder clicked his board fasteners off rapidly and staggered towards Jack, his swearing became more aggressive the closer he came, but Jack was already free from his skis, and checking his wife, who confirmed, "No problem, nothing broken, but watch out he's…"

Jack placed both gloves in fist position firmly in the snow half a meter apart, bending slightly forward and launching his right leg full power at a thirty-degree angle behind him. The scream echoed through the mountains, the ski boot connecting exactly as planned. This boarder's love life would be for some time – on hold.

He crumpled squealing in agony with both hands on his manhood. His pain was clearly severe, judging by the comments of passing skiers.

As the party arrived surrounding the crumpled boarders, Arno bent over and tucked his massive hand in the collar of the larger one.

"You are so lucky my friend got to you first, you surfing shit, you touch my wife, then I have to touch back." Arno's fist turned pressing his knuckles hard into the boarder's neck, a move he often used on the judo mat.

"I can't feel my balls, your mate attacked me." Now the boarder was looking for sympathy.

Arno pushed his head forcefully back into the snow, showing zero respect for the man's pain. He nodded at Jack with a wink of superiority.

In no time, the chateau friends were gliding towards the final one hundred meters of the last run; Carly and Stephanie were surrounded like a president in the open, even Nick and Simon stayed unusually close to their mother and her girlfriend.

Le Rotonde in the centre of Morzine provided the perfect table for the chateau team to eat good food and relax. Carly and Stephanie were still a little shaken from the afternoons experience, but the reassuring presence of husbands and capable friends made the incident pass quickly.

Never-the-less, boys do try to act like men, "Lucky we arrived late; hospital would have been home for those guys for a long time," Nick and Simon's comments further relaxed the ladies. By four o'clock, three loaded cars were winding their way back to Chambéry.

For the fourth time in three weeks, a local property agent had parked in front of the chateau, the company ad in the back window confirmed it to be the same *Immobilier*. The parking, as is common in France was scruffy, one wheel on the grass, and the often seen hanging plastic bumper, the result of an altercation at least a month ago; the car was empty.

"Do you think anyone will buy Crappy's old place Dad? This agent keeps coming back."

"Who knows Simon, it's a nice home, and anybody would be welcome after the last owner."

Jack's mind returned to understanding the letter from Mrs Swayland – an old client;

As they climbed the stairs, Jack was taken aback by the wonderful sensation that made Coco Chanel instantly recognisable.

Chapter 3

Marlon Crappy was becoming a regular at some of Marseilles more dubious bars, his Harley V Rod was often seen neatly parked to the right or left of the entrance doors. It was Claude's job to keep the bike looking immaculate, this he excelled in, always keen to keep his new boss happy and more so the flow of Euro cash, his wallet had never been such a pleasure to open.

The sound of the massive motor cruising up to the seedy back street bars pleased the owners. As the motor was switched off followed by the click of the metal stand the pattern became familiar, within seconds the daylight filtering through the door would disappear, then all clients, old and young, mostly male, would turn and take in the mammoth like figure of the man who liked to be referred to as, Sir.

The bar owners knew at least fifty Euros would be spent on every visit, more if *Monsieur* Marlon Crappy became interested in the regularly seen ex-convicts, or shady villains that seemed to gravitate to the enormous biker.

If they were crafty enough the owners or trusted barmen would glean the odd word or whispered sentence.

"It's a job close to the mountains, couple of days maximum."

"Could be some violence, quick stuff, nothing we can't handle."

"You're gonna love the females, they got all the right curves, best bitches you'll ever get your hands on."

The more Crappy frequented the bars, the more the deviants appeared on the scene. And the more intense his conversations became, the further he moved his low life contacts towards the bar's dark corners; from this point on their conversations remained private.

One rainy afternoon, Crappy was invited outside to inspect a large white delivery van, the company name on the side was so faded nobody recognised the original owners. He remained inside the back of the van with the driver for more than five minutes, regulars at the bar could not resist snatching quick glances whilst pretending to drink and gesture towards the depressing weather. Then the outside of the vehicle was appraised with equal interest. The bar guests assumed he needed something to transport his bike, what else would he need it for?

After what seemed like six months, but was actually three weeks staying at the hotel *Belle Epoque*, Crappy decided that his presence became a little too taken for granted; he was now fed up being constantly referred to as Sir. Living fell into a daily pattern, the same as prison life; he was forced to exist by the hotel routine.

The young African girl who cleaned his room talked far too much for his feeling, her accent was difficult to get, so she cringed when he moved too close. People unknown to him nodded or offered a quiet, *bonjour,* this was not good. His plans were going well, at least three, possibly four local thugs had agreed to do a job for five thousand up front and five thousand when the packages were delivered to Marseille. But he needed a place to go low key, a place where he could come and go without human contact.

Claude was given a new unexpected task.

"Find me a small apartment, no weird or noisy neighbours, safe place for my bike, only a month or two, need to think about something important."

Claude set about his new task with the usual enthusiasm.

"I know some agents; I'll set this up in no time."

For sure, the agents would pay a commission on top of the bosses usual fifty Euro thank you.

Claude sat deep in thought, waiting alone, tapping his fingers on the metal table to *Acc How long has this been going on*. He was not really a nervy person, but suffered from the constant pressure of, doing things right for his moody boss.

The Crocodile bar, on the Rue Frangy, a quiet back street of Marseille, had seen many owners over the years, for some reason it survived, but never made money. The newest owner, Rog, an Australian, had lavished Coates of paint on every possible surface, inside and out. Mostly variations of dark red, left in the storeroom by a less motivated previous owner. Rog seemed to love his property. Cleaning from top to bottom, morning till night.

Living above in a cramped apartment only fifteen meters square and always appearing like he had missed out on sleep for the last few nights. On this particular morning his choice of *Olympique Marseille* football shirt added nothing positive to his grungy appearance; what his clients loved was the Aussie accent and the constant references to, "the wankers," in all forms of the French administration. His French was at a good level, but only used for the delivery guys, all bar clients must communicate in Aussie!

The thumping low hum of the Harley alerted both Claude and Rog. In seconds, Marlon Crappy would appear at the door, a glass of red wine would be rapidly delivered by Jess, the permanently bronzed windsurf loving barmaid, and all other clients would pretend they were deep in conversation.

"G'day, Mr Crappy," Rog offered his hand, "all ok?"

"Good thanks, ready for a glass of wine." Crappy appeared to be in good humour.

Claude started talking before Rog had moved a safe distance away.

"Found a few good places, we can see them whenever you like, today maybe?"

Crappy bent his head sideways towards Rog, his expression clear and asking, *what do you want now, get lost.* "You looking for a place mate?" Rog now moved a bit nearer.

Crappy looked at Claude with a certain amount of anger.

"Any day now I'm moving out, my place up top will be free." Rog raised his eyebrows at Crappy who appeared thoughtful.

Claude could see his commission flying out of the window.

"Let's take a look." Crappy stood up and turned towards the stairs at the back of the room.

"Where you moving to?" The big man always full of suspicion.

"Been seeing a nice French girl, top bod, she sold her place in Paris, so bought a cool place around a kilometre from here, sea view, she wants me to move in, she a…likes tall blonde men, so I better go for it, prat if I don't."

Crappy was already at the bottom of the stairs.

Within ten minutes, Rog was back at the bar, Crappy had a handful of keys heading to check out the dimensions of the storeroom for his bike, and Claude appeared a little pissed off.

For the next two weeks; Claude saw very little of his new boss. He was glad he kept his regular job at the Cavalier; the Euro cash supply had dried up for the moment.

The day was slow and his over enthusiastic service for two suited businessmen caused them to whisper, he knew instinctively that they were not gay, but he was always motivated enough to attempt a conversion if the situation allowed.

His mobile buzzed in his jeans pocket, he hoped like hell for some good news.

"Claude, I need some help on my yacht, when are you free?" Claude mouthed an almost silent, "*Merde,* yeah, have to work this shift today, be there tomorrow morning, nine, ok?"

As Claude weaved his way through the wanna be sailors and dreaming tourists he approached the Sunseeker Predator and was visibly stunned. Since meeting his new friend, he had looked at the craft from a distance, but never this close. The glossy grey and black paint finish, the majestic lines caused him to shake his head in awe as the sun reflected off the many chrome fittings, he was a little amazed how clean the craft appeared, after hearing the gossip about it being moored in the harbour for several months. The older craft to the left and right made the Predators design appear more awesome and individual. But the new owner did not suit the sleek image.

The covers had been pulled to the back of the craft, but not at all neatly. It looked like somebody was in a rush and that somebody could be seen bending, gathering ropes, and crushing the covers as if he found the whole job a total waste of his valuable time. As Claude moved closer, he stared at Crappy's enormous rear, he smiled wondering how much more pressure the jeans could take, half of the man's massive bottom was on full display. The port of Marseille and Sunseeker could fall victim to their worst ever nightmare. A truly enormous, spotty, hanging butt fully displayed on the rear deck of a spectacularly beautiful yacht; no amount of Public Relations work could ever repair the damage.

"Yeah, Claude, what are you staring at, help me with these bloody covers, I've been pissing around for the last half an hour."

Claude launched himself onto the back steps, hands stretched out ready to assist, but also taking a snap look at the nearest group of tourists, luckily, they only had eyes for the Italian couple arguing over who would take their yacht out of the harbour.

"I am impressed Mr Crappy, you have a super yacht, what can I do to help?"

"You told me you were a good with boats, now's your chance to prove that, we're going out to sea, and if you're as good as I hope, I'll tell you about a job coming up. You can earn good money, but god help you if you fuck up, clear, you get it?"

Claude quickly realised how by a spur of the moment decision his life had changed. The money enticed him from day one, but Crappy always had an element of aggression over him, his eyes could change in a second, from calm calculation, to a potential killer's stare. He had already made the decision to accept this trait; maybe his judgement was clouded by the money, but compared to his dreary job at the Cavalier, this was a new avenue he intended to take full advantage of.

As Crappy moved awkwardly around the yacht, his weight caused the craft to lilt very slightly to one side. It was obvious to Claude that this man had no love of beautiful vessels, he did seem to have some appreciation for his Harley motorcycle, but the feeling that this particular possession was more nuisance than pleasure gave Claude a small knot in his stomach. What is this man intending to do with such a rare and powerful asset? Claude decided to block out the stories he had recently heard about, Crappy's violence to other prison inmates, *just do as you are told and enjoy the money.* This phrase kept repeating in the young man's head for motivation.

Crappy hissed open a can of Heineken, made a cheers gesture towards Claude, and dipped his head towards an open cardboard box on the rear deck. Claude observed at least twenty cans of beer and two bottles of vodka. He choose what he thought to be the best, only reaction to keep the boss happy, and reached in for a can of beer.

Leaning against the rear deck fridge Crappy stared Claude up and down, which made him uncomfortable, he lifted his can towards the big man, "To a good day at sea," but Crappy ignored him, turned and walked into the salon.

By the time Claude had emptied his can the owner had returned, his right hand cradled a plastic dossier, Claude caught a glimpse of photographs and documents, printed official looking documents.

"I'll take the buoys in, you take us out of the harbour, oh and don't worry I just paid a stupid sum of money to have this thing serviced, it works like an expensive watch."

Crappy pointed rudely towards the controls, Claude placed his can neatly into the cardboard box, walked over to the well-padded leather captains seat, slid on and suddenly felt like a film star, he gazed across the bow, then at the range of navigation screens, the wheel felt firm, as he expected from such a sporting craft. He quickly decided, whether good or bad his new life came with serious benefits, "keep dancing," he muttered.

Doing his best to appear at ease with the controls, but feeling a slight tremble in his hands, Claude knew he had to get this right, no margin for error. One wrong move may cause the moody one to explode, and in such a small place, and being a below average swimmer, he focused like never before in his life.

The soft drum from the rear confirmed that the motors were running perfectly. Crappy placed the buoys on deck with surprising neatness, disappeared for two minutes, and emerged back on deck in a dark blue summer shirt, then returned to his dossier. He appeared more like a man working in his office than a luxury yacht owner about to make his first foray towards the open sea.

Claude snatched quick glances behind as he cautiously manoeuvred the craft between the rows of yachts heading for the harbour entrance. He touched the tactile screens, played with the GPS; he had never been trusted with such luxury before. Crappy could never be described as level headed or even normally sane, but today he did exhibit the look of a man possessed as he turned over photograph after photograph, oblivious to Claude's best efforts.

The blue sky was increasing by the minute, so the hiss of another can caused the new captain to relax a little, the large man was immersed in his paperwork, and Claude loved every moment. His past experience with yachts involved more menial duties than sitting in the captain's seat. The dangers involved by working with a man like Crappy dissolved away; *my life is pretty good*, thought Claude who was determined to block out all pessimistic thoughts.

Marseille still appeared rather clear in the distance, but around two to three kilometres away now. Claude kept the pace slow and easy. Apart from a couple of fishing boats and a returning Corsica Ferries craft, the sea was uncrowded.

Suddenly Crappy placed his large beer scented hand on Claude's left shoulder, who looked apprehensive.

"Did I disturb your concentration? You look after my yacht well, good work."

Claude was visibly relieved, letting out a quick sigh.

"This is not hard work, compared to my bar job, give me this any day."

"Now we need to talk, come and sit with me, make this thing stop, drop the anchor, just stop it moving, do what boat people do, this is important."

Claude already knowing the obvious gave himself confirmation, Crappy was more comfortable on two wheels, a luxury yacht was just not his forte.

As the young barman approached the rear deck table his concentration froze on one grey dossier, simply because his name was scribbled in heavy green ink across the top. He began to worry what would happen next.

"Are you ready for the best paying job in your life?"

Claude was nodding, but he had no idea why.

"Yeah, but what do I have to do Mr C?" His voice had a slight uneasiness.

"I want you to hire a small car, white, the most common looking one you can find, if it's got a few dents, even better, I'll give you the cash, give the bar as your address, understand?"

Again, Claude nodded.

"This file has shots of some people I need to meet up with again, they live in Chambéry, in a chateau, your job is to make sure they are all still there, that's easy yeah, can you do this?"

"That's it, check on some people and where they live? Claude wanted to ask how much money he could earn."

"These kids, two boys, I think maybe fourteen, sixteen." Crappy held up two coloured photographs of Jack Rafters sons.

"I want you to check how many times they leave the chateau, school runs, the routine, sport, friends; I need to know where they can be found at any time, ok?"

Claude suddenly saw dark days ahead; Crappy could only have evil intentions for these young guys.

"The white envelope in this file has two thousand euros cash for you, and don't ask, I'll pay your expenses, you can stay at the, Formula Fix hotel in Chambéry, fine for a few nights. If you come back with what I want you get another two thousand, ok?"

Claude was late with his rent, had no car, owed money to some gay friends for the last holiday in Barcelona. This was exactly what Crappy wanted, a man financially hungry.

"When shall I go?"

"Tell the bar you're ill and go, I will expect updates."

Claude felt dazed, large sums of money were coming his way, he was for this day the captain of a Sunseeker Predator, but the knot in his belly became tighter.

As he stood, knowing enough of Crappy's body language which confirmed that the brief meeting was over, he could not resist glancing towards the file that now occupied his paymaster, bank statements with Arabic writing at the top, lower down the page, the words, current balance seemed to show a 7 followed by six zeros'.

The part time barman thought it best to become the conscientious captain again.

Within twenty-four hours, Claude was heading north out of Marseille. The Peugeot 206 has seen better times; the common touch parking as used in most French cities had caused its fair share of dents and scratches, exactly as the boss had insisted. The backstreet, *we rent for less*, car rental agency had lived up to its name, Claude paid less, but he wondered if the car could make it to Chambéry and back.

His new iPhone lit up on the passenger seat, the boss already wanted an update.

Chapter 4

The Burj Al Arab appeared larger in real life, dominant on the edge of the beach, and already visually fulfilling its position as the world's most luxurious hotel. The curve of the design so distinct, the pictures did it justice. The short helicopter trip from Dubai International Airport took around fifteen minutes and Hati relished every moment that this morning gave her.

She surveyed Jumeirah beach, the sands stretching far into the distance, eventually turning into a creamy-blue haze. The pale-azure-blue Gulf waters calm and inviting. How so much metal and glass simply grew out of the desert fazed her, she could not keep her head still.

The pilot held a static position for half a minute so that his passengers could take in Dubai and the tall slender wonders that made this city one of the most desirable holiday destinations. He gave a quick update.

"To our left is the Burj al Khalifa, all eight hundred and twenty-eight meters of it. The world's tallest structure. Soon beyond your hotel, The Palm, will come into view. Tell me if I can identify anything more for you?"

The fountains around the tower caused a misty haze, the sun dazzled across the glass panels, Hati was mesmerised.

Far below the Sheikh Zayed road was busy. Even from this height the vehicles looked exotic.

As they hovered towards the circular helicopter pad it appeared tiny from this distance so Hati firmed up the grip on her companion's lower arm.

The HH-65 Dolphin captain touched his dashboard button to bring the landing wheels into place, and could not resist a quick turn of the head towards his passengers. The reactions always followed the same pattern, beaming confidence as their luggage was taken from the Airbus to the chopper's luggage hold, once airborne the 'wows' and 'look at that tower', then periods of silence as the many tall buildings were appraised, the long beach line always caused, "Let's hit the beach today," type comments, and then the approach towards the tiny H, the passengers often fell silent, edging forward in their seats, almost willing the pilot to take it easy, focus ahead. If the day was windy, tension was high. The captain reflected back to one elegant American lady passenger demanding, "Captain, would it not be more sensible to land on the beach?"

As the rotors began to slow down three immaculately suited men appeared on the landing area, the following of a regular routine was obvious in their movements, one opened the passenger door greeting the guests in a rich Indian accent, "May I welcome you to the Burj Al Arab, the world's most luxurious hotel, my name is Ahmed, it is my pleasure to assist you in any way and, of course, escort you to your suite."

"It's wonderful to be here" said Hati whilst she eased her long legs onto the ground, a movement that was enjoyed by the hotel staff, even the pilot squirming left and right in his seat to obtain a cheeky stare.

Her companion focused on the luggage being removed by a small dark man in a perfectly pressed black suit, his every movement scrutinised almost as if his intentions were suspicious.

He enjoyed the warm gulf wind, but cussed himself. This flashy arrival confirmed he was just a little shit-a fake, no more or less. His mind was always elsewhere summing up his next move. A balding waiter took a pace forward.

"Please, Sir, Madame, may we offer you a glass of champagne, your journey is over."

The perfectly groomed man balanced the silver tray on a professionally manicured hand, the bubbles stopped one centimetre from the top of the Chrystal glass. Hati closed her eyes kissed her companion's cheek and gazed into the distance as she whispered, "Are we really here?" The only sound came from the hum of a Falcon private jet cruising high above the landing platform of the Burj Al Arab.

Claude paid the toll with his only piece of plastic money, a Euro card reluctantly issued by his account manager, a mean bitch of a woman at Savings and Credit Bank in Marseille. She emphasised his monthly limit could not exceed five hundred Euro's, and if he ever considered ignoring this boundary, the card would be cancelled immediately.

He pulled the card from the toll machine along with the receipt, slid both into his shirt pocket and floored the Peugeot engine full power hard left, followed by a hard right towards the brief auto route passage, less than one kilometre later, the turn off into Chambéry. As the new boss severely advised that Claude should be careful with technology, "*the chateau owners are very advanced*"; he thought it best to use the old method of navigation instead of his phone's superior features. The map on the passenger seat was full of red arrows tracing the route to Chateau Montjan. Claude decided to first take a quick look at the area around the chateau, get a feel for his surveillance operation, and then check into the Formula Fix hotel, an experience he was not particularly looking forward to, his gay friends told him to watch out for unexpected skin irritations that came up after a night's sleep!

He parked the car what he judged to be around one hundred meters from the chateau gates, pulled his jacket hood over his head, slid on sunglasses and eased a back-pack onto his left shoulder. The iPhone was placed in his right pocket, the baggy jacket allowed quick access when shots were needed.

As a black Range Rover cruised down the narrow road from the chateau gates, which clanged as if something mysterious lived behind them, Claude stressed and bent his head down towards the back-pack strap as if making adjustments. The man and two boys inside the car ignored the back-packer, they were late for school, and their father was being pestered.

Claude opened *notes* on his phone and tapped in *school run leaving at 1:15, Tuesday.*

He approached the chateau gates and peered through cautiously; observing white service vans parked at the side of what was most likely the descent to the underground parking, something like fifty meters away. *These people live well* he considered to himself. The brass panel to the right of the gate showed all of the occupant's names so Claude pulled out his phone, hit camera mode and clicked three times. He hoped that the glass camera lens above the brass panel would not record this moment. He could hear a faint conversation of two, maybe three ladies close to the chateau discussing the garden, but considered it wise to come back later, he needed to learn more about his current environment before taking chances.

Lying on the single bed, Claude flicked through the TV remote, only French channels and CNN were available; he had hoped for something spicier!

It had been at least one hour since he attached the shot of the chateau resident names to an SMS along with a confirmation of seeing what he thought to be the teenage boys Crappy was so interested in.

The Mondial pizza was not bad, but nowhere near the chef's superior quality as served at the *Cavalier*, Claude was not a fan of camping, at least not in this sense of the word.

Planning an early start for Wednesday morning he began to doze. The sound could have been the TV, but he was not sure, so quickly sat up, the boss was calling, the image of Crappy bending over on his yacht announced the call on the small screen, cheeky, but Claude needed all the humour he could surround himself with, the next days would be lonely and possibly dangerous.

"This lousy phone you got me does not work, I've been trying to send you a message for the last hour, fucking useless." Claude smiled; his wealthy boss had truly appalling tech skills.

"Did you get the attachment I sent, the owner's names?" Asked Claude in hope.

"I told you to be careful with that bloody phone, don't send that stuff, bring it back with you."

"I only got the message saying here it is, you forgot it, asshole." Claude was glad Crappy was a long way away.

He quickly considered a tech lesson over the phone would be a waste of time, and so suggested a better idea.

"Mr Crappy, all is going ok here, maybe best if we don't talk too much, know what I mean? I will do everything, you'll get all you need the minute I get back, ok?"

"No fucking choice, this phones not working, do what I told you, don't spend much."

The line went dead, and the shot of Mr C's bottom left the screen. Claude stretched back on the small bed, and tried to clear his mind determined to be the first visitor on his floor at the hotels shared shower next morning.

"Why not take my Wrangler dad, friends at school are asking to see it, I'll drive, you bring it home?"

"Not a good idea, the car's in your private life, and that's where it stays, school is school." Jack Rafter slammed the door of his Range Rover, he already fended off this question at least ten times before. His sons breathed heavily considering silence to be the best response.

The jogger at the bottom of the road appeared heavily dressed for a warm spring morning, his ear phones showed he was oblivious to traffic, and also glued to his mobile screen; As the Rafter's car passed, he stopped, opened *notes* and touched in *school run, leaving at 7.40 Wednesday morning.*

By Friday afternoon, Claude had filled several pages of *notes* with the comings and goings on the Rafter family. They were certainly the most active people in the chateau. Two attractive ladies were regularly seen jogging around the grounds. Claude managed a sideways shot of them, which clearly promoted their large breasts, long legs, and athletic poise, as this was taken from a small side road, the emergency exit – entry, should the main gates be blocked, he considered himself lucky to be left undisturbed behind a massive cedar tree. He was sure the ladies were Anna-Tina Geisinger and Eva Critin. Crappy will, no doubt, like these shots he considered. The turning parabolic dish on the top of the chateau roof worried Claude making him too scared for a possible entry into the grounds.

Marlon Crappy displayed a miserable mood day after day, he only grunted at Rog, and appeared to suffer from an even greater lack of conversational skills than normal whilst Claude was away. He did his best to hide, either in the apartment above the bar, or creep down the back stairs avoiding client contact. The roar from his Harley quickly fell silent as he headed off to the port. Rog noticed the vodka bottles in the storeroom vanished on a regular basis, but considered that the rent paid weekly in cash more than covered a few bottles of cheap Polish Vodka.

The large man was lost. His days consisted of darting between the yacht and his small apartment, he was lonely, girls looked towards the ground as soon as he came close, followed by hissing and tutting after he passed. He awoke with a hangover every morning; life on the outside had to be better than this. Did he trust Claude too much? Why was the Chambéry visit taking so long?

His life felt as unstable as the prison days, with no end to the waiting. He needed some form of pleasing solution, some comfort to ease his insecurity.

The lawyer's brown case was never far from his side. He pulled the metal box out, opened the lid and sighed licking his lips when he saw the thick pile of Euro notes, his sour mood eased briefly. In five minutes, his plans were made.

As he peered through the security glass windows of Rolex Marseille in *Rue Grignan*, passers-by considered a robbery was about to take place, the staff inside were even more convinced. When he pressed the door buzzer, the manager was called, he quickly considered one man, even this big could never get away from the crowded area easily, plus the metal detector remained silent.

"Please come in Sir, welcome to Rolex, what can we show you today?"

The ladies were just how Crappy liked them; well groomed, large bosoms, full red lips, and the manager reminded him of Claude.

"I saw a nice watch in the window, gold," his enormous greasy hand pointing vaguely behind him.

It was immediately clear that this prospective client had never stepped foot in a luxury timepiece store before.

"Please be seated sir, I will show you a couple of models." Crappy placed his briefcase between his legs as the manager retrieved two of the gaudiest examples from the corner window.

The Rolex staff were not at all surprised that this customer choose the model favoured by others of his style, large, gold, heavy, a vulgar, a *look what I can buy*, announcement; although they were pleased that yet another piece of gold was required to enable the clasp to fit around the massive wrist.

The early afternoon hour still allowed time to make yet another purchase; no horses were sparred as the Harley approached *Boulevard de Plombières*, Toyota Marseille. Crappy certainly felt more at ease in these surroundings. The customers and staff were typical French minimum effort style, *buy if you want, but if you don't, who cares!* After making sure the salesman took him seriously by pulling his left shirtsleeve halfway up his forearm Crappy offered a cash incentive for rapid delivery, it worked, the sandy coloured Land Cruiser V8 would be registered and ready to drive away in five days.

The bad man's mood now improved, he owned a few things, luckily, he decided against the possible purchase of a large Apple computer, like the one the receptionist used at the *Belle Epoque,* simply because he had no idea what to do with it, Claude would be consulted when he returned.

By nine thirty the next morning, with a mild hangover drifting gradually away, the man with a shiny new Rolex was sitting on the captain's seat of his very own Sunseeker predator, he kept watch on the inquisitive tourists that wandered aimlessly around the gangways checking out the yachts, his often created the most attention and comment, or was this due to his dimensions?

In the room below his padded chair two ex-cons were fitting a new door to the yachts guest cabin, Crappy insisted that the door must be impossible to break, even with tools, and is fitted with an electronic entry code, one that only he knows. As these seedy contacts were from electrician and carpenter backgrounds, he guessed the job would be done well. As usual he tried to buy their discretion by paying cash, payment in full for materials plus one thousand shared up front, and another one thousand if the job was a good one. The big man's patience was, as always, in short supply, he was half way through a bottle of warm vodka.

Claude was due back any day. Three thugs who agreed to do a job for Crappy were becoming irritating, threatening to go for other offers if he could not move things along, and his lack of knowledge regarding modern mobile technology frustrated him, how the hell could his massive fingers type on such a touch sensitive screen? Plus, "What the hell's an attachment?"

He alternated between Yacht and bar many times each day.

"Give me one more week, and then we should be good to go." Crappy sat with his back against the wall in the now *reserved* corner of the Crocodile bar. Ari, a dual nationality Dutch-French thug was harassing the always down beat giant on when he could expect to get paid, and see some action.

As the spring sun came through the bar window Crappy saw several long scars to the side of Ari's neck. No doubt a gift from an earlier job that got rough considered Crappy. But he actually liked this feature, the more aggressive his team appeared the more confident he felt about success.

Rico, the wary and reserved partner of Ari sat a couple of meters away to the far side of the window. The sun coming through caused Crappy to grimace which allowed Rico to evaluate the huge man. In the back of his mind, he intended to relieve Crappy of whatever money he had, the obvious difficulty being, how does a man of a mere seventy-eight kilos', even assisted by a partner of eighty-five kilos' defeat a mass of at least one hundred and thirty kilos with a reputation to nose chop a man to the ground in a split second.

Rico decided to play it nice, the waiting game, until he could see a chance.

Rog knew full well that Crappy was a bad one, but he'd always been close to bad ones, growing up in a rough part of Adelaide taught him, if you treat them right dividends can follow, and he was more than happy having this particular contact renting his apartment.

It was late evening. Due to the warm spring weather Rog was kept busy serving local drinkers on the terrace, his Aussie charm frequently baffling the French clients. He heard at least three times, "How can this man be so cheerful? He seems to work the whole day!"

From the far end of, *Rue Frangy* a dirty-dented white Peugeot came spluttering towards the terrace. Rog recalled Claude leaving in such a vehicle some days ago, so lingered between the tables awaiting the arrival of what he found to be, "An irritating little poofter."

"You look well shagged mate, love life too much for ya?"

Claude ignored the typical man comment as he climbed out of the car, frowned at his bosses dusty Harley, gave a cold shudder to Rog, and took a thick blue file from the passenger seat marching towards the bar door. Behind his back Rog whispered, "Wee queer."

Crappy ignored Claude's jovial smile of achievement as he walked towards the table, his eyes were fixed on the blue file.

In a deep calm threatening voice Crappy whispered, "You got what I needed?"

"Everything, best I could do, they're a busy bunch."

"I'll pay tomorrow, on the yacht, not here."

Claude gathered his hands terribly neatly, Crappy turned away in disgust.

The surprised young man left the file on the table and turned towards the bar. The five-hour drive had made him thirsty.

Propped up with silk cushions on the bed in the Predator stateroom Crappy flicked through his helper's papers. All was written in a clear and neat format, as he would have expected from such a tidy man.

Jack Rafter's boys lived a life of luxury; they were driven back and forth to school every day in their father's Range Rover. When they jogged outside of the Chateau grounds a large American man was always by their side, he was as quick in reverse as forward, something about him shouted military. Claude heard and noted his name on several occasions, Dan continually pushed the boys to perform, this left Claude with no doubt regarding the man's nationality.

Their father sometimes joined the group, but he always appeared focused on business, on more than one occasion Claude saw him stop and respond to a phone call, stock markets and statistics were quoted with a great deal of precision.

The list of chateau residents confirmed the names most detailed in his brother's belongings.

Crappy stroked the printed shots of Anna-Tina and Eva, "Umm, nice, real grinders," he grunted.

By ten o'clock Crappy had made his mind up, the Rafter boys would be target number one, if that went south, the sexy ladies would be target number two. He began to feel good about the potential pain of these bastards, like him, losing a loved one.

Chapter 5

"You're spoiling me, what have I done to deserve this?" Hati looked radiant; the tight black dress was so thin that the curves of her body clearly confirmed she could only be wearing one piece of clothing. She stretched her toes enjoying the warm sand under the table. The Majlis Al Bahar restaurant was living up to its reputation well, only a table on the sand was promised, as simple and stylish as that. But the warm gulf air, second glass of champagne, and promises of 'more shopping, after the business tomorrow' caused her to reflect on her family, they were trying relentlessly to get out of Syria, and she was living the life of a diva. Another quick sip helped to ease away thoughts of her past life.

"I promised you a special time, because you're a very special lady, and this is just the beginning."

Hati reached across the table and stroked her companion gently on his cheek. He responded by caressing her bare foot with his, they simultaneously smiled at one another, showing perfect teeth and the glow of a day on the beach, this was a couple that appeared to be seriously into one another, nobody else mattered. Their waiter cocked his head to one side, not the first time he witnessed such over-affection.

"Are you ready for tomorrow?" Pierre Perroquet changed the evening's sultry mood as only a criminal lawyer could. Hati pulled her feet back under her chair and stopped smiling. Suddenly, the Dubai holiday became something much more serious.

Marlon Crappy pinned photographs, crude drawings of cars surrounded by stick human shapes, and trivial scribbles over most of the wall above the tiny plastic covered desk. He had transformed the once scruffy flat of Rog into a crude mission room. He gazed for minutes at a time to the faces of Nick and Simon Rafter, then he licked his lips when staring at Eva and Carly; his mind imagined again and again the feel of his massive arm flexing around the boys' necks, then his arm would change position to fondle the ladies, no resistance would be possible, his back up team would ensure this. The pleasure and revenge sensation possessed his mind day and night, sometimes when Rog was making small talk, it became so obvious that Crappy was in a dream, he grinned, mouthed small words and pulled strange faces, but made no reply when Rog stopped talking.

"Well guess your mind is busy these days, new bike and car to look after, and that tick tock…wow." Rog shook his head and slid behind the bar while Crappy stared down, still making small movements with his lips and slight shakes of the head. Having worked as a loner all his life, he found putting a team together a complex challenge.

The large man still displayed being on the outside as a new experience, always suspicious, or at the least awkward with everybody who came into contact with him. His disastrous people skills often resulted in people drifting away to a far corner, or conveniently developing a fit of some coughing type ailment plainly to leave his space.

By now, being a free man for almost four months, the local people were used to his mood swings and strange facial expressions. His contacts fell into two groups, the ones who accepted him as a permanent fixture in the area, offering a simple *Bonjour,* nothing more, and the ones who were happy to use him for a cash incentive, whatever the job happened to be. The numbers of helpers were growing by the day, just as the wads of cash in the silver metal box were diminishing.

Claude had never worked so hard in his life. The alliance with an ex-con would never be perfect, but it paid well. He still retained his job at the *Cavalier*, he also cleaned the Harley, Toyota and yacht belonging to his out-of-the-ordinary boss. Sometimes he received two or three fifty Euro bills at the end of the day; he learnt quickly that getting paid in the evening usually resulted in his intoxicated boss failing to count if he passed over the right reward. Claude always insisted, "It's better to do this in the corner, not here." Crappy never even considered the devious reason behind this manoeuvring.

As the Mediterranean sun became powerful and the days grew longer the *team,* assembled by Crappy displayed more and more unease; Claude was by now on first name terms with three unpleasant and aggressive men. He could put up with Crappy, which was now like a daily routine, but the others made him uncomfortable. He heard whisperings about, "That cash box – think we could get a look in that flat of his?"

He considered informing his boss, but that may cut off his flow of cash, so he fell back into that uncomfortable and calculated decision, and kept his mouth shut, for good or bad.

Knowing the time to travel to the chateau was close, Crappy decided to pay his thug helpers a small incentive purely to keep them on the line.

He was becoming so frustrated trying his best to hide his new possessions around street corners, in a garage, or a safe street recommended by Claude that he sometimes forgot about the old leather case. On one occasion, he left it under the table in the Crocodile Bar for half an hour. It was spotted by a local deviant, but when the man considered what Crappy could do to him if caught; he considered no valuable papers or cash would be worth the amount of pain that Crappy would enjoy inflicting.

As usual all residents of Chateau Montjan were busy. The ski season was now over, and the expected warm days were still in short supply. Jack reminded Arno and Dan about their planned security reviews, which seemed to become a little sloppy as the year moved along.

Boris was consulted as to when he would be back and available for a check of the system.

"Sorry Jack, the security business is one of constant surveillance, you're not seriously saying that no checks have been made in the last months?" Boris sounded edgy.

"I thought Arno would do it, he thought Dan would...well you know." Said Jack.

"No way, Jack if I'm not around this is far too casual, I'll be back at the latest Friday, let's meet in the morning at nine, can't believe this!" Boris sounded unusually impolite.

Jack, Arno, Dan and Boris sat silently in the office of the chateau penthouse, coffee was poured, and all the guys stirred like they were drinking mud, or were they just a little concerned what could show up. The USB key was loaded and, as always, Boris floated off into his own world, tapping the keys at a pace the other men could only dream of.

Hazy glances were exchanged between the three whilst they also awaited the appraisal from Boris.

"First I'll start checking the cameras, from the wall mounted one's nothing unusual, but as he always does, our gardener spends far too much time talking, every camera shows him enjoying a conversation, he's not our PR man." Said a frowning Boris.

An air of relief was evident, if the gardener was their biggest problem, security was working well.

"Now let's check the tree cameras." Boris took rapid sideways glances as he typed in each cameras code.

"These are the long-range shots, towards the garden corners, apart from our own family and friends jogging, nothing special."

"Tree's by the gates, the lenses need cleaning…um is this the postman, no, this person's wearing a hood, and the time shows early afternoon, the postman comes around ten every morning. Zooming in…this creep is holding a phone, looks like he's taking a shot of the residents name listings."

Nobody said a word; the big guys in the room edged their shoulders forward. Four minds were racing, all asking that same question, "why would a man, hiding with a hood be so interested in who lives at the chateau Montjan?"

"Bloody property agent, you know how many cards we get with promises of a serious buyer looking at this place." Arno opened his hands attempting to trifle the situation.

"Let's hope you're right, because that Swiss bastard, Lasalle had a big family, we don't need this all over again, and well, do we?" Said Jack in a very deep and focused voice.

Boris was shaking his head as he flicked through more screens. He had the usual twitches of a geek, circling forefinger, eyes blinking like he missed a shot of some calming potion.

"This must be him again, trying to cover up behind a tree, same pose; you can just make out his phone if I go for maximum zoom."

Arno's initial attempt to calm the room had not worked; unsurprisingly all faces were serious, showing a high degree of concern.

"Now I think back a guy with a hood on, head always bowed down, poor jogging style did appear often when I took the boys to school. This is beginning to piss me off." Jack exercised his hands and stood up hastily.

"I'm checking on the boys, quick SMS, Boris what do you think is happening here, you are a security specialist?"

"I need to check all the cameras, the small details may show more, but rack your brains, anything unusual, we need to be painfully thorough, and let's do this sooner rather than later."

All of the men were now standing, shuffling aimlessly around the room. Jack received an, *all ok* message from his boys, as everybody else was in the chateau, for the moment a tiny sigh of relief was possible.

"Let's pick Simon and Nick up together" offered Dan, Jack nodded in agreement.

Eva Critin truly loved where she lived. The neighbours were a well-groomed mix of handsome-interesting men, and elegant women, the odd tech genius and two young brothers that made even Eva wish she had taken another path in life and decided for children.

As Eva spent time alone in her apartment, she often considered her dark past, that of an operative in the French secret service, the *sûreté*. By using her political contacts, she had been able to break up the destructive attack from the French tax office which would have ruined the chateau owners financially. What exactly happened to Harvey Lasalle, the Swiss billionaire who orchestrated the attack so that he could take over the chateau was never cleared up. She assumed high politics kicked in and people were removed for never to be clarified reasons. Living with this memory was acceptable; she had to, but the back of the head worry that one day she may be placed again in that, no negotiation corner, haunted her on a far too regular basis.

The knock at the door was a welcome distraction.

"Eva, hope I'm not disturbing you, may I come in?"

Eva knew a great deal about men. A good second career could have been a male-mind reader.

"Of course, Jack, but why do I have the impression that this visit is not for a dinner invitation?"

"You never disappoint, can we sit, may need a favour…again." Jack's voice tailed off.

"You talk Jack, I will get a coffee and sorry but have a feeling it needs to be a strong one."

"The security cameras we bought last year, they all work fine, but we just checked over the last months recordings."

"Cameras never lie, unfortunately." Eva shook her head gently as she placed the coffee on the table. Jack's eyes widened whilst checking out her perfect hands.

"Look Eva this may be nothing, but after last year's situation, well, we have to be on top of anything."

"So, what are you telling me exactly Jack?"

"At least two fairly clear shots of a man with a hood on, in one he takes a photograph of the nameplate on the gate." Eva dropped her head, "oh my."

"And one where he tries to hide behind a tree, again taking shots of something towards the grounds."

"Boris is doing a complete security check now." Added Jack.

"What do you expect of me?" Eva stared stylishly towards the chateau grounds, her large green eyes wide and slightly angry.

"You did a wonderful job for all of us the last time our future was threatened, maybe check out if Lasalle passed his evil intentions onto a family member-friend?"

"Easier said than done Jack, my contacts usually demand an eye for an eye, something in return, tell me what I can offer?"

Eva cast her mind back to the last conversation with the minister, would he really expect the chateau men to do something sinister for him?

"Absolutely no promises Jack, I'll make a couple of calls, these types of favours can cause a backlash."

"Thanks Eva, best we can expect for now…we" Jack so wanted to say something supportive, but his mind blanked.

The last glance between Eva and Jack was not so genuine.

The atmosphere in the chateau that evening was calm. Jack joined his boys for a quick half hour workout in the gym. Arno made the difficult decision to keep the day's events away from Stephanie. Dan called old team friends in LA, Boris and Anna-Tina scrutinised the security cameras for the smallest of clues regarding the maybe prowler.

Eva however was on another agenda. After three attempts to call her old boss from the *Sûreté* episode of her life she was becoming frustrated. He was now a minister and a busy one. Eva recalled his complex financial dealings, even in the days when offshore banking was a distinct advantage, with generally no questions asked, this man managed to set up structures that even well-versed accountants found difficulty in fully understanding, especially the reasoning between complexity versus advantage.

At the fourth attempt, she was lucky.

"Eva my darling, the woman who always captured my heart, you must be looking simply wonderful these days, how is the *Savoie* treating you?"

Raising her eyebrows Eva was in two minds about continuing the conversation, she remembered the man always being drunk after mid evening.

"I am sorry to disturb you Pascal, but I need a small favour." Eva heard him swallow hard.

Cutting into Eva's flow, the minister sounding worse by the second.

"You can ask me anything, if you come back to my penthouse like the last time, I will make it special."

Eva shook her head, whatever or whoever was threatening the chateau, no favour was worth this experience again.

"Pascal you remember what happened here last year?"

"I do, of course." The clink of bottle on glass was heard by Eva.

"We appear to have a prowler hanging around the gates, taking pictures. Have you heard about a situation, I did ask you to keep a close eye on Lasalle's contacts."

"Lasalle's contacts are broken, once he died, they fell apart like an amateur acting group, you have nothing to worry about."

"Are you sure?"

"Did I let you down the last time, Eva did I?"

"No, I owe you for such a special favour." Eva quickly wished she had not said this.

"I must stop now; my number one line is flashing, good night Eva."

For at least twenty minutes, Eva sat silently in the darkened lounge mentally repeating every single word of the conversation, she rarely did this, but her female radar caused this reaction, and as the minutes passed, she could not release her mind, the words kept coming back again and again. Her hands were moist as she tapped her fingers together.

The high-pitched ring shocked her, increasing her heart rate. The same Paris number she called half an hour before showed up.

"With Eva."

"How are the men, your team in the chateau looking these days, Eva? I may have a job for them."

"I…um…sorry what exactly do you mean, a job?"

"Don't play games, please, you know very well what I mean, are they ready, it would be such a shame for all of those nasty tax matters to rise up again, remember our conversation about deals with the devil? Well, Eva, answer me please."

"I suppose they are, certainly all super fit but…"

"No buts, you will hear from me soon, I wish you a nice evening."

Eva could not sleep; she rubbed her beautiful green eyes constantly, turned over and over again in her large bed, the sheets pulled at her tight stomach, and she kept berating herself for calling the minister. If she did manage to doze a cold shiver snapped her awake. Now the favour was being called in, and she knew this man would pursue it to the bitter end.

Her greatest worry was for Jack and Carly Rafter's boys, with one phone call she had probably changed their lives, what had she done? No backtracking option would be available, this situation would get worse by the day, the minister's reputation was dirty, to say the least, and Eva Critin was the only person responsible, and living in the chateau.

Strangely for Jack, Arno and Dan, Eva was nowhere to be seen in Chateau Montjan for several days, her car stayed parked, collecting dust in the garage space, faint lights showed at night, but her door remained closed, the tiny scribbled note, *sorry heavy cold, please leave me in peace for a few days,* fooled nobody.

The chateau men felt something in their stunning residence was going wrong…again.

Chapter 6

The private office that came with a Burj Al Arab suite was extremely well appointed down to the gold-plated iPad, meticulously clean, and the reclining chair felt so much more comfortable for Pierre Perroquet than the one in his Marseille office, a wobbly wooden inheritance when his father died. That office offered views over roofs and prefab buildings to the Mediterranean, if you were prepared to stretch your neck a little.

Now easing back in the soft leather chair, a broad panorama of Jumeirah beach faded into the distance, the gulf waters were a rich mix of pale blue and light green, and as he looked further a grey mist covered the far horizon. *This,* he thought, *could be paradise.*

It was still early morning, but he had been awake and moving around for hours, partly because his mind was churning over since his eyes first opened at five-thirty, and partly because his nervous system demanded coffee. The early morning hotel service lived up well to the reputation, simply discreet with calm and perfect execution. The waiter spoke in a hushed voice fully aware that this suite was occupied by two people, and the lady was obviously enjoying the luxurious king size bed one floor above. The tray was placed with silent professional ease.

Perroquet tried his best to enjoy the view as he chewed his thumbnail, it was truly spectacular, but his eyes were constantly drawn to the only file on the desk. The childlike signature of Marlon Crappy still bothered him. Sometimes his attempts to copy the signature looked authentic, and sometimes not. Within the next few hours, he would experience the perfect test. The coffee calmed him, the chocolates pushed to one side, and again the view took his attention away, but not for long, he was determined to get that signature right.

He had probably read the brief document more than fifty times over the last two days, but things had to be faultless this Saturday morning, no second chance would be possible, and any doubt would result in unanswerable questions. His eye's flicked between the views and the document. The stress was far less in his Marseille office.

"Don't worry; it will all be ok, promise."

Hati touched Perroquet's shoulders which helped to calm him as her soft hair tumbled forward caressing his ear and cheek, even so early in the morning she smelt exquisite. Her delicate hand pushed the file to one side as she eased onto the desk, the pose was almost erotic. Perroquest immediately considered another love making moment before they left, but quickly dismissed the thought, better to save the passion for the evening. Hati deserved better being so deep into this complex plan with her boyfriend of one year. His eyes took another quick shot over to the signature as Hati left for the shower; she had quickly assessed the tension in her boyfriend's face.

He noted down the most important questions to ask his lover when she returned.

When did she last check the tracking system placed in the old brown leather case?

What was the last update from her property agent friends in, Chambéry, did she find any more useful information in Gerard Crappy's apartment? Does the agent make the regular promised checks?

Standing close to the full-length windows, forehead pushed against the glass and hands in pockets, Pierre Perroquot realised he was not enjoying this view, or the hotel for that matter, at all. It was all a feeble excursion to take his mind off the morning's business, just like reserving the suite, the helicopter arrival, extra glasses of Champagne for the flimsiest of reasons. What he was about to do could end his legal career, throw him in jail, possibly the same jail Crappy just came out of, maybe Hati also. He could even become the victim of a revenge attack so violent that his weak heart could let him down for the last time. It was hard to admit, but he was simply a back street sleazy lawyer, but now he was too deep in to pull out, D-Day had arrived.

Never had a meeting been so frequently analysed in his life before, and being so far away from his birthplace, legal friend network, and daily comfort zones he felt a little out of his depth.

Casting his mind back, he remembered this plan formulating quickly, maybe too quickly. He stayed up late the night he received the inheritance dossier for

Marlon Crappy, an old debt payback from a legal colleague, it appeared simple and straightforward to accomplish, a career criminal with a very low intelligence level who was about to inherit a fortune. Perroquet concluded in no time that the money would be wasted if passed onto such a dumb lost soul, he convinced himself Crappy would blow it on women, alcohol and overrated possessions, gone in no time. He actually created a mental block, one so clear and realistic that he decided the very same evening this convict would have to be content with the cash, simple enough, and even that had been pilfered. Once the deed was done, Crappy would never be able to find him, Perroquet would utilise his dubious Marseille contacts to set the man up for yet another prison term, the fabricated crime, rape-assault-violence all would be easy to construct around such a character with his well-documented vicious past.

Having seen his fair share of legal cases won and lost for the most illogical of reasons, he was now determined to clear his head, he was making this issue far too complex, seeing bears at any moment. Today will happen, it will work perfectly, Hati will fall deeper in love with him and they will live happily ever after, he hit his head gently against the glass attempting to knock these thoughts in, for once and for all time.

Hati was out of the shower, the sound of her opening and closing cupboards and humming loudly on the upper floor irritated Perroquet, so he grabbed his notepad.

"Darling, when did you last check the tracker in the case?"

Hati eased herself elegantly down the stairs.

"Last night, here in the room, I told you in bed, but you looked heavy-eyed."

"Well." Perroquet barked like he was in court interrogating a witness.

"He's still in Marseille, same places, that tiny street or the marina, nothing changes."

"And your friend, the agent, has she checked his brother's old apartment, anything new?"

"She always checks the place, remember I even went once, it's empty, and we have all the paperwork. Please try to relax Pierre, tonight it will all be over, we can arrange the trip home."

Hati stretched out her tanned arm and placed her hand to the side of her boyfriend's neck, stroking gently.

"I'll try; I just want this day over." With that, he turned his back and walked into the office.

The early summer months are warm in the Arabian Gulf, so the sight of the White Rolls Royce Ghost was welcoming as the guests from Marseille stepped through the automatic doors. The nearby palms moved majestically in the warm wind, as at least three beaming hotel staff members calmly, almost silently moved around the vehicle offering to assist with the lawyer's case. The chauffeur wore a stunning, exceedingly well pressed white uniform. The rear doors were opened simultaneously for the guests to slide inside; the chilled air caused Hati to sigh in a raised voice.

"Wow, this feels good."

Pierre Perroquet managed a forced smile holding his Louis Vuitton case upon his knees; he stroked the latches with his fingers as both car doors made a soft clunk.

Hati pushed up the centre arm rest to be closer to her man, pulling his right arm onto her bare leg, at least now his smile looked more comfortable.

The car eased away silently, Perroquet took a very deep breath, and bent his head towards the one person who could calm his tension, Hati responded warmly, as always.

"I'll let you know when we are close to the bank." The driver's announcement went unnoticed.

Marlon Crappy excelled at nothing, maybe only violence; he was certainly not a great planner. When sober, he more realistically assessed his competence, which was less and less often these days. He spent countless hours; sometimes late into the night putting together the preparation for a kidnapping, but it was only his plan, based on extreme levels of violence, brute force, the things he was best at, if things went wrong, his only solution would be a clumsy run and hide strategy, with no doubt even more violence along the way.

Claude was as faithful as ever, his wardrobe was bursting with new shirts, and he always showed the same level of commitment since the first day, picking up his bosses new Harley, constantly polishing the Toyota, and now the newly acquired BMW-X5, Crappy appeared to hold image concerns. He looked after all of the toys like they were his own, but the ex-convict's mood swings were getting worse. Crappy was drinking more, appeared to have some sort of female friend, although she had never been seen, and, Claude knew *a job,* was imminent.

One evening after consuming close to one and a half bottles of Vodka, plus a few glasses of wine with his closest associates at the Crocodile bar, Crappy felt weary, he grunted as usual, "Going up." And left for the apartment.

Lying on the bed staring at the wall which was full of drawings, pictures of the chateau owners, families, the childlike scribbles of cars with doors open, and arrows pointing away from the car, Crappy realised he had not checked his cash box for many days, he stretched his bulk to the side of the bed, reaching underneath for the brown leather case. Pulling it against his chest he felt this movement had spun his head, so he shook it to clear his vision, but the problem persisted. He was seeing double.

Resting his head back on the pillow he reached deep into the case, but could not detect the metal box. His breathing increased, he started cursing, his hand was darting from corner to corner of the case, and his fingers were scratching the inside, so he rose trying to see what his hands could not find. Through his blurred vision the open metal box was visualised a couple of meters away on the plastic table cover. He coughed, pushed himself up with one hand, leaving the other still deep in the case, making two unsteady steps towards the box.

"Fuck me; I can't do this again, ever."

A thick wad of bills laid neatly inside, tied together with an elastic band, he stroked the metal, closed the top and fell backwards on the bed, but his right hand felt injured, something was causing him pain; he forcefully pulled the case open with his left hand and managed to release his other hand cautiously sliding it up the side of the case, attached to his bleeding fingers were red and green wires, very sharp and very thin, connected to a small plastic device; as his forced concentration cleared his vision he saw a tiny screen with 6 flashing numbers, after a few seconds they all changed, he made out the words, *security tracker*. As his eyes felt heavy an immediate decision was made to give Claude the biggest tip ever if he could explain what this stupid little device was for and why was it buried in the bottom of his case?

"Could we see a little more of Dubai please, we seem early." Pierre Perroquet's voice was weak, childlike, and not at all that of an experienced lawyer. Both the driver and Hati turned their heads at the same time showing surprise at this request.

Perroquet tightened his grip on Hati's hand and gave a quick nod of confidence; the driver waited for the right moment and spoke.

"Certainly sir, would you like me to call the bank, suggest maybe we will be delayed a few minutes?"

"No…no not at all, we must be there on time." Now the voice conveyed seriousness and control, more like a lawyer.

"Of course, sir, no problem at all."

Hati became worried, and the driver saw it in her eyes, as he hid behind tinted sunglasses.

The Rolls remained silent for several minutes as the guests admired the modern architecture on route.

Hati desperately wanted to release her hand from the vice like grip of her boyfriend, but she realised he was unaware of the tension being applied. As she turned hoping her smile, raised eyebrows and piercing green eyes would, as always, relax him, his grip became even more firm. Even the cool air from the climate system in the Ghost could not reduce the perspiration that Hati endured between their hands.

Perroquet has no idea his beautiful girlfriend was attempting her best smile only a few centimetres from his cheek. His eyes were fixed on a large green sign displayed on a building in the distance, Al Rahudi Bank.

"I'm one hundred percent sure this is a device to track the owner of the case, you can see it's been sealed into the leather, your powerful hand broke it out, where the hell did you buy it? Not normal is it!"

Crappy had the look of a killer, his head was still pounding from last night's alcohol, but his eyes showed pure hatred, and Claude subconsciously edged backwards.

"A lawyer gave it to me, a dirty scum street lawyer, greasy haired shit, they always wear those fucking shiny Italian suits, and he's going to tell me why this is in the case."

Claude looked confused and relieved; Crappy's anger was directed at a lawyer, not him.

"Do you know where to find him?" Asked Claude in a doubtful voice.

"He's got an office here, not far away, you wanna come?"

Claude started shaking his head; he cast his mind back to the first meeting with Crappy at the Cavalier bar. Crappy burst into anger because Claude moved too close to the man's private papers and that was a crowded place, what would Crappy do in the privacy of the lawyer's office?

For a reason he didn't understand Claude said, "yes," almost as if he dare not refuse his boss's offer.

Within a quarter of an hour, the BMW pulled up in a cobbled side street close to the Rue Montgrand, the invalid parking spot went ignored by the incensed driver. An old passing couple felt motivated to explain the French parking code, but the coughing-spitting Crappy made this advice seem an unwise choice today. Claude's hand was shaking as he attempted to close the car door, it took three tries. Crappy kept silently fingering the remote and walking several meters in front of Claude. The big man moved like a pro boxer heading for the ring, it was clear pending violence made him calm and put him into the right mental gear.

After three attempts on the door buzzer which Crappy hit harder every time, it became obvious the office was empty. Claude hoped this moment had come and gone without incident. As Crappy bowed his head considering his next move a voice caused his head to shoot left.

"Looking for Maître Perroquet? Afraid he's away this week, can I help?"

Crappy detested enthusiastic young men from the legal profession, not one of them had changed his life for the better.

"Where is he?" Crappy leaned forward and looked the young man up and down.

"Oh, he's far away, in Dubai on business, can I help with something, I'm looking after the office in his absence, is it an urgent legal matter maybe?"

Claude felt the urge to offer support.

"Maybe we should come back next week boss; this is a very personal matter."

Crappy brushed past the young lawyer heading for his car, Claude gestured by raising his shoulders and walking backwards towards the vehicle.

The screech from the tyres told the young lawyer that this was a dissatisfied client, which he knew was not unusual for the legal practice of Pierre Perroquet.

Crappy bottled up his confused state of mind, what else could he do? Claude said little in the car during the ride back to the bar, but both men were puzzled as to why a tracking device, if this was indeed what they had found, would be attached to a case owned by a man like Crappy. Sitting in a dark corner of the Crocodile bar, the large man drank glass after glass of red wine, Merlot, the other bar residents sensed his mood so nobody came close, only Rog silently filled the man's glass when empty.

Being a man with very little education, Crappy struggled to put this jigsaw together, he mouthed words, tracker, shit lawyer, Hati, but nothing came together. He tried his best to reconstruct the meeting in Perroquet's office, but it seemed an age ago. The silver box filled with crisp Euro notes, he recalled signing several legal papers but no copies were given to him, and the lawyer saying something about, "Money making people happy," Crappy also remembered his urge to leave the office as quickly as possible.

Claude shuffled across the barroom, weaving through tables and staring at his boss, as he moved closer the large bald head turned in his direction, if Claude had ever seen a sign of pending danger, this was as clear as he had ever seen from the monster, but he still moved on sliding a chair out so he could sit facing the man.

He took a deep breath; it was not enough, so another one, and another, Crappy's expression turned from anger to surprise, people just did not come so close when he behaved this way.

"I think I know something, and sorry I'm not interested in your money or private things, really not but…"

"For fucks sake say something you little prick before I smash you through the floor."

More deep breaths and Claude began to shake a little.

"Please don't do anything crazy, only hear me out," Crappy offered a quick nod, no more.

"The day you told me about a situation in Chambéry, on the Predator, you asked me to go and note when that family living in the Chateau left, came back, you remember?" Another quick nod.

"I saw your bank statement that day, I could not help myself, the Arabic writing took my attention."

"So, what," Crappy downed another glass of Merlot.

"The lawyer gave you the case, so he must have known about the tracker, I think-assume he also gave you the bank papers?"

"He did." Said Crappy with an interested tone.

"You own a bank account in Dubai?" Now two nods followed.

"Why would a Marseille lawyer need to be in Dubai?"

Crappy's fist split the round table in two, the empty wine glass ended up meters away, Claude pushed his chair back quickly enough to save his legs and Crappy stood up.

The giant had travelled mentally from confused to little doubt about this particular lawyer in the last ten seconds, the more he played it over, the more he was sure, Maitre Perroquet could only harbour selfish intentions for his largest bank account, but he had absolutely no idea what to do about it.

Immediately his planned kidnapping fell to the second priority, only the trusted Claude could help sort this catastrophe out.

Chapter 7

The banks windows were lightly tinted, but Perroquet could clearly see people moving around inside, most were Emirati local's wearing the dishdash. Hati had been assisted out of the Rolls by the chauffeur, now Perroquet's door was opening. With a very deep breath he edged out onto the pavement, stretching his back as he stood, but his stomach felt tight. He couldn't help himself, his mind was cursing in French, asking what the hell he was doing in Dubai on this Saturday morning? Will this work?

"Tell me sir, shall I wait here, meet you somewhere, whatever you wish, really my pleasure to assist."

Hati responded because her boyfriend was looking lost, staring at the large green glass door of Al Rahudi bank.

"Just leave us here, we will probably do some shopping after this," Hati doing her utmost to belittle what was about to happen.

The chauffeur softly closed the car door then marched with great authority to open the bank door for his guests. Perroquet remained silent, ignoring Hati's gentle caress on his back.

Due to the white suited chauffeur's persistence of following the ultra-polite routine for his clients, several bank customers took interest in the couple entering, the locals knew immediately that the white uniform belonged to the Burj Al Arab staff, so casual interest lingered, at least for a few seconds.

The reception counter was a monument, a heavy looking structure of polished black marble, with computer screens sunk into the top showing the faces of six managers and directors, their names and position in the bank. A fine-looking collection of well-presented bankers.

An Indian lady of around fifty, with impeccable make up, and skin to support it, exquisitely groomed black hair and an above average confidence level greeted Pierre Perroquet and Hati. Guessing she was at least twenty years younger, Hati cocked her head to one side and enlarged her powerful eyes, offering a confident pout.

Perroquet appeared trance like, oblivious to everything around him.

"Welcome to Al Rahudi bank" said the more senior lady casually flicking her loose hair back in clear challenge to Hati's piercing green eyes, "How may I assist you today?"

As if awoken by an electric shock, the lawyer from Marseille twitched, starred straight at the receptionist and calmly spoke in a slow deliberate manner.

"My names Marlon Crappy, I have a meeting with your director Maqbool Hameed."

Hati gave this moment silent praise.

"I understand sir, he is prepared and waiting for you, my colleague will escort you to his office."

The receptionist glanced to the left where a locally dressed man approached.

The young Emirati male looked immaculate in his flowing dishdash, he was a short jolly fellow with a permanent smile, his hair and beard were trimmed to perfection, he shook the hands of Hati and Perroquest formally and gestured towards the lift in the far-right corner of the reception.

"Please follow me, Mr Hameed is looking forward to meeting you Mr Crappy, I do hope your journey here was agreeable?"

The young man's accent was more Californian than Arabic.

"Yes, everything has been perfect, we do enjoy being in Dubai."

"I am proud of my home and happy to hear you enjoy my city."

He pressed the top button whilst enjoying a quick glance at Hati's very red lip gloss.

It took only fifteen seconds for the lift doors to reopen. Perroquet appeared more relaxed than Hati had seen in a while. The young man led them along a wide glass sided corridor, a variety of locally dressed and more normal bank attire suits could be observed as they walked, Hati guessed the staff were fifty percent male and fifty percent ladies, she showed interest in the offices left and right as if appraising the organisation, but Perroquest focused straight ahead assuring himself that the imposing door at the end of the corridor would be the place where his best ever legal performance would be mandatory.

"Then call the fucking bank for me, I have most of my money there, and I need it soon, the cash will be gone in a while, it's all my money."

Claude gave a half-hearted reply to Crappy's rage knowing he would sound more convincing than the swearing pig in front of him.

"You don't have a code to access your account?"

Crappy's blank expression was a pretty clear answer.

Claude was street wise enough to assess that a simple call to the bank would be useless, they would ask a multitude of security questions, which no doubt Crappy did not have available, probably causing more problems in the end.

"You must have more information than just a bank statement? Credit card maybe, any codes?"

As he spoke Claude began to take in the reality of the situation, of course the lawyer gave Crappy the minimum; if his intentions were as it now seems, why give more than a simple statement. Keep the large idiot in the dark, and steal his real money. *Clever plan!* thought Claude.

"I think an email would be better, we attach a copy of your identity card to prove who you are, the statement, I'm thinking, do you have your brother's identity card as well? He opened the account. That's more proof."

Crappy felt useless, he had never been able to open a bank account due to his criminal past, now he owns a massive one, unfortunately in a far-off place, with no way to access the funds.

"Just do something; I don't trust this little legal shit."

Claude demanded all of the documents, ID cards, statements, and suggested he leave for the *Belle Epoque,* he could use the hotels computer, scanner, and prepare a proper official looking file.

Leaving the apartment in a rush, Claude was surprised that Crappy gave him the BMW keys; he felt a sudden urge to help his lost boss, not forgetting his mercenary need for a strong future cash flow.

Crappy fell back on the bed with a bottle of Vodka held to his chest, he shook his head in frustration cursing, and thinking over how he would brutalise the lawyer when he caught up with him.

A local businessman and major client showed up at the *Cavalier* two to three times every week, and occasionally at weekends, he treated the place like his own home. This time he had a local hooker in tow, she was dressed in the minimum of clothing and pretending to be smitten with her new lover, and he was lapping it up. After a boozy lunch during which the petting embarrassed some of the older clients, they, unfortunately for Claude, choose to get cosy in the hotel's office, the hotel was full, the secretary was off for the weekend, and the door was unlocked. Claude imagined the office desk would be *the place.* But no way could he interrupt this moment of true passion, so he offered to help in the bar and kept a close eye on the closed office door. His irritation showed, but he was not man enough to either inform Crappy of the situation or chance a conflict with the hotel's big spender, and the time was passing.

Maqbool Hameed was short but wide, Gucci shoes and his suit looked expensive, made from a very light, but comfortable looking fabric, with a black and grey peppered moustache making him appear like an ex-military man. His pose exuded confidence, but his handshake was lacking sincerity, some sort of heavy cologne hit both of his guests. He was judged by Perroquet to be from Lebanese descent, speaking initially in French but then switching to English for no particular reason. As most of the paperwork, documents in the director's office were in either Arabic or English, the lawyer assumed the French was a simple courtesy, to open the meeting with a familiar greeting.

The office was unnecessarily large for one man, although he seemed comfortable and suited to his surroundings, a career banker without doubt. The wooden panelling, which covered most of the walls shone like polished teak. Sheikh Mohammed, the ruler of Dubai's picture took pride of place behind the banker's large black and silver chair. The floor length windows reminded Hati of the, Burj Al Arab.

"I hope you are enjoying Dubai? I see you are staying at our best hotel, a good choice, and sorry, I could not help seeing the Rolls pull away, they treat our most respected clients very well."

Perroquet has recited his opening dialogue over many times, but was having a little difficulty kicking off, so Hati stepped in.

"The hotel is everything we expected, and more actually, we are tempted to stay longer, the service is just…simply it's paradise."

Instantly the lawyer gave a very small shake of his head, if the director believes we could stay longer he has reason to delay things, *shut up, Hati,* he thought to himself.

"Pleasant as Dubai is, I am afraid we have a very tight schedule, I must be back in Marseille on Monday, have a client arriving from New York, planning a possible takeover of a French firm, I'm already deep into the case."

Hati was impressed with this delivery, but had no idea what her boyfriend was talking about.

Gradually Maqbool Hameed reclined into his padded chair; he nodded calmly like an old man watching a chess game, as if the result was a foregone conclusion.

"Please excuse me, I know this is a difficult subject, but I would like to offer you my sincere condolences for the loss of your brother, a dynamic and talented man, we were hoping to build a long relationship with him, his business was growing rapidly, he had the gift to make money quickly, we could have been good partners, but life can be so cruel."

Perroquet bit his lip faking a lost look.

"It was a tragedy for the whole family, as you say his career was…well so special, we will never fully get over this."

Hati stared at the ground, shaking her head pretending she was close to tears, adding a well-timed cough for effect.

"I must say I was a little concerned that it took so much time before we received the official notification of your brother's death, normally close relatives respond to our letters, and considering the amount of the deposit…it has been can I say, a little unusual."

The lawyer knew instinctively that this was a shot across his bows, a cautious banker moving in and around the issue, saying just enough to demand a clear explanation. Out of the blue the deposit looked set to stay in Dubai.

Hati knew she dare not look at her boyfriend.

The atmosphere in the office was polite, yet tense, the next words from, *Marlon Crappy,* needed to be beyond perfect.

"My brother's death was like a bombshell, and followed by complex circumstances, you know he was an accountant, I'm a lawyer, and it doesn't get more complicated than that, it took time to sort out a number of issues, French administration is a nightmare."

The bank director said nothing, only offering a small nod of agreement, but it could have been to the contrary.

"I see you have the dossier I sent over, trust everything is in order?" The lawyer was moving up a gear.

"That depends on your wishes Mr Crappy, as you are now the sole signatory for this account."

This was a good sign; clear confirmation that the senior banker accepted the dossier sent by Perroquet, he was indeed now the sole signatory.

"Sadly, my affairs are all based in France, I really do not have need for such a far-off banking network, my world is different, less international than my brother's."

"This tells me we are about to lose a valued patron, unless I have been misreading my clients for the last thirty years, it's a great shame when the first meeting also turns out to be the last."

Both Perroquet and Hati saw the meeting moving more in their favour.

"Dubai is nice, very nice indeed, but a great distance away from my world, I now need to put my brother's money to use more locally, I mentioned the project with the American arriving next week, we may become partners, my personal investment will be large, hence an urgent need for funds."

"Very well Mr Crappy, as you say, Dubai is not Marseille, do you intend to close the account?"

"Sadly I do, the funds are crucial, required as security in fact with my bank manager in Marseille."

Hati recalled the recent meeting between Perroquet and the squirming, over scented man from, Marseille Trust, she had never met such a scheming rat of a man before in her brief legal career. Her boyfriend agreed the man's reputation was tainted, but his choices were limited for such a large transaction.

"Paperwork and more paperwork Mr Crappy, our world is full of administration these days, KYC, know your client, money laundering questions, I do hope your bank is on our approved recipient list?"

"*Merde,*" said Perroquet under his breath, this, he had not considered.

"Would you please excuse me, I will bring my assistant in to start that paperwork, she's far better with this than I am."

As Maqbool Hameed strode across his office, both Hati and Perroquet could not help turning, watching his deliberate steps, simply wondering if he was really heading for his assistant, or possibly checking them out.

Claude was stressed; his voice had now risen a couple of octaves. He left the bar at regular intervals to check the office door, apart from a soft moaning sound apparent as he placed his ear close, no change; his urgent tech needs remained unavailable. The thought of calling Crappy came and went. A tirade of abuse down the phone would only stress him further; he counted five missed calls, and his nerves were already causing a jumpy facial twitch.

His fingers picked at his knuckles, fiddled with his shirt buttons, he misheard client's orders, he even sipped a glass of Rosé when bending down to fetch bottles from the fridge under the bar, but it didn't help.

His colleagues giggled behind his back, joking that he was jealous about the rich client taking a girl into the office, "It should have been him!"

Finally at three thirty an embarrassed looking man, with a sweaty forehead curled his face around the office door, the client looked left and right, for the moment the corridor was empty, but Claude was locked on, he stared almost willing the man away. The bar client repeated his order for the second time; he was amazed as Claude walked calmly away, tutting as the lady quickly rushed after her lover towards the stairs.

He ignored the odour in the office; he had to, closed and locked the door, nervously tapping the key board, and opened the envelope with Crappy's documents, spreading them on the newly polished table.

He scanned everything Crappy had given, the bank statement, ID card of Crappy and his deceased brother. His fingers constantly missed the right key; his stress level was higher now than in the bar. The colleague tapping on the door asking, "When is the office free?" did not help his concentration.

Claude knew the secretary enjoyed a quick glass whilst working, so stretched his arm towards the small fridge door while typing, chilled Rosé would calm him, and drinking from the bottle when in private was not a crime.

Confirmation all scans were loaded showed up, so Claude opened, *Thunderbird*, to start the email.

For extra drama, he typed a bold heading.

Attention the bank director, you are about to be defrauded, Marlon Crappy is not for real.

He then explained a vague story about a lawyer who was not a real lawyer, a man who actually was the owner of the account, but lived in southern France. Then the urgent need to make contact with the true account holder. The bottle of Rosé was close to drained, so the text read well one time, not so good the next. Claude came close to forgetting the most important line.

'Do not send any money from this account until you speak with its real owner.'

He checked the banks contact email and typed slowly, calling out the address letter by letter, he verified the address again, all looked perfect, he added, *Muscat branch* under the heading for clarity.

Including Crappy's mobile number, his own, and requested, please use these first; this is a general business email so not always private.

Another click to check the quality of the scans, they were good enough, so he emptied his bottle and hit, *send.*

Leaving a time for the weight of the mail to go through, confirmation came up in the outbox.

Claude printed a copy to show the boss what a fine job of financial security he had enacted, and headed to the bar intending to slate the junior colleagues, and take another glass of Rosé to further calm his shaking hands.

As Pierre Perroquet and Hati sat silently hoping for the best, but also giving space for some negativity it came as an unwelcome shock to hear a lady's voice behind them.

"We need to make a check on your Marseille bank dear clients, are they part of a network? I can't find a partner bank listed in Marseille."

Turning like surprised cats, caught in a corner, the visitors from Marseille had worry etched into their faces.

"No, it's a private bank, no network, old established owners, could say the Royals of the city...why?" Said Perroquet as he rubbed his fingers together nervously and Hati tried to appear confused at such a silly question.

"Please give me the bank's IBAN, Swift, whatever you have, I'll check again, maybe they route things via Paris."

Perroquet clicked his case open; the first document on the pile displayed all contact details for Marseille Trust.

"It's a well-known bank; I cannot believe you could have problems transferring my money to their branch!"

Perroquet mustered his most enquiring lawyer's face. The secretary gently took the document, gave a small bow of the head and left the room. The couple from Marseille heard Maqbool Hameed whispering with his secretary in the doorway, it lasted seconds, but felt longer, much longer.

"We have missed the deadline for international transfers today, I'm so sorry; these things appear to take longer than ever these days, so much more control and administration."

The banker stood behind his desk holding a clutch of official looking papers; both Perroquet and Hati noticed the banks green header at the top.

"Would you please sign these papers for me Mr Crappy, this confirms your intention to close the account, I imagine even if your Marseille bank is not possible as a recipient, it is still your intention to close the account?"

"Yes, it is, but I am a little confused, do you have a problem with my bank?" Perroquet swallowed hard.

The director still standing, sighed as if he was becoming a little bored with the sequence of events.

"My dear Mr Crappy, your brother transferred the funds into this account from one of the most respected-security rated Swiss banks, now you are asking for me to authorise a large transfer to a rather small, seemingly unlisted French bank, I would be doing a poor job of bank Due Diligence-governance if I did not check such requests out formally, it's my legal responsibility, ultimately my job could be on the line. Banking compliance is the new bane of our lives."

Perroquet felt that the bank manager was stalling, scared he would probe further, but he could not understand why, what was missing with his presentation, was this just routine, or had something suspicious been flagged.

The money had to be transferred to this specific account because no questions would be asked; he arranged legally buried favours for the manager, a weak link of a friend, but also the only option.

"How long will this take?" Hati broke her silence to calm her nerves.

"Let's move forward my dear clients, please would you sign this in triplicate, Mr Crappy."

Three identical documents were positioned on the outsized desk in front of Perroquet; the manager's eyes darted between his client's faces and the papers; his stare was irritating.

"Your pen or mine? I know lawyers can be touchy regarding the signing of such documents."

Perroquet appeared to miss this question, his eyes focused on the line at the bottom of the first page, his name, for the moment, was printed clearly. The silence was heavy, only lasting for a few seconds.

"Oh, it's the signature that counts; you know how you love signing documents darling."

Hati again filling in for her boyfriend's hesitation.

The sweat between his fingers made the pen difficult to hold, so Perroquet passed it to his left hand, took out his handkerchief and pretended to stem an itchy nose.

Hameed stared at him saying nothing. Perroquet bowed his head and whisked off his best, Marlon Crappy signature, his urge was to keep momentum, so he shot his pen to the next document, and the last, attempting his finest swish of the hand to make all signings the same, but he was sure the last lacked something.

"Ok, so can we move forward?" Perroquet appeared tense.

"I must say you do appear a little stressed Mr Crappy, we are doing our best, you being a lawyer, this must be familiar territory for you?"

"Oh, he always works this way, and next week is very important for our future." Hati gave a warm smile to Hameed. Again, the banker offered a condescending smile as if any moment he could pull the carpet from under their feet.

Hati made light conversation regarding the visit of a businessman from New York, Perroquet replied with simple grunts, "Um, yes, right," type responses; they were again alone and the next ten minutes seemed like a whole afternoon passing by.

Claude parked the BMW half on the kerb, clicked the key fob to lock four times in rapid succession, almost tripped into the bar, ignored Rog, and climbed the stairs two at a time.

He knocked and entered the apartment without waiting, which he immediately regretted.

"Where the fuck have you been, I called twenty times, more I think," his crude boss was half naked, bleary eyed, and the room smelt like a zoo cage uncleaned for many days.

"It's done, don't worry, the bank has everything, the money's safe."

"So, what next, I want that money here, not there, how can we do that?"

Crappy rose up and dragged a denim shirt on.

Claude let out a deep sigh, he truly wanted to believe what he had just said, but knew the situation was close to skewered. He suddenly reflected how much he could gain if the Dubai deposit could be transferred back to France, his mind began to race, at least he did own a bank account, Crappy did not, he lived from the cash in the silver box, which he had to replenish in the near future.

A plan began to form in Claude's mind, but first he better look up an old gay friend, who just happened to be assistant manager in one of Marseilles more shabby banks.

"My dear Mr Crappy, Madame, it gives me pleasure to confirm that the entirety of your account will be transferred tomorrow morning. I do apologise for the timescale taken, please feel comfortable in the fact that we do have to be vigilant when large sums of money are involved, and your Marseille bank does route international transfers via its associate in Paris, which shows up on our preferred list."

Maqbool Hameed considered his confirmation a formality, but could not understand the look of overwhelming surprise on his guest's faces.

"Very good to hear, so can I assume the funds will be in my account early next week?"

"They will, and I shall send one of my senior account managers to the Burg al Arab with transfer confirmation tomorrow morning, will you be in the hotel?"

The last thing Pierre Perroquest needed was a local bank official showing up at the hotel asking for a client named, Crappy. He missed this completely and registered in his own name. Hati showed her think on her feet skills again.

"We may leave tonight, now things have been sorted out, you know how important next week is for our business, why not leave us confirmation on the banks secure site, I can check wherever we are."

Hameed began to confirm by nodding, he looked a little embarrassed. "Your age puts me in the technology dark ages Madame, of course, I will keep your access open so that you can download the documents."

The lawyer and his close companion offered generous thanks and long handshakes to the bank director as they were escorted out of his office, the same young Emirati man displaying warmth as he ushered them towards the lift.

"We seem to have a small problem! You are staying at the Burj al Arab?"

Both Perroquet and Hati nodded and said, "yes," at the same time.

Now the lift descent lasted minutes stopping at every floor, the bank felt like a shopping mall, people entered and left at every floor; the young local man remained politely silent, staring down.

The Marseille visitors both swallowed hard at regular intervals pretending to enjoy the action around them, their performance was not convincing.

"Sorry but why did you ask about the hotel?" Said Hati with a sharp turn of her head.

The young man ignored the question as he looked at the exotic Indian lady sitting behind the reception, she raised her hand attempting to command attention.

"Ah Mr Crappy, we took the liberty of calling your hotel, simply to arrange a car for you, it's a warm day, they have you listed as Mr Perroquet, am I losing my mind?"

"Crazy but this often happens to us, my name is Perroquet, I always book the hotels, it does confuse the staff, sorry." Hati again demonstrating her off-Piste skills.

The Indian lady gave a shrug in a could-care-less fashion, the young Emirati man smiled faintly, as if he had heard this one before. The same hotel chauffeur stood on the outside about to open the Rolls Royce door. Hati slid over the back seat effortlessly as Perroquet moved in beside her. They simultaneously remembered forgetting to thank the young man in the bank for his kind assistance.

As the Rolls pulled away Maqbool Hameed was seated at his desk, almost mesmerised by the signature of Marlon Crappy. Next to the file lay the authorisation document for a priority transfer in excess of seven million euros to Marseille Trust.

The director of, Al Wasi bank in Oman was about to do a client search, as the email which just arrived from southern France bothered him, real or not, he felt compelled to look a little further into this unusual communication. The account number quoted did not match their system, and no employee in the bank had raised a security alert, however he faintly recalled a conversation with a bank colleague some months ago; this odd client name rang a bell.

Chapter 8

It was an exception for Claude to arrive at work early, especially on a rainy Marseille Sunday. The financial incentives from his scary cartoon character boss made any hour possible, but the dreary bar job was routine and called for nothing extra.

Apart from the cleaning girls talking loudly together and a delivery van driver singing a *Sam Smith,* song whilst supplying the bar cellar below, the *Cavalier* was quiet. Claude snuck into the office and opened Thunderbird to check the mails, and while they were downloading, he replaced the bottle of Rosé in the office fridge. Requests for reservations made up the majority of new mails, loads of spam, then a couple of requests for invoice payment, *last reminder*, but nothing from a bank in Dubai. Claude began to feel a little gutted, he'd tried his best to help stop a possible emptying of the account, and he was convinced his actions were the best at the time, but for this morning, no news was bad news.

He knew the monster waiting for him back at the apartment would explode, which did seem logical, he would also go into meltdown if somebody stole seven million euros from his account. Claude imagined he could play with at most another hour before the cleaning girls transformed into breakfast waitresses and started setting up the bar for Sunday morning, *le petit déjeuner.* He knew the Mid-East worked on a Sunday, plus Dubai being a couple of hours ahead, a mid-morning call would be feasible, so began planning his opening lines. He noted all of the relevant information from the file deciding to present himself as Marlon Crappy. Whatever the outcome, he attempted to convince himself that his boss could only thank him for such an initiative, he could even report his efforts had halted the transfer, and that would ensure a sizable thank you from the silver box. He again focused on his telephone dialogue.

Hati thanked the concierge for, "Such wonderful speed and efficiency," and rushed towards the shower to report their travel plans. Perroquet was nursing a stiff head, the celebratory champagne had flowed the night before, so cold water directed on the temple and neck helped to provide a little relief.

Hati was never a big drinker so thanked her common sense when she saw her boyfriend's groggy stance.

"We're booked, Air France tonight, first class, leaving at, around one o'clock, we arrive at, *Charles de Gaulle* 6:15 tomorrow morning, how's that for cool?"

Perroquet cleared his throat and turned the shower jet off, "Have you checked on the transfer yet? Should we leave if it's still not sent?"

Hati looked disappointed, she was trying her best, but the doubt had ridden with them ever since they left the office of Maqbool Hameed, she would have preferred her boyfriend checking if the funds had been sent, but as usual it fell on her shoulders.

"Can we enjoy a coffee, and then I'll log in."

Perroquet gave an unsure nod and switched on the hair dryer hoping the noise would kill off any further positivity from his lover. He was sinking into a depressed state; his nervous system was now losing out to the effect of last night's alcohol. He was sure the bank director would have delay issues with the account closure.

Hati stroked the ornamental bottle of Coco Chanel, gently pressed the spray and stretched her neck as the mist tingled on her body.

"We have the day to enjoy the beach, share a jet-ski, come on darling, it will be ok, he was just being a typical dull-suspicious banker, and they're the same all over the world. I'll check soon and tell you everything is ok."

"I want to see that transfer in Marseille, then, and only then, can I relax!" Perroquet appeared to be suffering, and the chance of becoming a multi-millionaire was not evident in his current frame of mind.

Claude was ready; he refused the temptation of the Rosé bottle, choosing deep breathing and a rigid back instead. The bank documents were spread across the table, he was ready to go.

The dialling tone sounded far away; his grip was tight on the handset.

"Good morning, Al-Wasi bank of Oman, how may I direct your call?"

Hearing the word, Oman, fazed Claude a little.

"Yes, good morning, this is MARLON CRAPPY," Claude spoke as if the person on the other end was deaf, "I wish to check something on a large deposit I have with your bank."

"Of course, sir, hold for one moment please."

Claude glanced towards the fridge.

"This is Priyanka Choudhry, private account manager, may I assist you?"

"Yes, you may, this is, Marlon Crappy, shall I give you my account number?"

"Just one moment Mr…Cratty."

"My name is, C.R.A.P.P.Y."

"Please excuse me sir, the line is not good, a moment please."

At the third attempt, Priyanka managed to alert her director via the internal system, who was now rushing to her office.

"Hello are you still there?" Claude heard the sound of the coffee machine; breakfast preparation had begun and it disturbed him.

"Please give me a moment sir; our systems are a little slow today."

Claude locked the office door.

"Good morning Mr Crappy, this is Mohammed Fasi, Director of private client accounts for Oman."

Claude still wondered why nobody mentioned Dubai. But quickly realised he had to endure whatever formalities they threw at him.

"I just need to check my account is safe, I have reason to think someone may be trying to steal from me. Have you received the email I sent?"

"That's a serious situation Mr Crappy, but sorry, I must identify you before we go further. Let's start with the account number."

Claude pulled the bank statement closer.

"It's Global Currency Managed account number, 9090 6341 7733."

"I assume you have your security ID pin in front of you?" Said the bank director.

"Fuck no," whispered Claude away from the mouthpiece.

"I don't, I lost it, could be the person I am worried about took it." Claude was spitting in the air, shaking his head in desperation.

"Then I am sorry Mr Crappy, this was given to you when you opened the account, we explained the importance of the code numbers when you need to call, or log onto the account."

"My date of birth is March nineteenth, nineteen seventy-nine."

"Again, sorry Mr Crappy, the same person who took your security id could have also taken your passport; we cannot help you unless we hear this information."

Claude felt useless; any more waffling could cause added problems, and this was looking bad enough.

"Please tell me, is the account, ok?" He tried a last shot.

"Um…well…ok Mr Crappy, I can only tell you that this account is safe, nothing further."

"Yes, yes, thank you so much, then it's, ok? I will tell, no sorry I mean I'm happy, thank you again Mr Fasi, wish you a good day, good bye."

Mohammed Fasi and, Priyanka Choudhry shook their heads in unison, something strange was going on; the bank director requested a file note, "Any client requests regarding this account must be authorised by his signature only."

Now he must take up contact with Marlon Crappy some other way, as the person who just called the bank failed to convince him that he was the account owner.

Hati's long red nails delicately touched the laptop keyboard; Perroquet hovered behind her but refused to look towards the screen. The connection, like all services in the Burj Al Arab, worked perfectly.

The screen turned green, the colour of Al Rahudi bank, Hati tossed her hair back confidently whilst typing in the six-digit code. The next screen flashed and opened the account access page.

Hati blinked, stroked her cheeks and stared intently;

Account closed zero value in all currencies.

"Darling he sent the money, he did it, really, look."

Suddenly, Pierre Perroquet lost all sensations of a hangover. He placed his shaking hands on Hati's shoulders.

"No, are you sure?"

"Read and react, my legal lover."

The bed was far too far away for the moment, so as Hati was dragged from the office chair towards the carpeted floor, tears filled her beautiful eyes. Two minds raced along with their heartbeats. The tangle of belief against disbelief flowed through the love makers. The passion was nowhere near real, just that the moment called for this act, sort of stress relief in the purest form.

Peirre Perroquet considered how much the best bottle of champagne would cost in first class this night, while Hati dreamt of how many babies she would mother, girls, boys, she relished the thought of a stress-free childhood for her children, the opposite to hers. The lovemaking continued until the two fell side by side, exhausted, speechless and still harbouring tiny doubts as to the transfer showing up, back home.

Four thousand five hundred kilometres away a young gay barman was powering his bosses BMW up and down the backstreets of Marseille, enjoying the calm of a Sunday morning, but more so the thank you for the wonderful news he could deliver. His hands already moist from imagining how many fifty Euro's bills he would earn for this piece of security work.

Marlon Crappy stared coldly from his apartment window; Claude took three attempts to park the BMW parallel in the row of dusty old Renaults and Peugeots. The body language, an art learnt from many years surveying the exercise yard, told Crappy his young helper was positive about something. He decided to listen instead of threaten, maybe his money was safe.

"I actually spoke with the bank director, the account is ok, his own words, he told me it was safe, seven million Euro's is still sitting on the account."

Claude glanced at the silver box on the table top, confident his exaggerated claims would enlarge his reward.

"That's good news, now I need to know how we can get that money here, my little box is feeling light, you know what I mean?"

Claude diverted his gaze away from the silver box whilst hunching his shoulders.

"How about transfer it to my account here? Even I know banks will not give out large sums of cash these days, I guess you don't want to visit Dubai?"

Crappy's inadequate understanding of Claude's idea caused him to begin cursing the day he became wealthy, life in prison was much less complicated.

The big man turned away from Claude and opened the silver box.

"Here, two hundred go and fuel the BMW up, what's left over is for you."

Claude left the apartment in a huff, the car would be fuelled with one fifty, he would keep his fair share, after this morning, he deserved it.

The suite at the Burj Al Arab remained occupied for the day, room service provided a constant flow of champagne and local snacks, three more love making sessions tired the newly wealthy dreamers who fell into an alcohol induced sleep. The alarm was set for eight, enough time to shower, pack, check out and enjoy the opulence of the Rolls Royce Ghost on route to Dubai International airport.

Crappy spent the day on his Predator, it was the most private place to try and work out a plan. His anger still raged towards the people living in a Chateau, they have to pay for taking away his brother, Claude would never replace him. The pain grew when he considered how much use his brother would be at this moment, he could arrange the money transfer in an instant, accountants do things like that, but he had no idea, and could only hope his trust in Claude would not backfire.

He flicked open the silver box, the once thick pile of crisp Euro notes was looking depleted, he began to regret buying so many possessions, then his sulk lightened, hold on, he is still worth millions, but how the hell can he touch it?

He stared at the old and crumpled bank statements from Al Rahudi bank, somehow, he had to get his hands on this cash, and soon.

As his mind thrashed back and forth, he reflected on the past months, the ridiculous events taking him from prison thug to multi-millionaire yacht owner. By now, all of the new possessions were more burden than pleasure, the constant invoices delivered to the Crocodile bar for mooring the Predator, the fuel for the cars, and paying Claude, the rent for an apartment above a bar, not much bigger than his prison cell. Why did this happen to him?

He foraged through his paperwork, it all looked worn and dirty, his hands had made the administration grubby. His eyes were attracted to a letter from the lawyer, the man who organised his new lifestyle. A letter confirming, he was the legal owner of a yacht moored in the harbour of Marseille.

He slapped the table with a massive soiled-sticky hand.

"Yes, you bastard, you are the one who can help me get what's mine."

Crappy decided, whatever the cost, Maître Perroquet is the man who can transfer his money from Dubai, after all he provided all the paperwork, this is what lawyers are good at.

Crappy called Claude to check if Perroquet was in town, professional assistance was needed to transfer his money to Marseille.

The giant began to relax, this was the solution he had been searching his head for, now he could plan revenge on the Chateau owners, suddenly his complex list of worries appeared to dissolve a little, things were looking better.

Chapter 9

"Then I suggest we take the boys further afield, maybe try surfing around Biarritz, great hotels, food, they always complain about the lack of waves in the south." Jack Rafter, Mr attention to detail and family pacifier attempted to suggest holiday plans to his wife.

"Sounds fine darling, please make sure the hotel is close to the beach, all the best places in France are a nightmare to get to in full summer."

"I'll sort it out soon, leave it with me." Jack's voice trailed off; he was heading to the front door.

Chateau Montjan was not a large place, but the money lavished inside and out by the mix of international owners turned it into a jewel of a home. A residence bursting with the latest security, where every single owner subconsciously scrutinised visitors, from the DHL guy to the property agents, who regularly tried to obtain sales mandates.

Jack considered the meeting that he was about to take part in, a quick check all is ok, nothing new here run of the mill routine, then he could return to his financial business. The UK Final Leaving Decision vote on a Brexit was moving closer, a major decision for Europe, and one that could affect his business for years to come.

As he arrived at Arno Van Bommel's open door his mind could not have been further away. He recognised the slow deep laugher from Dan Lancaster but was more focused on his iPhone, checking the STG v Euro rate. Entering the lounge, he guessed he was the last arrival. Eva Critin was seated in her favourite dark green high-backed chair, Arno always saved it for her, Dan, Boris Von Phren and Anna-Tina Geisinger well-spaced out around the low Japanese coffee table, the decoration always took Jack's eye, it seemed to change at every visit.

Jack could not help noticing, the guys looked relaxed and thoughtful, Eva and Anna-Tina appeared to be at a bereavement, so he sat slowly determined to keep his silence. This meeting already demanding more attention than he expected.

The men in the room mostly into their forties, well experienced, travelled and street wise, quickly measured the lady's demeanour as Eva had called the meeting, all eyes fell upon her, clearly things need to be said this day, the silence was palpable.

She started with a small shake of her head, as if she doubted her ability to deliver the necessary news.

"Eva, this Chateau seems to be a dream, yet sometimes kinda nightmarish, none of us are in a rush, tell it like it is babe." Dan's Californian charm did change Eva's body language; she smiled a very sweet thank you towards him.

"I don't want to recount those terrible days we experienced last year, it's too fresh in our memories."

Eva took a deep breath.

The whole room heard Jack's, "Oh no."

"No Jack it's not Lasalle, we know he's gone, not his family or friends either."

Anna-Tina took hold of Boris's hand, she didn't look at him, her hand said it all.

"Somehow I had a feeling this would come back to bite us; would I be right in guessing politics and Paris are involved." Jack tried to ease back in the chair, but his posture was plainly stiff.

"My dear Jack, not only you, all of you are my very dear friends, I love you like family, it was never my intention to harm anyone here, I did what I could to help us through."

Arno was unaware his knees were jumping up and down, like a young footballer about to take to the field for the first time. Suddenly his legs froze.

"Eva, we are a sort of team now, like it or not, it's what we've become, tell us why we're here."

More silence followed, but not for long. Eva's eyes turned cold and darted from left to right.

"The minister in Paris, the one who helped us and made the tax attack disappear overnight. When we thought all was behind us last year, he called one night, drunk, but he's often like that in the evening. Not a long conversation, but you know how some moments live with you forever? Well, he told me, Eva, when you sell your soul to the devil, one day, maybe sooner, maybe later, I will have a project for your new team. Keep them alert, fit and ready. He also reminded me that I could never truly leave the secret service."

Jack's silenced phone had vibrated three client calls, but his mind was elsewhere, client questions and problems were not his current priority.

"So, what does he want, what does he expect?" Jack's voice calm, deep and thoughtful, like a doctor delivering the bad news.

"I really cannot say, I am so sorry Jack, your boys, I never…" Arno interrupted.

"Tell us what you know, the creep has a plan, guess we have to do some dirty work for him, then he lets us off the hook until the next job, fucking parasite."

"All I know is he sort of intimated something, he said it could be soon, the next weeks, of course he won't say too much." Eva was now visibly calmer; her old job skills were showing through.

Boris had been silent cleared his throat.

"Where is his office? Get me close, I'll tell you more about his plans than he knows, promise."

The room atmosphere lightened a little, Boris was back in town, his considerable, but unrequired skills of late now came back with a vengeance.

"Not that easy Boris, he is far more senior these days, I'm sure he has plenty of chaps like you around to keep him safe." Said Eva.

Jack, Dan and Arno all smiled a superior smile, they were sure Boris was the best in his league, no anaemic tech-teen on a miserable French salary in Paris could outfox him.

Eva raised her voice attempting to control the meeting, "His reputation has always been soiled, when I operated from Paris, he was always under somebody's spotlight, a payoff here, keep a witness silenced, it's the only way he knows, and now he's gone up the political ladder, that's not good news."

"So, our lives are put back one year, we wait for the call, keep the dirt away from our loved ones, arrange a grubby deed for this scumbag, and pretend we're all happy and contented."

Jack shook his head in doubt.

Dan eased forward, hands together, "Can we be practical, he's not gonna get us to do his shopping, bodyguard him, he already has that covered, this is plain shit, and we're the guys digging it for him. He's got us by the balls, and I dream one day I have his balls in my hands."

The two ladies in the room showed little embarrassment over Dan's American stance on the issue, knowing he was spot on.

"I presume holiday plans are on hold then?" Said Jack with raised eyebrows.

"No fucking way is this little A-hole using us, we will never get off the hook, whatever we have to do this time, you can guarantee the next time will be worse." Arno's massive hands gesturing as he spoke.

"Taking out a minister? Complicated, even my old team would think twice about that mission." Dan was looking very serious.

"Eva," Jack raised his index finger to his lips, "You must know other senior people in Paris, this guy has to be shut down, we are not his garbage collectors because he smoothed over a corrupt tax inspection for us."

"Jack, don't forget how Gerard Crappy died, those Russians were never caught, we were next to his Sunseeker Predator, it appears the minister has some shots from the helicopter that buzzed over that day, shots of you guys, maybe a bluff, can we chance that?" Eva certainly chilled the room.

Boris held his hands up, as if under arrest, "Eva, this snake keeps reminding you about still being in the service, let's take advantage of that, tell him you want to see him again, but you must get me into the building, his flat wherever he keeps his blackmail files, I'll clear it away like the ultimate housekeeper, it will be buried-forever."

Eva reflected on what she had to go through with the minister to orchestrate the last favour, now she was being asked by her closest friends to suffer his touch again.

A picture of Jack and Carly Rafters boys took prominent position on Arno's sporting wall. The whole Chateau had deep affection for the young guys; they were loved by all like family, not merely neighbours.

Eva stared towards the boys faces; they seemed to will her onto the proposed Paris visit. As she dropped her gaze every person in the room sat fixated on the ex *sûreté* operative.

"This is the only way to break him, we get to him first, none of us are equipped to carry out a rotten deed, except you Dan, and then what? Return here as if nothing has happened?" Jack was obviously trying to form a plan, and it didn't take long for his friends to back him up.

Dan spoke first, "Jesus I'm sorry Eva, if I saw you entering my office, I'd say yes before you asked anything."

"I wish it were that simple Dan." said Eva with a dismissive shake of her head.

"Well beautiful lady, seems our options are limited, you have to set this up Eva, you know we will support you to the end, simple case of cut out the cancer before it takes over." said Arno.

Eva had a look between flattery and confusion.

The room was now full of more positive people, but less so with Eva, she reflected on another night of *passion* in the minister's apartment, it was more like rape, and she vowed to never let herself sink this low ever again the last time she closed the penthouse door.

"This needs some careful planning, he's not stupid, and I can't call up and invite him to dinner." Said, Eva wishing she could backtrack.

Jack could only think of his family, he hoped trips to Paris would be for pleasure, not to terminate a senior French minister! But his pissed off attitude was evident.

"Eva, you're the only person in this room capable, sorry, no question, you're back in the service, Dan, Arno and I will guarantee your safety, Boris maybe, Anna-Tina also can enter his tech world and either close him down, or at the least destroy any evidence he has, leave us on safe ground."

The lady who had just re-entered the French secret service stood up, placed her hands neatly across her lower stomach and addressed her team.

"I will not let him hurt us, you are all my friends for life here, all I have, and this poison cannot enter our lives again. Leave me for a day or two; I will plan everything, just like in the days I tried to escape from, I'll tell you when to pack for Paris."

Sunday evening Jack Rafter surprised his family by spending most of his time in the office, the excuse being, would the UK leave Europe, would a Brexit really happen he was left undisturbed, Carly and the boys understanding his concerns. In reality, he was exchanging emails with Dan, Arno and Boris, all trying to put some substance towards a mission soon to be planned in Paris. They were, these days, business men, not hit men, without question the minister had to be broken, but how?

Boris kept intimating he 'may' have a solution, but his replies were so vague that the guys were clueless as to what he meant.

It had been some time since the uninformed wives of the Chateau had seen their men so sombre at dinner, conversation was hard, the guys all blamed business reasons, bloody politicians and too much regulation, for this night, it worked.

As Jack tossed and turned in his bed, he realised he would be lucky to enjoy another hour or two, the light was coming through the curtains, a night of planning, thinking it through had bothered not only him, but Arno and Dan also; Boris always slept like a baby, a true tech head.

Jack tried one more time for his favourite position; he knew he had to clear his mind.

Thirty-six thousand feet above the Chateau, an Air France Airbus was about to commence the descent towards Paris, *Charles de Gaulle.* A stunning lady with piercing green eyes, bronzed legs and a twinkle in her eye was pestering her boyfriend.

"What difference will a couple of days make, it's not high summer yet, the Intercontinental will have rooms, and you know the shopping is far better than Marseille, please darling, I think I deserve it!"

Chapter 10

Claude was feeling harassed, the tourists were arriving in Marseille, which required longer hours behind the bar, and the terrace was often full for lunch and dinner. His cruel and bitter friend was acting like a nut, one moment demanding help from the stressed young man, the next hiding on his yacht. He worshipped alcohol which caused him to miss Claude's calls, only to then call up later, and threat what he would do if ignored.

It was close to 9:30, the Monday morning coffee crowd were slowly arriving, sitting in the sun, yawning as if the weekend took its toll and catching up on the weekend events. Screens were beginning to replace newspapers. Claude has stocked the bar, cleaned all of the tables and bar top, now time to again try calling the office of Maître Perroquet. Marseille lawyers were not known for early starts, so Claude hoped his bosses' manic need to see the lawyer would soon blow over, this was a meeting he preferred to avoid. He hoped the weird one had forgot about the tracker in the case.

The same message played, "I am away on business, if urgent contact my colleague, otherwise I'll come back to you upon my return."

Claude hesitated as he touched the screen; Crappy would explode for no reason when he heard the lawyer was still away, the effect of a weekend's alcohol clouding any possible logic. He relaxed when the phone of Crappy went over to the *orange* message service. Claude promised to try later, and returned to the swelling terrace.

Paris traffic was heavy. Hati and Pierre Perroquet could not make out the taxi drivers nationality, his French was fine, but the accent was Germanic and a little clumsy.

As they passed the Opera house the driver cursed a bike courier who almost drove across his bonnet, insults were traded with exaggerated waves of the hands, the drivers accent went downhill, they were relieved that the Intercontinental lay just around the corner on Rue Scribe.

Perroquet gave a derisory tip as they followed their luggage into the hotel, he was sure the driver used some eastern bloc swear word behind his back.

Hati approached the check in desk like a celebrity, after the sunny days and close to successful mission in Dubai she was looking good, and knew it, her walk turned quite a few heads, the boyfriend fiddled with his mobile, and still no news on the transfer, his deep frown caused the reception staff to focus solely on his stunning lady friend.

"We need a suite for two to three nights, if you have something overlooking the Opera that would be nice."

The lawyer gathered himself together, "and the best deal would be appreciated we have stayed before, and will certainly do so again."

The receptionist ignored Perroquet choosing to stare at the reservation screen; she tapped her fingers together as if finding free rooms would be a chore. Hati felt her patience was being tested.

"You need the room for three nights?"

"Yes, that's what I said." Hati wondered why hotel staff persisted in pretending rooms were scarce, she was confident her preferred room would be available any second.

"Yes, we do have one more left, may we offer you coffee, the room is being cleaned, perhaps half an hour."

Both Perroquet and Hati exchanged sarcastic glances together. The check in form was signed, an insincere "thanks," was whispered by Hati as the couple left the reception.

Within twenty minutes, a sweat young Parisian girl with a shy smile had located the handsome couple. The small key folder in her hand was waved like a prize had been won.

"Please may I show you to your suite?" As the lift doors opened on the third floor Perroquet felt his mobile vibrate in his pocket, he resisted the urge to check, he knew this was an SMS, and he only wished for one SMS this morning to make him a very happy man indeed.

Once the girl had left the suite Hati moved into overdrive, "What do you think for lunch, dinner oh and shopping darling, today or tomorrow? Now we're in Paris so…"

Perroquet nodded in agreement, but said nothing as he slid his mobile out of his pocket. His girlfriend was busy arranging clothes on hangers. He exhaled deeply as he read the first screen, then quickly pressed to open a full screen SMS.

His scream almost burst Hati's eardrums who spun around in terror as if her boyfriend was suffering a seizure.

"Look, read this," his hand shook as he held the screen towards his stunned companion.

The transfer you expected has arrived from Dubai, regards, Luke Marseille Trust.

Hati tried her best to match Pierrie's scream, she failed, but it did impress the cleaners in the corridor who assumed the new arrivals were testing the clean bed.

As they embraced, Hati glanced over her lover's shoulder; one magazine on the coffee table caught her eye. The jewellery stores of *Place Vendôme* would be hit before lunchtime, the fashion stores of *Printemps* after lunch at *George V.* Perroquet was still fixed on his phone screen.

"The last time we went to his office some irritating little prick offered to help us."

"I remember the day, but can I ask what you need a lawyer for?" Said Claude sheepishly.

"I'm running out of money, you know how much I got in Dubai, well I need it here, that Chateau situation is on my mind, and lawyers can sort out things like that." Crappy looked at Claude whose head was bowed towards the floor.

"They need an account to transfer the money to, you don't have one, this is why I offered mine." Claude was getting a little cheeky. The young man's eyes had moved, but not his head Hounding Crappy was sometimes fun.

"Lawyers work together; they always do special deals that we have to be thankful for; I know that from my time in…well, I know how they work." They both knew where Crappy had spent, *time*, but the subject was never mentioned.

"So, this paperwork pusher can do something to get my money over here."

Claude began to realise, maybe his chaotic paymaster was smarter than he gave him credit for. Lawyers always have a variety of bank accounts where transfers can be held, property sale proceeds, company purchase funds, his late father was an insurance administrator, and Claude recalled him mesmerising the family over dinner recounting the vast sums they sent to lawyer's accounts when settling claims.

With renewed and as always mercenary enthusiasm, Claude jangled the BMW keys.

"You drive, I drive? He said he was available when Perroquet was away, let's try."

Lawyer's offices in France often fall into two categories, the swanky far over the top historical buildings on tree lined avenues where all is polished and shining every day of the working week. Hugh heavy entry doors decorated with brass or gold coloured ornamentation that makes the visitor embarrassed to touch. Where the fees begin as you enter their underground parking. Or the somewhat lesser weather-stained buildings frequented by pigeons, with old wooden windows, grubby discoloured name plates, and entry buzzers which only work if you press with all your body weight.

Maître Perroquet had elected for the more economical choice.

Claude felt pessimistic that anything remotely upbeat change could happen this morning, why an assistant lawyer would help the oaf to sort out his personal financial problems seemed a little farfetched.

The luck of the post lady leaving through the main door as the unlikely two arrived did surprise Claude; she sang a friendly *Bonjour*, pushed the door open and leapt onto her bike.

Crappy primarily appeared in Claude's life as a large bodied buffoon, a wacko, someone to fleece and keep happy, but moments came and went whereby Claude considered more respect was due.

The speed with which Crappy grabbed the door realising entry to the building, the element of surprise, and of course the prospect to examine the lawyer's office in his absence, impressed the young barman. Clearly his devious side outpaced his daily stupidity.

The giant began to move like a burglar in the night, maybe even a tad slimmer, a quick wave of his right-hand requested *stay behind me*, Claude followed almost in awe, like a high-class burglary was under way.

As they reached the first floor Crappy spotted a small pile of neatly stacked letters resting against the office door of Maître Pierre Perroquet, obviously the place was empty, but who let the post lady in?

The two men stared at each other, then both dropped their eyes to the letters. The ex-con formed a fist to hit the door, hesitated, then lowered his hand and grabbed the pile of letters. Yet again Crappy's brisk action astonished Claude who heard a door open on the higher floor. A large finger pointed towards the lower stairs, then Claude felt a sticky hand pushing his back, they made noise but reached the front door and left before seeing any other person in the building.

Claude wondered why this just happened, but as usual, kept his mouth shut.

A somewhat more cheerful Pierre Perroquet slid his hand up and down Hati's back as they walked towards *Place Vendôme*, Paris felt good, the cooler air after Dubai was refreshing. Parisian girls certainly wore less than Dubai females. They talked in nervous bursts still recounting the uncanny events which put them in Paris on this day. *S*uddenly Hati pulled her boyfriend's hand, *C*artier was bursting with possibilities, and her eyes darted across the meticulously clean heavy glass windows. The fatigue of the long flight washed away in a few short steps. The happy multi-millionaire hoped his dubious banking friend in Marseille did not forget the instructions, "Boost my credit card the moment the funds arrive."

"You can help me opening these bloody letters, you know my English! I hope for his sake nothing looks dirty; all lawyers are fucking liars."

"So that's why you grabbed them," said Claude with suspicion all over his face.

He watched Crappy throw around ten envelopes across the plastic covered table, above their heads the wall was still covered with the plans to kidnap two young men in Chambéry, Claude wondered if it would ever happen, he considered his life was getting more and more complicated, the pay for reward scale had to be improved.

Crappy sat on the bed, so Claude eased a wobbly old wooden chair a cautious meter or so away. At least three of the letters displayed postal stamps in Arabic. The simple-minded giant showed a quick recognition of this, he lifted his eyes to Claude as if saying, told you so. The first letter opened was from a local client, a garage owner complaining about the size of his lawyer's bill. The relish, or possible brewing anger showed all over Crappy's large round head when he slipped his index finger into the first letter showing a recent date from Dubai. He almost ripped it in half, pulling in irritation; the envelope fell to the floor.

"Why do my bank statements go to this lawyer's office? I've never seen one since…"

Claude knew the answer to this rather stupid question, but simply hoped to control the pending rage; he would never get out of the door in time. Even from his position across the table he could see an account balance of 7.000.000 euros, another column displayed quarterly interest of, 52000.500 euros, Claude wished his boss would throw those 'crumbs' his way.

"He has no reason to receive your bank statements; they should be coming to you at the *Crocodile* bar."

Another letter was pulled angrily from its covering envelope; Claude noticed a postmark of Muscat Oman. The letter style and presentation were very different.

The cold shiver that vibrated down Claude's back was only the start of his reaction, his mouth became instantly dry, and tension pulled at his forehead, his tight chest halted his breathing, he subconsciously wiggled his chair away from the plastic covered table. He could smell the same horrible odour from the office where he typed the email to a bank in Muscat; he had to leave this room.

"I think I'm going to throw up, sorry this is all too much for me."

Crappy was looking worryingly pissed off.

"What, don't fuck me around now, you know my reading is not so hot, you're supposed to help me."

Claude was limping towards the door, one hand on his stomach, the other across his mouth.

"Ok then, fuck off and throw up, fucking poofs." This was the first time Crappy had acknowledged his helper's sexual persuasion.

Most of the letters were from agitated clients displaying worry over the time Maître Perroquet spent away from Marseille, *why were their cases constantly delayed without result.* Two more envelopes remained. The ex-con was now more relaxed, Claude's sudden departure had left him no choice, the small pile of paperwork confused him, he applied his own minimal logic, why would the lawyer receive *his* bank statements when the balance showed all of his money in place. He cast his mind back to Claude sending the documents from the *Belle Epoque* office, maybe this was the best ever deed from the man he just insulted, maybe an apology and a couple of fifty euro bills from his dwindling pile would bring him back. So, he decided to open the remaining letters.

The first drew his eyes to an overlarge signature from a man called Maqball Hameed, Director of Al Rahudi private bank in Dubai. The letter was short and simple,

Dear Mr Crappy,

I look forward to welcoming you in Dubai, my staff and I have pleasure in carrying out your wishes to the letter.

We pride ourselves on being one of the best and most modern banking networks, this we will happily demonstrate during your stay.

My secretary remains at your disposal for any assistance when you arrive in our wonderful city of Dubai.

Crappy's limited education concluded he was being invited to meet his bank manager in Dubai.

The last letter showed a Marseille postmark, yet another bank, Marseille Trust, Crappy's mind was in reverse gear, he imagined this can only be another local client harbouring doubts over their lawyer's service attitude.

Chère Pierre,

I am happy to be of service to you again my friend. I have opened the account; as soon as the funds arrive, I will increase your credit card limit to the one million agreed.

Send me a text from Dubai when you know the date that Al Rahudi bank will be closing the account and making the transfer.

Glad to be in business again, just like the old days in Paris.

Luke Dardain
Director
Marseille Trust

Marlon Crappy had little trouble understanding this letter.

His roar caused clients in the *Crocodile* bar to dip their heads as if the floor above was collapsing on them, even shoppers dawdling in the street looked up towards the apartment window.

Children tightened the grip on their parent's hand.

Something large and dangerously aggressive caused people to quicken their step, move away from a weirdo that was too close for comfort.

Claude had not thrown up, but choose to hide in the bars cramped toilet. The scribbles on the walls took his attention, maybe for the humour in some of the short messages, but nothing made him smile due to the echo of a one hundred and thirty kilo beast somewhere above the tiny room, the roar still repeated in his tight head. The window was too small as an escape route, the stairs remained silent, no one had left the apartment yet, so Claude made a calculated rush for the bar's main door. Within nine seconds, he was out and in the open street, several people gazed at him as if he was the lucky one who escaped whatever was going wrong inside. He walked long and fast, after four blocks he slowed down, his back was wet, he forgot his sunglasses so his watering eyes blinked in the bright sun. Passing a cheerfully decorated wine shop he paused, a special offer caught his eye, red Sancerre, three bottles for the price of two. Why oh why did he work the shift that day Marlon Crappy booked into the *Belle Epoque*.

The BMW sat opposite the main and only office of Marseille Trust. The driver's stare took in the three floors which made up the bank's offices. It was one in the morning, the occasional car passed but the street was quiet. Crappy wondered which office Luke Dardain occupied, it didn't really matter, he would find him anyway. Another hour passed, now the street was dead. A sweaty hand reached into his jacket pocket. Claude's was the first number to show up in the phone book.

The barman rolled over in bed, he guessed this call would come, but he had nowhere near enough balls to pick up, he waited for voicemail to take over, the deep rough voice he knew so well cleared his throat.

"Claude it's me, that day I ripped your shirt in the bar, bit stupid hey, well I got stupid again yesterday, and I am sorry, not good what I said, I owe you, also need your help mate, no mean it, I really need your help, call me please, I'll put things right."

Claude's mood eased, he rubbed his head, seems like he's off the hook, at least for the moment.

Crappy drove back to the *Crocodile* bar, his mounting anger towards Maître Perroquet evident in his rapid breathing. Somebody would pay dearly for stealing his money; nobody dare screw Marlon Crappy.

Chapter 11

Jack Rafter filled his days with family matters and business. During the night the demons came and kept him turning and thinking. What exactly would he and his close neighbours be required to do in Paris? How far would they fall if things went wrong? Yet again the dream of moving to France, living in a Chateau, hearing his sons speak a variety of languages sparked a level of doubt, was it all worth it? But this was not a decision he could turn back. A solution had to be found, and this would most likely be a painful one.

Foreign number plates accounted for half the drivers on the auto route to Annecy, the campers with the standard retired couple gazing bewildered at everything that passed amused Jack, wondering if he and Carly would ever end up in a large white camper van on route to some dull destination when their hair turned grey, no not a chance in hell!

He glanced at the file on the passenger seat, Hervé Besson, a local Notaire, turned out to be one of the best business partners Jack knew in the region. They referred clients onto one another, from Jack the Brits and Dutch who had inheritance-property type needs, from Hervé the more international maybe Russian, Canadian or Far Eastern, recently even American contacts looking to invest in Europe. The respect had built well, they both had confidence in the relationship, and the monthly meeting was arranged at the Imperial Palace hotel on the lake of Annecy.

Jack parked in the last parking place he could find, decided the sticky air would make his jacket a pain to wear, so rolled his sleeves up and hoped Hervé would do the same.

"Bonjour" came from left and right as he entered the hotel, the reception was calm so the girls tried for customer contact; the baggage guy cleaned his shoes on the back of his trouser leg. Clearly some sort of seminar was in full swing, well presented short skirted girls and busy young men in dark suits cradled

folders on which Jack noticed the words, *marketing tomorrow's ideas*. He mentally wished them luck.

Knowing Hervé enjoyed the occasional smoke, Jack guessed the terrace would be the place to find their reserved table, he was right; Hervé lifted an open left hand towards his friend. The table was perfect, on a corner next to the terrace wall; a light breeze lifted the umbrella so Jack smiled thankfully, he could avoid the smell he detested, cigarette smoke. Hervé gestured towards Jacks shirt, "Good plan, it's a hot one today," they shook hands warmly as the waitress waited patiently.

Two glasses of dry white and two Perrier were ordered; Jack suggested they hold on ten minutes or so before they needed the menus, as the waitress turned away both guys checked out her confident walk, a complimentary raising of the eyebrows was shared by the men.

"Moving on from the local scenery how's business?" Asked Jack.

"Well, the Brexit decision has cooled the UK buyers for the moment, also sending shudders around the rest of Europe, lot of questions coming in, but people are holding back, and as you know Sterling is suffering."

Jack quenched his dry mouth with a quick sip of Perrier.

Hervé seemed to have something on his mind, the third cigarette was lit from his silver lighter, Jack could never remember more than one, maybe two being used, even over a long lunch session.

"Are you ok, Hervé? Get the impression some issue is bothering you."

A brief silence followed, and then Hervé nodded as if he was obliged to explain.

"You remember all that shit you and your neighbours went through last year, the orchestrated tax attack." Jack sighed and narrowed his eyes.

"Oh do I."

"Did you know Gerard Crappy had a brother?" Jack immediately sat bolt upright.

"The mother produced two of those bastards?"

A short silence followed allowing Jack to reflect.

Casting his mind back to the long conversations with Hervé, at the time he was scared that the family home could be sequestrated by the tax office, so his friend proposed ways to block this, he helped all he could.

"Should I be worried?"

"I don't know." Hervé shook his head as the waitress offered the menus.

"Look Jack, maybe this is nothing, occupational hazard for me, but I hear a lot from colleagues. Some lawyer with a dirty reputation in Marseille is involved. Crappy, the brother, left jail in Marseille earlier this year. The guards were happy to see him go, he has a reputation for violence. He inherited that yacht plus a lot of cash which his brother stole from the Swiss financier, Lasalle."

Jack held his head in his hands watching the bubbles in his Perrier.

"So, we have a jailbird, a wealthy one, who I guess thinks we killed his brother, is it that bad?"

"This is what I know." As Hervé started talking Jacks mind flashed back to the security cameras around the Chateau, somebody was watching them, they were already being stalked.

Hervé continued, "The lawyer has always been on the wrong side, odd guy, he has some doll of a secretary who keeps him, shall we say protected. The talk on the street is he kept most of the inheritance for himself, gave the dumb con a yacht and a pile of cash. As the brother has no bank account, or real address it's hard to keep a track of what he's up to. The most specific thing I heard is that the accounts were in the Middle-East, and the lawyer and his girlfriend recently made a trip to Dubai, still not back yet."

Jack had already texted Dan and Arno telling them to keep an eye out for intruders until he got home.

"I really expected a more pleasant lunch, not a possible life-threatening situation."

Hervé looked embarrassed, he had to tell Jack this gossip, but he was sure his friend and family were in serious danger.

"Jack, I will try to find out more information. If the lawyer has stolen his money, he could be in the most danger. The brother was a lunatic in jail, massive guy who dropped other prisoners with one chop of his hand."

"That does not improve our situation Hervé, are you telling me we could be number two on his hit list?"

"Hold on Jack, it's possible he makes no connection with you and your neighbours at the Chateau."

"Remember Eva, the ex Sûreté lady, neighbour?"

"Do recall a Chateau diva."

"That dirty minister in Paris, he has some bloody shots of us on a boat close to the Predator that day, we look as guilty as the guys on the jet-skis, the ones who did do it."

"Oh my god Jack, this minister can access anything I can, if he decides to use Crappy against you."

"Can we just close this off now, I've gone from positive business man to worried sole in the last half hour, can things get worse?"

"I'll do all I can to get more information my friend, it's the least I can do, you look like you're leaving?"

Jack was unaware he had stood up.

"Sorry, have to get home; my friends should hear this immediately."

As Jack glanced at the drinks, Hervé waved his hand. "All mine."

The handshake was quick but solid. Jack almost crushed a tiny Italian man who considered he had priority through the terrace door.

"*Merci-au revoir,*" was wasted, the reception girls saw a man in a big hurry.

Pierre Perroquet was a little shocked when he checked his newly boosted credit card account, so he enlarged the screen, but nothing improved, it was painful in small or large print. *Cartier* made the largest hole; several debits from *Printemps* followed up a close second, the champagne lunch at *George V* could have financed a small, but reliable car from a backstreet garage in Marseille. He wondered if the permanent smile on Hati's face since the early morning massage would last, more days in Paris would result in him reducing her credit limit.

Three knocks at the suite door announced breakfast; two waiters slid the trolley towards the centre of the room, in no time the table sides were opened up, a small but fresh bouquet of roses placed in the centre, coffee poured, the Financial Times folded to the right of one plate. The more senior waiter offered his open hands to ask if their presentation was acceptable. Hati did her best to exhibit the dazzling gold bracelet as she gave the note to her boyfriend who was still watching TV in bed. His real signature far swifter than the fake one in Dubai. Twenty euros were folded into the note and passed over. Hati pouted as the waiter checked the tip ignoring her new jewellery.

"I have a wonderful idea darling, look a shop dedicated to bikinis, imagine our favourite beach, *Tahiti plage,* I haven't bought a new bikini in years."

Her manicured hands presented a magazine showing a shop window full of large breasted models in very skimpy beachwear. This suggestion for another day of shopping failed to impress the lazy lawyer, after managing to wobble out of bed, grab a coffee cup and a bowl of cereal, it was clear, the thought of another day on the streets of Paris did little for him.

"We have to get back, I need to check with the bank, some of this money needs to be invested, make it grow, not only spend it." The positive smile fell away as Hati realised this brief holiday was drawing to a close. Her last resort, a change of tack.

"Let's change your old watch, I saw you lingering by the Rolex window." His head was already shaking. Hati slipped her bathrobe off as she slammed the bathroom door.

Perroquet hit the concierge button on the phone pad.

"Can you get us two seats on the first departure to Marseille tomorrow morning?"

Jack had never been a driver who obeyed the speeding limits; today he was pushing his luck. The turn off to Aix-les-Bains shot by at 160, as he climbed the hill Arno's number lit up on his car screen.

"Waiting for you, all quiet here, where are you?"

"Around twenty minutes away, seen my boys?"

"They're in the gym with Dan."

Jack breathed a sigh of relief.

"Is Eva in?"

"Jack it's me, we are ALL waiting for you."

"See you." Jack touched the screen and swore at an Audi driver.

Jack's son Nick waited in the garage.

"Dad you come back from a meeting to go straight into another one."

"Sorry bud, promise we will go away soon." Jack wondered how much more hollow he could sound; a trip north was the next voyage for him.

Arno's door was open, but silence filled the apartment. The faces that greeted Jack sent a clear message. No one welcomed the messenger, he had to speak first.

"Look I don't want to worry you all, but just had lunch with a well-connected Notary business contact."

"You mean those guys who can access more crap about you than your bank manager?" Dan threw a sarcastic *told you so* glance to his neighbours.

"Yeah, those guys." Conceded Jack.

"Guess what, Crappy had a brother." Eva looked sour and Boris stopped tapping his iPad.

"He came out of jail earlier this year, inherited a pile of money, no doubt what his brother stole from Lasalle, plus that handsome yacht. He could be looking for revenge, who killed his brother, or he may be targeting a lawyer in

104

Marseille, the street talk is that the lawyer stole a big chunk of what Crappy was supposed to inherit."

"Fuck a princess. Sorry ladies" Arno apologised, "So, the new axe above our heads is, will some jailbird decide to come after us, or if we get lucky a scum bag lawyer gets it first?"

"That's exactly the way it looks, again sorry, I had to tell this in person." Jack was still standing.

Several conversations had started in the room, just quick simple comments, the theme all the same, "How long have we got before he turns up here?"

Within half an hour, the neighbours had returned to their own homes. The logistics of hitting a senior minister in Paris, or being confronted by an ex-con with a penchant for violence plagued all of the Chateau resident's minds. The wine cellar along with the sleeping pills started to look a little depleted.

Chapter 12

Hati ignored the poorly parked Toyota Land Cruiser; it was crudely slotted into a tight row of cars roughly fifty meters from the office entrance. The two men inside exchanged a quick glance of recognition as her heals clicked along the pavement. She was not at all happy to be back in Marseille. Paris, Dubai even the airports smelt better than the back streets of her hometown.

The office files were still piled high, the promise of 'a quick tidy up', from her boyfriend's colleague had not materialised, but she was glad to see such a small stack of mail on her desk. An SMS from her lover promised *maximum 20 minutes,* she felt depressed to be back, so began conjuring up ideas for the coming weekend, Pierre would give in as soon as she stroked her blouse open, her large nipples always reduced him to putty.

The black BMW turned into the ramp descent as the flashing light confirmed the electronic door was lifting. Crappy raised his head, so did Claude, the thick black hair of a well-known Marseille lawyer recognised by the Toyota driver.

"Give him ten or fifteen minutes, then we go in." Claude nodded as he quenched his dry mouth from the plastic bottle, it didn't help, his lips felt like sandpaper.

Perroquet climbed the steps from the car park with enthusiasm, a couple of hours in the office, and then onto a boozy lunch with his friend Luke from Marseille Trust, the promise of, "Investment funds that outperform all others in their class," appealed to him. He was sure the moaning clients of his legal practice would soon be a problem of the past. He was humming to *Coldplay.*

"Hi," was the best Hati could manage; her displeasure at being back, plain and obvious.

As the door buzzer sounded, she hit entry without bothering to ask who was there.

She tapped her nails on the table, showing boredom and staring towards the door, a quick recall of the warm Gulf waters drifted through her mind.

The footsteps sounded quick and familiar, the smiling post lady did little for Hati's mood.

"Welcome back, see you did some shopping." Hati managed a weak smile as she generously bowed towards her right wrist.

"Not much today, left a big pile a few days ago." The disinterested lady stretched her back in surprise at the post lady's comment.

"Not here, must have been another office, three letters on my desk, that's it."

"Check again, left them against your office door, anyway sorry, busy day."

As the post lady eased through the door she paused, turned and popped her head back around.

"You know, I wonder what makes you do this job, last time I came in, a monster of a man arrived, could hardly fit through the door, he looked like an assassin from a scary movie, and the smell! I'd be terrified of dealing with types like that. *Bonne Journée.*"

Perroquet stared out of his office window, he heard the whole conversation, Hati had no idea what to say; the trip to Dubai flashed through both of their minds, maybe the bank director should have held onto the deposit.

"Do you think it was him?" asked Hati with a quiver in her voice. She saw Perroquet shaking his head in disbelief but he said nothing. He could feel his heart-rate increasing. For five full minutes, they both remained silent and played the same scenario over and over, fingernails were chewed with eyes enlarged like never before.

The second-by-second vibrations from footsteps on the stairs caused the lawyer to stand, his legs started to shake. Hati displayed a look or terror; she stared at the brass handle as it vibrated, then the vibration got stronger.

The door was smashed open with such force that files slid from Hati's desk, she turned her head away in the hope she could avoid eye contact with the monster walking in. Her left arm was taken with such force that she was instantly dragged across the table, as her best effort at resistance failed; she placed her right hand forward to steady herself.

"That looks new and really fucking shiny, paid for with my money, YEAH?"

Perroquet stood in his doorway, both hands shaking, fiddling with his shirt buttons.

"Please don't hurt her; we've done nothing wrong; I can explain."

Crappy let the terrified girl slide back across her desk as Claude almost hyperventilated on the last stair outside the office door.

"Your post lady is as stupid as you, I read your mail, you've been to Dubai to steal my money."

Hati backed away from the desk attempting to put the maximum space between her and Crappy, she saw the lawyer sweating profusely, his eyes displayed a sure and clear image of pending horror.

"Explain now, it better be good, I need my money." Crappy's eyes confirmed he could kill at any moment, his head moving left and right between his prey.

"We went to Dubai for my business, nothing to do with your bank account." Perroquet looked at Hati for the usual support; her shaking head confirmed she lost that talent a few seconds ago.

"Then why does my bank send letters to you, and not me?" Claude wondered why he choose this path, the bar job never turned out this nasty.

"My fault, I was confused where to send your mail, I hoped to see you so this could be arranged." Perroquet was clutching at straws, and Crappy knew it.

"Last time I ask, where is my money?"

"It's safe in the bank, we can check if you want." The lawyer was playing for time, hoping somebody in the building heard their plight.

"You're a dirty little fucking liar, like all your legal friends, now sit at your desk and call your friend Luke, at Marseille Trust, let me hear it."

Perroquet was amazed how much the monster knew, but Luke would not understand his situation, the speaker phone would seal his fate, his heart-rate was now causing him breathing problems.

"Look let the girl go, we can sort this out."

Crappy was clenching his teeth staring at the ground; he produced the silver box from under his jacked and launched it at Perroquet's head.

The empty box crashed onto the parquet floor, Hati tried to scream, but only a whimper came out.

The lawyer's right eye and nose had been cut open by the box, the blood dripped in large spots onto his tie and blue silk shirt. Before he could gather himself and focus from his left eye, Crappy had pushed his desk hard up against his chest. Hati now sat in the far corner like a punished child who disobeyed the teacher, she sobbed with her head between her knees. Claude chose to remain outside the office. Crappy produced a ball of wire from his pocket; he grabbed the lawyer's desk with his left hand, shoved it across the room, and pulled the bloodstained tie up and then made a swift right turn. Perroquet twisted like a broken toy, his back now towards Crappy. Without resistance his hands were pulled together, four turns with the wire feeling tighter every time caused him to cry in pain. Crappy moaned like a lion waking up.

"I'm gonna get my money, the box is empty."

The desperate whimpering of Hati continued, her lost voice confirming she could offer no help at all.

Within seconds, Crappy was standing over her.

"No please, your money is here, we can get it." The voice so weak, Crappy ignored her offer.

She too screeched in agony as the wire was turned around her wrists.

"Claude, I'm taking their car, they go in the boot, my yacht is the best place for these criminals."

Claude knew his service would be required; he just hoped to get away without touching the victims.

"Please think this out, they will die in the car boot, its summer, the harbour is full now, it's too busy."

Claude's head was resting against the door but he still refused to enter.

Crappy considered the logic from his partner.

"Ok we stay here today, take them tonight when it's dark."

Three more agile minds considered a day in the cramped office, bound, and one person already bleeding. The ex-con only thought about when his money would be returned.

After three hours, the air conditioning was battling to keep up with the Marseille summer heat. Colleagues in the building had passed the closed door, but the silence inside caused them to walk on without interest. The plastic tape over the mouths of Hati and Perroquet looked dirty, the monsters constant pressing, and the odour from his hands made Hati nearly vomit. The cuts on the lawyer's face had cauterised. He relaxed his head against a cupboard, his suit ruined with blood spots. The slightest noise caused the lunatic to lift his hand in threat of a chop. Claude shook as he attempted to make coffee, longing to return to his job at the hotel.

A brief phone message from Luke Dardain at Marseille Trust caused the whole room to focus, and caused Crappy to kick the leg of Perroquet as he checked the wire handcuffs. The mobile of both Perroquet and Hati were passed over to Claude, "make the things silent, no noise."

"See, lying little bastard, he wants to spend my money like you." Said Crappy.

The faces of the onetime happy lovers tilted forward facing the ground, too afraid to make eye contact. They both considered how they would make it through this day, blocking out the threat of being stowed on the yacht, that thought was just too frightening to consider.

Claude was dispatched to bring water. He asked himself how he could escape this nightmare as he stood in a line of lunchtime buyers. They appeared happy enjoying the work break, he looked ashen. The cheerful girl wondered why his hand shook as he offered the ten euro bill. She put it down to a probable user and greeted the next customer. The street was busy, so nobody took much notice as Claude slipped the key into the large oak door. Back in the office Crappy was standing close to Hati, she was crying. Something happened in the ten minutes he was away, but he dare not ask what.

The afternoon went on forever and as the sleepy Crappy fell in and out of brief slumbers. Claude pulled the tape off the victim's mouths, he lifted his forefinger to his lips almost praying they would remain silent, the blinks of appreciation thanked him for the good deed.

Contemplating another eight to nine hours together in a warm office, sitting on the floor, and needing a pee break soon Perroquet whispered to himself, it was nothing of value, but it helped his confidence and occupied his mind. His whole life became ruined this day, practising lines, offers of getting the money for his assailant, anything to get away with his and Hati's life was the best hope.

His paperwork pushing life has never called for violence, he realised his pathetic body was no match for a giant who lived for physical confrontation; he was as helpless as the day he was born. His lover sat in another room; he heard her soft murmurs. Why did he not keep the cash in the silver box, which would have been ample? Stealing the Dubai account was a poorly calculated idea, he called himself stupid at least thirty times in his mind, becoming a lawyer should have been a ticket to wealth, not sitting in blood-stained clothes on an office floor; Hati's voice caused him to lift his head.

"Please don't harm us; we are claustrophobic, not in a car boot, please."

Crappy eased himself off Hati's office chair bending over towards her.

"You're what?"

"We both suffer from claustrophobia, we will die, really."

Crappy had no idea what this word meant, so considered it a weak ploy to confuse him.

"Don't steal people's money, that's why you have class, whatever the fuck it is."

Claude knew it would be a waste to explain this condition.

The office prisoners were dozing, the heat and stress, lack of food made them feel weak. But the man sitting on the secretary's chair looked possessed, like a crazed and desperate street mugger. He ordered Claude to check the car boot, "Make sure it's empty, we take them down when this place is quiet."

Claude hoped he could avoid contact with other workers in the small office building; he did, but could not understand why he returned to the smelly office. The pleasure of Hati's perfume long gone.

The stench of urine woke the lawyer, he realised he was sitting in his own excrement, *could this day get any worse*, he considered to himself. As the evening sky turned darker Crappy became agitated. No activity had been heard on the other floors for over two hours.

"Claude we're going, you hold the doors open, and I'll bring these two, move it."

The stairs sounded like they could collapse at any second, the sweaty hands of Crappy held the prisoners by their collars, his body stench caused Hati to almost choke, her coughing lasted from the office to the car park.

"Please, I can't take this." The once beautiful girl shook with fear.

Claude placed himself between the car boot and the rear door, he almost willed Crappy to let the girl sit on the back seat.

"You in there." With one turn of his right arm, the monster threw the lawyer into the car boot, the thud confirmed he received yet more damage to his fragile head.

"No, he can't take it."

"Shut it, last time I tell you." Crappy pushed Hati's neck violently towards the cars back seat, slammed the door and crashed his large hand on the boot lid, the clunk echoed around the empty garage.

"You drive, I'll sit in the back next to her, get us close to the yacht, they know me at the port, tell them we need to unload some stuff, make it work."

Claude drove as best he could, but could not help being disgusted with his actions; he had no hunger despite the last meal being some fifteen hours earlier, and his hands felt as dirty as his bosses. He quickly decided if things went wrong at the port he would run for it, not caring if his heart gave in, or even his legs, just keep running away from this torture, never to be seen again in Marseille.

The lawyer woke first, his eyes were still running, his nose dry, a strong chemical smell filled his burning nostrils. He turned his head to see Hati opening her swollen eyes, moving closer to her the chemical smell became stronger, she shook her aching head. They both recalled the rag pushed into their faces before they lost consciousness.

The mattress felt firm, as they both tried to focus, looking left and right. Through a small round window, a blurred image of ropes and dark blue buoys gently rose and fell, it quickly became clear they were now the unwelcome guests on a luxury craft somewhere in the port of Marseille.

Chapter 13

Several ambitious, well-presented men did their best to make eye contact with the stunning lady in first class; her head remained bowed, she was clearly having none of it. The train was moving at top speed towards Paris, most seats were full, but nobody dared to occupy the vacant seat next to Eva Critin. Her full concentration was devoted to an exchange of mails between her tablet and Jack rafter's mobile.

Like I said many times, don't take too much risk, set it up for us, Boris tells me he may have the perfect solution, we are ready when you need us. Jack read the message to Dan, Arno and Boris who all nodded in agreement, he then hit send.

Eva's face had interested men from all over the world; she had that special, rarely seen perfect formation, large piercing green eyes, cute nose, lips large enough to hold a man's attention to the point of embarrassment, a smile that dropped jaws and hinted at sexual desire, and a confident voice that purred from a long elegant neck. Her hands matched the package as she delicately typed her message.

Don't worry guys, this is what I do, remember? But please give me space, this has to be faultless, if he suspects, sniffs anything wrong, we may never meet again, serious but true. A large hug to all at the Chateau, I will be in touch, Eva.

Jack read with seriousness in his voice, the guys in the room took in the reality of Eva's mission knowing their call to duty would arrive sooner than expected.

Gare de Lyon was busy. Eva disliked such populated places; Chambéry was calm compared to this metropolis. Parties of summer tourists speaking rapidly in Italian and Spanish caused her to weave left and right, her wheeled suitcase clipping their rudely piled backpacks. She breathed a sigh of relief walking out of the building. The east of Paris was not famous for its clean air, but outside smelt better than inside. Glancing up at the clock tower; it reminded her of the trips to London walking under Big Ben. Surprisingly, for a Parisian taxi driver, the young man jumped out of his car and gently placed Eva's case in the boot. He stared at his passenger thankfully, clearly happy that she outpaced the fat Chinese couple also heading for his cab.

"No tours, I know Paris better than you, Boulevard Haussmann, the Marriott Opera."

The driver knew this was no simple secretary so obeyed with a quick, "ok," in the mirror.

Eva's mind was alternating between confidence and doubt. She had always operated on her own instincts, men constantly offered advice but she never took it. Her decision to stay single confused the many admirers who enjoyed the occasional lunch or dinner. Her guard never truly let down. As too familiar streets and buildings passed, she wished life had turned out simpler. The evening *apero* at the minister's apartment then a cosy dinner was not her perfect date. Babysitting four screaming children would be more appealing.

The Marriott appeared on the left to Eva's surprise, the journey faster than she expected. In no time, the porter hauled her single case from the trunk, the driver was told to, "Keep the change." Her entry caused the usual lapses in conversation around the hotel lobby. Within ten minutes, Eva was in her room and staring out at the tourists on Boulevard Haussmann, she now had to kill five hours before the mission commenced, and the only people she loved and trusted were now five hundred kilometres away.

"Don't piss us around Boris; we're all in this together, what's up your sleeve?" Jack's attempt at a French shrug was not convincing, causing Dan and Arno to shake their heads a little in obvious amusement.

"I'll tell you all when I know it's definite, still waiting to hear from an old school chum. I went for the tech world; he joined a pharmaceutical lab in Rotterdam."

"What the hell, a lab rat? No room for baggage on this trip man, this is our baby." Said Dan with a look of derision.

"It's a long shot, but if it works…our lives will be much easier."

Boris had certainly stirred up a great deal of interest in his mysterious contact, so the guys decided to give him space, after all his performance last year saved all of their necks.

Eva's face was serious as she inspected her choice of clothing. A dark grey blouse, the buttons spaced well enough to keep a man's interest. Black skirt, short enough to exercise a man's eyes, mandatory high heels, subtle red lipstick, and hair formed into a tidy tail. Should the evening require, she could release her hair followed by a gentle shaking of the head, for this, the minister would certainly become crude and commence his usual suggestions, "Shall we leave soon for a nightcap on my balcony overlooking avenue Foch," or, "any underwear I have to get excited about Eva?" She could already hear his dirty laugh.

The small flick-knife was tucked deep into the Gucci bag; Eva grabbed her plastic key and left the room.

The taxi ride to avenue Foch took forever, meeting at six for drinks navigating Paris traffic gave Eva too much time to think. Cruising up the Champs Elysées brought back memories of her time in the service, every meeting-mission called for a trip up or down this infernally busy road, and here she was again.

Little had changed in the minister's elegant building; the floors were polished to perfection requiring careful navigation for Eva's heels. The lift carried a strong almost overpowering reek of perfume, far too much for Eva's discreet use, she realised the Saudi family; owners of the whole fifth floor were in residence. As was normal for the elite club of senior ministers, no names or identity showed up on the plate next to the door buzzer. Eva checked her appearance in the hallway mirror; she looked flawless, she sighed a small yet sad 'umm' asking why the man on the other side of the door could not be her dream, instead of her dilemma.

It took exceptional effort to create a genuine smile as the door opened, but Eva pulled it off.

"Why do we always leave it so long my beauty?"

Look in the mirror; check your breath, thought Eva.

"I have no idea Pascal, time passes so quickly, we should not leave it so long from now on." Eva swallowed hard and forced the smile to stay in place as she entered the apartment.

The decoration had not changed, gaudy paintings, mostly nudes in crude poses, covered the lounge walls. Greek statues, in a selection of awkward sporting poses took up space on the marble tables, and the trophy wall still exhibited pictures of the minister posing with a dead rhino, plus pictures of his ugly children at the same hunt, two hefty girls and a lost looking boy, no doubt confused as to why his father killed such a magnificent beast and appeared so proud of his actions.

Eva felt his hand stroke her back, now the smile failed.

"I am so dry Pascal, oh for a glass of champagne."

"Have a bottle chilled in the kitchen, sit down darling, I'll bring it." The sound of dreary classic music started up, "truly no idea," whispered the minister's date.

Eva eased onto a single seat, doing the best to cover her toned legs with a small amount of material.

She heard the rattle of ice-cubes in the bucket before the minister appeared at the door, as he smiled, she noticed his teeth had been whitened; his once reserved smile now a brasher dazzle of tiny sparklers.

"I booked our favourite place, corner table overlooking the Seine; it's one of the few places I can use these days, security."

"Yes, tell me more Pascal, not easy to read about you in the press these days, one can only guess you've moved back into our old business?"

"A new position really, I'm responsible for internal security, but all angles, banks, terrorist transfers, this sort of thing, but they keep me rather undercover, for the obvious reasons."

My god thought Eva, how can I break this to the guys back at the Chateau.

She resisted the offers to sit closer, deciding the hard-to-get act would most likely produce better results.

After twenty minutes of small talk, the driver called to inform the minister that his car was ready and waiting.

The staff at restaurant *Bords de Seine* greeted the minister with a large dose of arse licking, so much so that Eva almost lost her appetite. The man was enjoying his popularity, especially the over-the-top references to his, 'Healthy look' and, 'always arriving with such stunning partners', this made Eva long for the company of the guys back at the Chateau. They were real men, tall, handsome, physical, simply the opposite of her rotund date this evening.

Drinks were poured, napkins placed, and Eva knew some ground had to be covered.

"Tell me more Pascal, the men I live with, what do you want from them?"

"Well, my Eva, a direct question, let's say at this stage the possible disappearance of a very irritating banker, an American, he's dirty, but has friends in high places, so I have to remain distant from this."

Eva took an unusually large gulp of champagne trying to work out her next question.

"Any idea when?"

"No."

"Where?"

"Again, no."

"I have to work on them, motivate them, which could be difficult."

"Eva," the minister again displayed his new dentistry, "Getting men to do what you want, come on, that's the easy bit." Eva bowed her head towards the decorative plate.

The chicken was tender, salad dressing light and slightly spicy, but the small potatoes were ignored. Her companion cleared his plate whilst talking about 'sexually interesting' travels of late, Eva's thoughts wandered.

The constant grovelling of waiters, plus the occasional friend sucking up to the minister told Eva that full attention was missing, so she released her hair with a gentle sway of the head, now his body language changed, head to one side. His mind became focused.

"Two more glasses of the best champagne." The waiter raised his eye brows at the clicking fingers.

"How long are you in Paris, Eva? I would love to show you my new office, maybe tomorrow, introduce my secretary, although she's no measure of your beauty."

Yes and no went through her mind; the office visit? yes, the night? no.

The next hour passed with ease. A beautiful lady from Chambéry tantalising with her blouse buttons, touching the man's hand, pouting her lips to the best effect and most importantly keeping the best champagne in the restaurant flowing. The memorable bleary eyes now showing as the minister sank a little in his seat. Now more smug, but alcohol was taking over. He became garrulous with mentions of, "How he could now take people's lives away with a simple phone call." Eva gave polite nods at the right time. Suddenly he realised the lady seated opposite no longer worked for him.

"I have more of this at home, shall we…"

"Only if we see Paris at night from the balcony? Chambéry does not compare, I insist." The nod of agreement was a little wobbly which caused Eva to feel more confident, he was on his way and would most likely pass out before Eva had to endure his dirty intentions.

The driver stared more in the rear-view mirror than the windscreen on the short journey back to avenue Foch, Eva took his attention, seeing the minister in this state was a regular nightly occurrence, but this lady had much more class than the hookers and lost divorcees who for some strange reason succumbed to the man's charms.

Eva resisted several attempts to fondle her breasts, touch her thighs, promising another glass of champagne would make her feel, "excited."

Resting his back against the lift mirror the minister suddenly spoke with a fair degree of soberness, "Why are you in Paris darling? The last time you left me without saying goodbye, no call for weeks, now you want to see me for dinner, out of the blue."

Eva felt a chill of doubt, why this question?

"I did work in Paris, remember Pascal? And still have a wide range of shared friends; we always have so much to catch up on."

The minister's moment of interrogation left as quickly as it came, his eyes struggling to read the digital floor announcement, and then looking back to Eva for confirmation they would not be confronted with the Saudi security guards.

It was eleven thirty and yet another bottle of quality champagne was almost drained. Paris by night was a vision. The lasers from the Eiffel Tower holding Eva's attention as she shot quick glances to her drooping date. His eyes were more closed than open. All Eva wanted was tomorrow's office visit, access the way so her team could get in and out, check the level of security, the secretary, build a clear picture, maybe even if lucky, spot his computer password, that would make Boris a happy man and save a wasted, maybe unavailable, half hour to hack in.

The groping arm around Eva's right breast caused her to panic a little, the man still had some energy, she had hoped he was running on empty by now.

"Shame to waste this vintage, the more I drink the more I get turned on."

The well-chosen words worked, the man threw his head back as he drained his flute.

"Now to bed." Was said with little conviction as he banged his glass on the table. Eva held his hand as he almost tripped over the balcony door frame.

The bedroom decoration was possibly worse than the lounge. The red bed cover from another age, slippers neatly placed underneath. A book of French poetry on the bedside table next to thick reading glasses. The walls covered by an almost carpet like layer of light grey paper.

"You jump into bed, I'll do girl things in the bathroom, be with you in minutes."

Eva waited a good ten minutes before she heard the reassuring sound of a drunken man snoring.

She tip-toed through the room, dimmed the lights and slipped onto the balcony. The night lights of Paris were still magical; she emptied her half glass into the flower box and took out her phone;

Hi Jack, enjoying Paris by night, alone at this moment. If all goes to plan, I will get into his office tomorrow, get all the detail I can; must go in case he wakes up, more tomorrow, Eva.

Jack read the message in bed, knowing the ping of a reply would be too dangerous at this time of night.

Chapter 14

The noises above their heads were unfamiliar to Hati and Pierre Perroquet. They wanted to scream for help, but fear of the unknown and further violence from their monster captor restrained this urge.

The tiny round window confirmed the craft was beginning to move, the white yacht slipped out of sight, now images of blue sky and the occasional mast came and went. The chemical smell had now been replaced by body odour. Congealed blood on the lawyer's head made him look more like a homeless person, instead of the once tidy man from the legal profession. Hati wriggled trying to release her hands which only increased the pain.

"My hands are dead, I can feel something like liquid on them, you the same?"

Her companion gave a nervous jerk of his head, "It's blood, the wire is cutting into us."

"Why is this happening to us? Our life was ok before this lunatic came along, let's give him the money and live on." Hati turned on the bed, her eyes asking for help.

"I'm trying to find a way out, he's stupid, some angle, there must be a way." The lawyer's words did nothing to comfort Hati.

Claude watched Crappy at the controls; this was a disaster waiting to happen. The Predator narrowly missed scrapping a sailing yacht's bow; it weaved excessively right and left with over-steer. His large hand rested on the power lever, one slight pull and Claude would jump overboard. Somehow, they reached the harbour entrance. Children on the high stone wall called to the yachts captain, hoping for a wave from the bizarre looking person who appeared nothing like a sailor. The power lever was pulled surprisingly gently, the Predator majestically lifted in the surf; the engines purred confirming a great deal more power was on tap if needed.

The cold stare from Crappy told Claude that the guests below could expect further pain any moment.

The five hundred euros in Claude's back pocket gave him little comfort, silence money thrown at him last night after the victims were safely locked away. He now realised the higher the gift, the more skewered his life became. A flashback to the day he met up with Crappy in the port caused him to swear aloud, "You dumb shit," he said it twice to reconfirm his misery.

"You take over, keep going straight, don't want any other boats around, got it?" As Crappy eased off the captain's chair he took a small note from his pocket, Claude knew this was the code for the door below. He wondered how much more blood he would see today.

The beep sounded four times, and then the door opened silently. The sight of Crappy caused a sharp intake of breath from both bodies lying awkwardly on the bed.

"Enjoy the night?" asked Crappy without a hint of sincerity.

"What do you want us to do? Please say, can we use our hands, they're bleeding." Hati spoke but Perroquet remained silent.

"I'm gonna let you enjoy some sea air, nice, when I think how you treated me."

The prisoners showed little confidence in the lunatic's offer.

He pulled the lawyer's shirt, lifting him in one movement off the bed. Hati managed to manoeuvre her legs to one side doing all she could to block the man's touch. As she stood her head felt dizzy, the lack of food and water caused her to slip, she bounced off the side wall causing Crappy to grunt, the movement of the craft did little to help her balance. Perroquet was still being held tight as Hati edged along the bedroom wall.

"Move out and up the stairs." Crappy pushed his two captors as if they were cattle leaving the barn.

Claude turned nervously, his attention switching between a passing sail yacht and the sad dejected couple staggering up the stairs; Perroquet missed the last step, he stumbled next to Claude again hitting his face on the deck. Hati cried and the monster behind her sniggered.

"I promised you fresh air, now sit against the side here, I don't want you seen by anything passing."

"Can we please use our hands, they are bleeding, it hurts so much." Hati's plea caused Claude to mouth something with his lips. Crappy took a worn pair of pliers from his jeans pocket and bent forward between his prisoners.

"If you dare to fuck with me, do anything stupid, I'll tie it around your necks and throw you over, got it?"

The relief of the wire being cut caused a weak sigh from the dejected looking lady; she slid against her boyfriend who was trying his best to bring life back to his blooded hands.

"I hear the current is strong out here, can you swim?" The ex-con smiled as he stared at Hati's slender legs.

"No, not really good, why?" Perroquet asked but knew their lives were on hold until the money was returned.

"Because if my money is not back with me tomorrow, the next time you two bastards see land will be when you're washed up on the beach." Claude stared at their hands both moving as if life would never return, the faces tired and sunken. In the space of one day, they had travelled from the position of beautiful people to lost desperate pawns, and the person who would decide their fate cared little about human emotions.

"What do you want us to do?" The lawyer's voice as weak as his shaking legs.

"You're a lawyer, you do dirty sneaky things, seen it all my life, you call your friend at the bank and get my cash, and I want cash, get it."

"I don't know if he can do this so quickly."

"Then get ready to taste salt water."

"Ok I'll do it; I need a phone." The lawyer felt so weak he was caving in, but Hati supported this offer with a small shake of her head.

Claude reflected on the current news runs where the police examined phone records to put crimes together, so declined to offer his mobile concentrating on the controls instead.

Crappy slid his greasy hand into his back pocket and gave his mobile to Perroquet.

"I wanna hear this."

His bloodstained hands shook as he held the phone, placed it on his upper leg and tapped in the number for Marseille Trust. After three buzzes, a lady answered.

"This is Pierre Perroquet, put Luke on please."

Her voice was full of doubt, "Mr Perroquet what happened? We were waiting for you, the meeting."

"Just put Luke on."

Within seconds, the familiar voice came on, but it sounded anxious.

"What the hell, I came to your office, did something happen? I saw blood on the floor, Hati's desk, what a mess, where are you?"

"Just do what I tell you, we have a big problem, I mean a very serious one. I need all of the money in cash, you must help me, I need it immediately."

Luke could hear the sound of seagulls, wind, he tried hard to imagine what sort mess his friend could have landed in.

"It's not easy to get that sort of cash ready quickly, I mean millions, how can I…"

Crappy caught snatches of the conversation, the waves lapping against the Predator made it difficult to hear all; he bent over close towards the small screen.

"Get the cash ready now, the girl will pick it up. If I don't have my money by the end of tomorrow Marseille will say goodbye to one of its famous lawyers, and his bitch helper. Call your friend on his mobile when it's ready, get it?"

"I'll do my best, sorry Pierre can …" Crappy cut the conversation off with a touch of his thumb.

The coastline was now a distant blur; other craft passed, but always a safe distance away. The bobbing motion caused a sick feeling for Hati, who had only drunk water in the last twenty-four hours, food, when your life was held in the balance lost its attraction.

"You two are going back to the room, you better hope your friend gets my cash."

Both were surprised when the monster forgot to tie their hands. The four beeps confirming the door was locked again made them relax, but they had no idea why.

Claude was pacing around a small circle at the back of the main deck when Crappy came up the stairs. The shaking of his large fat head made the young barman uncomfortable.

"And now?" Enquired Claude, gingerly.

"Why did you lie? You said my money was safe in Dubai."

Claude glanced at the swell of the waves; jumping was not an option.

The back of the boat suddenly got a lot smaller as Crappy moved closer and looked down on Claude menacingly.

"Maybe I made a mistake, I'm a barman not a business man, I tried my best to help."

"I've paid you a lot of money since we met, I told you that day, I don't like complications, now look at the mess!"

The slap from the right hand caught Claude unaware; he was too busy thinking about his next excuse.

He tripped over the chrome divide and fell towards the salon table. The sound of him hitting the wooden deck made the prisoners below jump in shock; they listened expecting a further thud.

"I gave you a new job, paid you tax free with my fucking cash, now you sit on my yacht like a little bird, scared to help me."

Claude was dazed, he knew this might happen one day but never truly expected it. The motion caused him to fall back, his head bumping on the chrome support of the captain's seat. A hazy image of the Sunseeker logo took his attention. A tiny drip of blood from his lower lip changed colour as it landed on the teak deck.

"You let me down one more time; I swear I'll kill you fucking rat."

The prisoner's one floor below heard every word. Perroquet considered whether Claude could become an aid, Hati was thinking the same thought. For the rest of the afternoon, the monster's helper kept the craft turning in large circles, but land always in sight. Crappy came and went from his master cabin, the smell of alcohol stronger every time he passed. By six fifteen, Claude was asked, over politely to, "Take us back to the port, but slowly,"

The cries from below confirmed the couple were again being restrained. Claude felt his swollen lip whilst wondering if the call would ever come from the banker, maybe he disappeared with the money?

The Predator was gently slotted into its mooring. Fortunately for Crappy, the owners to the left and right were rarely spotted in the port, seemed they were too old to sail now, and the kids only ever came two or three days a year. As the light fell away Claude received a fatherly pat on his back followed by a soft voice.

"Would you mind getting us some fast food, for them also, we all need to eat."

KFC was a busy place, kids were screaming, parents were fed up, all glowing from a day on the beach; Claude touched his lip constantly, more from embarrassment than anything else, he was a gentle creature and detested violence. He ordered the same menu for four people, extra fries to keep his boss happy, and munch on the way back. As he left the restaurant three Gendarmes passed at a snail's pace in front of him, should he, could he, three armed men could easily take Crappy who, as far as Claude knew, never carried a gun. One of the Gendarmes turned his head on Claude, he was too neat for a normal policeman, for sure a gay spotting a potential partner for the night. Try as he might no words came out, they sauntered past, and more crowds surrounded the confused young man. The Gendarme tried one last glance, it was wasted, Claude increased his pace, suddenly he saw the light, stay as the happy helper for now, if the funds arrive tomorrow, he could gain well, if not get out, move to another part of France, good barmen always found work, the yacht world certainly brought out the worst in people. As Claude stepped on board Crappy attempted to smile, a welcome to his young helper, his face asking if all is forgiven. Now Claude was the man with hatred in his eyes.

Chapter 15

Eva slipped out of bed keeping a towel wrapped around her torso, the drunken oaf, still suffering bouts of snoring, allowed her at best three to four hours of sleep, but her body was unsoiled. She turned on the coffee machine, performed a set of stretching exercises on the balcony and returned to hear the minister's alarm play a grating violin tune.

"Eva, you're still here, last night must have been good, yes my darling?"

The look that came back could only be delivered by a woman. He rubbed his forehead, thanked Eva for the coffee on his bedside table, and then tried to remember what actually happened before he fell asleep.

By eight thirty, they were both looking tidy and ready for work. Eva managed to avoid his suggestion of a "delayed start," making up a late morning meeting excuse with an old girlfriend in *Montmartre*.

The driver appeared amazed that the same lady he dropped off last night was still on talking terms with his superior, he had never witnessed this before. At least, ninety percent of the journey was filled with the minister on his mobile, nothing of real interest to Eva, mostly clarifications of today's meetings with his secretary.

Eva recalled the building being a dull colourless administration centre years ago when she was in the service of her country. Nothing much had changed except for the door security, they were younger, dark skinned and cocky. One attempted a deep voiced *Bonjour Madame,* which Eva totally ignored thinking they would be no match for her men at the Chateau, the minister's mind fully occupied with his agenda.

The workers on the fourth floor greeted their chief with courtesy; they were a serious bunch, reasonably well dressed for the paperwork pushing types. None of the ladies matched Eva's height or natural beauty. The hum of jealous gossip followed her along the corridor.

The minister's false charm from the night before had long been forgotten, he now pushed his office door open, walked in front of Eva and barked at his secretary.

"I told you I may be late; you changed the early meetings, I hope? Oh, this is Eva, former Sûreté, in Paris for a couple of days, don't worry she's secure."

Marine had a solid handshake, Eva judged her to be in the early fifties, certainly took care of herself. The glasses were chosen with care, they suited her small face perfectly giving her a look of confidence. Her blonde hair well cared for. For sure, she was single.

The minister was already in his room and on the phone.

Eva accepted the offer of coffee which gave her time to evaluate her surroundings. Somebody loved office plants; both the secretary's room and the ministers were ordained with many exotic varieties. The first door to enter the secretary's room and minister's door were old, the handles worn and creaky, not a problem for her Chateau team.

Marine did her best to small talk Eva, "Why did you leave a place like Paris for Chambéry? Do you miss the service? You look far too young to be retired, even for this country." The ladies chatted in a relaxed way leaving Eva hoping she would keep the job after a visit from her team. Entering the minister's office, Eva was met with frosty stare as if this was forbidden territory. The closer she moved towards him the more uncertain he appeared.

"Are you staying long? Thought you were meeting a friend."

"You invited me to visit your office, have you forgotten last night so quickly?"

The man was still baffled as to whether he performed or not.

"Sorry my darling," he rose from his chair and placed his arms around his old girlfriend.

Eva's response was much warmer than he could ever remember. She pressed her thighs against his, her nose rubbed against his cheek, she held him resisting his uncharacteristic efforts to pull away.

Marine politely pushed the door closed.

"Ok Pascal, you're a busy man, let's speak soon."

The peck on the cheek was rapid, the man collapsed into his chair, stunned at what just happened in his ministerial office.

"Ciao." Said Eva as she pushed the door open.

Marine managed a confused smile as she watched her impressive new contact leave the office.

As Eva quickened her pace towards the lift, she mentally repeated the access code for the minister's computer. Just as Boris had suggested, "these types often keep in under the keyboard."

How she actually pulled this off would bother her for the whole day.

The message arrived on Jack's mobile early afternoon. He was relieved that Eva made it through the night without damaging her pride. The script was short but clear, useful details about the minister's office would help Boris to prepare. A great deal had been achieved during the brief visit, and now he must update the guys.

Arno and Dan were found in the garage, both bending far into a Porsche engine bay. The moment Dan heard Jack's footsteps he dodged out of the car bonnet and gave Jack a look of relief.

"Really sweet looking at all this metal Arno, but for me as long as it starts and moves off, I'm happy," then he winked at Jack with a look of boredom.

Arno was still engrossed with Porsche design.

"Listen guys," said Jack with his usual serious stance, "Heard from Eva, typical undercover communication, but the way I read it, she has what we need to get into his files, time to start planning our visit to Paris."

Arno bit his lip whilst sliding his hand along the bonnet.

"Let's hope we can be as efficient as her, this whole thing keeps me up at night, and yeah I know we have to stop him, but I still really hope we are not jumping out of our league."

Several seconds of silence confirmed the men were all evaluating a daunting mission, one that was too vital to fail.

Jack shook his head in doubt, "Where the hell is Boris? Without his help, we just can't do this."

"Oh yeah, our Boris," said Arno, "see that old Volvo, well, a weird geeky looking guy arrived last night, stupid bloody east of Holland accent, I tried to speak with him but gave up, good that Boris arrived and rushed him to the apartment, he's up to something, but what…"

The confidence in Boris and his unusual methods caused zero doubt for his friends. He was a top tech specialist, whatever he was up to, it probably would benefit their mission.

Eva decided to stay in Paris for the next few days. One brief and slightly frosty coffee with her minister friend confirmed more of his plans and schedule. He liked to spend time away from his office duties. The mornings were his preference for *away meetings,* at which time his secretary took advantage and arrived late. The likely strategy would be for the Chateau team to arrive very early, before first light. The late workers during the evenings would cause problems; the night was too dangerous with lights and suspicious movement when the streets were empty. Delivers at the rear of the building started early, as did the garbage collectors. Several access points were utilised and most appeared to be via doors, without any appearance of security in place. Eva was forming a well-crafted mission for her men, and it was getting close to zero hour for their arrival in Paris.

Jack's wife Carly, showed amazement, "You're going to Paris to watch the European football tournament? I thought you all hated football, I always hear you saying how limp they are, falling for no reason, you're not serious!"

"Darling, it's business as well, you know I have clients there, Dan has never seen a soccer match, and Arno wants to keep us company." Jack hoped saying less was more convincing.

"Next thing you'll be telling me Boris wants to come as well." Jack shrugged, luckily his mobile killed off the conversation.

As Jack paced through the garden, fencing off a client who 'really' wanted to invest in, *the next Indian Amazon,* he noticed Boris patting the roof of his friend's Volvo, he shouted *"Bon voyage,"* as the car cruised away.

The two men casually walked towards one another; Jack noticed a mischievous look on the young Dutchman's face.

"Do me a favour Jack, stay away from my cave, I have bottles of something seriously special in there, and I don't mean wine, when we leave for Paris, best we go by car. Don't worry I think we have the perfect solution, fragile, but will do the job. Our target will become another of France's early retirees, but a disabled one!"

The bond between the two men was evident, causing Jack to narrow his eyes playfully towards Boris.

"One day, this will seem like a dream, I do hope it ends well."

Chapter 16

Marlon Crappy stared at the mobile phones on the Predator's salon table. It was 9:30, the sun was already strong. The prisoners in the guest cabin had been fed and allowed a bathroom visit, but no call had been received from the man at Marseille Trust. Claude had called the bar telling he was sick, making the simple calculation that Crappy would pay much more than his minimalist boss at the hotel. Soon he would have amassed a few thousand euros and if the time came to leave the lunatic, he could move on with a handsome profit. Hoping the money would arrive he doubted that Crappy could count in thousands, so what's the problem if a few wads go missing?

The morning dragged on, Claude busied himself cleaning the Predator windows and front deck, and this also allowed him to check out possible escape routes if things went wrong. His all too regular excuses to walk around the marine police building, "Check everything is calm," were missed by Crappy who was busy listening to his captives, his agitation, as usual, calmed by the vodka.

At exactly 11:46, cosmic played on Perroquet's mobile, it was the same number he called yesterday, so the monster spread his chest in anticipation. Claude stared at the phone like it could explode any second.

A massive sweaty finger moved over the *slide to receive;* he then lifted the phone to his ear.

"Hello, hello," the director of Marseille Trust sounded nervous.

"Do you have my money?"

"Can I speak with Pierre Perroquet?"

"No fucking way, where is my money?"

"Your money is here."

"Ok, I'm sending the girl to pick it up, don't ask her anything, just give the money and shut up, understand?"

The aggression in the voice led Luke Dardain to refrain from asking further questions.

"She's coming this afternoon, if anything goes wrong, I will be coming over, and you don't need that, I'll kill you in your own fucking bank."

Dardain gently placed his phone on the desk. He had a thousand questions to ask Hati but reasoned this may not be a good idea.

The bulging leather bag under his table had been delivered minutes ago by a local drug baron. His fees of one hundred thousand euros, for such an urgent need seemed reasonable, his choices were limited, banks these days could not produce such large amounts of cash, they were never asked in fact.

He hoped his friend would be released and the lunatic he had just spoken to would not see the loss.

The code awoke Hati, Perroquet already heard the steps coming down the stairs.

"You got ten minutes to look tidy, you're getting my money."

Crappy leered as Hati eased past him entering the bathroom. Her nervous system was shot, but if she refused, what could the monster be capable of next? Try as she might, her bruised wrists did not respond to the cold water, they were still swollen with the cuts just managing to hold together.

She missed the smell of quality perfume, tied her hair in a messy tail and opened the bathroom door.

Her boyfriend's eyes were trying to say something, but the fear of Crappy noticing caused her to gaze away.

"Claude, use my car, take her to the bank, and bring my money back. If you get any clever ideas, think again, you can either earn big from this or wait for me knocking on your door."

Claude had already made his decision.

The bright sun made Hati wince as she arrived on deck, the large designer shades purchased days before in Paris had disappeared. Her slender legs felt unsure as she squeezed past the belly of her captor, and again his odour made her hold her breath, four steps further the sea air reassured her. As she peered through narrow eyes Claude attempted a nervous smile. He was standing at the bottom of the rear steps car keys in hand, appearing eager to get off the boat. As Hati took his hand to steady herself for the large step onto the walkway she noticed the bruise on his left temple, there was no doubt in her mind who was responsible.

The walk to the car was brisk. Occasional laughter from yachts moored left and right agitated her, why are they so happy when her life is hanging on a thread. Claude wanted to talk, he wanted to talk so much, but what could he say?

"How are you feeling? Don't worry, all will be ok when he gets his money."

Eventually as the car left the port Hati turned to Claude.

"Why are you helping him?"

"Don't ask, just don't ask, ok?"

"He's a psycho; he could kill all of us." Her voice shook as she tried to gain Claude's interest.

"Do what you're told, and it will all be ok, now shut up."

Tears edged down the once beautiful face, she looked wrecked and wondered if she could produce the energy to carry this off, and obviously Claude was not going to waver.

The Marseille Trust building looked how Hati felt, grey, uncared for, one letter from the bank's nameplate had slipped, the stains on the wall told this happened some time ago. The joy of shopping, no limit, in Paris felt like a lifetime away, and Hati was convinced she would never see the beautiful city again.

Claude held her door open but she was reluctant to get out.

"Come on, let's do this." The cold tone of Claude did not help.

Pulling her blouse sleeves hard Hati attempted to hide the damage from the wire handcuffs, Claude noticed and showed a quick moment of concern, it passed in a second.

The receptionist clearly expected them, she pointed towards a door behind her desk struggling to make eye contact, they marched in as if no time could be wasted.

As Hati's head spun she walked close behind Claude and suddenly came face to face with Luke Dardain. The effect was like a mirror, confused, eyes lost and showing the result of little sleep. Dardain managed to speak.

"Something has gone very wrong, I imagine?"

Hati could only offer a single shake of her head.

"The police are capable of helping; they know what to do in situations like this." The bank manager was trying but knew it was in vain.

As Hati wiped a tear away she wondered if her boyfriend was suffering; Claude noticed the bulging leather bag next to the desk. Something told him this man was as bad as they come, his eyes moved too quickly, more like a pickpocket than a bank manager.

The paintings of historic buildings in Nice and Cannes did little to improve the office demeanour, it was purely a facade for a dirty money mover, and Claude wanted to get out as soon as he could.

"Look you know why we are here, just give us the bag and this is over, no more bloodshed."

Claude looked between the bag and Dardain, Hati kept her head low.

Reluctantly, Dardain lifted the bag and offered it to Claude. Hati asked herself why she had to do this, of course she thought, insurance, Claude might just run for it, she would return for her lover; Crappy was possibly acting stupid but under that veneer a calculating creep of a man terrified her.

No words were spoken on route to the Predator. Claude locked the car doors; Marseille had a vast selection of street robbers who would love to lift the valuable bag from the back seat before the driver could react. The port was busy since they left, many yachts and powerboats had come and gone. An old man with a neat pony-tail was playing a saxophone at the end of the Predators mooring row; he smiled cheekily with a quick gesture towards his wrinkled cap which was already showing a decent pile of small change. Even a quick wolf whistle from the instrument at Hati's perfect legs produced no reaction from the glum pair. As they stepped onto the Predator's rear deck some fifty meters away a New York accent grabbed the musician's attention, "Real good, always loved the sax." Four euros clinked into the hat.

The monster was wedged between the control screens and the captain's seat; he stared at the lost looking pair arriving on the rear deck, as they climbed up the stairs his eyes dropped onto the black leather bag, his expression remained midway between a madman and simple lost soul. There was no sign of Pierre Perroquet which concerned Hati, had anything happened to him whilst they were away?

"Claude, put the bag on the table, draw the cover over, it's windy, you bitch come with me." Crappy yanked her wrist.

The door code sounded faster each time, Perroquet sat up hoping like hell for some good news. Hati was pushed into the room; she collapsed like a child on the bed. Crappy was already thumping back up the stairs.

"Did you bring it back?" Perroquet asked gently.

"Yes darling, what else, you know you can count on me."

"What's he doing?" Even more sheepishly.

"Probably counting it."

"Oh my god, what if he discovers we…"

Claude zipped up the plastic cover which caused the outside world to cease, the bulging bag sat firmly in the middle of the table.

Crappy pulled the zip open with amazing gentleness, as his helper stretched his neck peering into the bag. Pile upon pile of crisp fifty euro bills sat in front of their eyes. The smell was difficult to discern, somewhere between burning paper and plastic, but strong. Crappy cast his mind back to the first time his hand delved into the silver box, that seemed so insignificant compared to this visual pleasure, he pushed the bag to the end of the table and began stacking neat piles next to one another. He was visually childlike as the piles grew, some notes displayed the archway covered with an orange hew, some showed the map of Europe, which Crappy smiled at, he recognised France.

He moved around the table as if protecting his kill, Claude stayed a respectable distance away.

When the bag was empty, he placed it under the table.

"Claude give them some water, here's the code." The man was shocked, one moment he was trusted to look upon millions of euros, the next faithful enough to know the prisoner's door code, as he passed the table he took in so many images of 50, he couldn't wait to come back to the salon.

It took several hours to count the piles of crisp paper, both men working at the same pace, surprisingly Crappy only drank water, the first time Claude had ever witnessed such sobriety in the man. But as the counting came to a close the monster's mood was flashing red, the signs were always the same, enlarged eyes, increased breathing rate, he was going downhill rapidly, so Claude eased back in his chair. Experience had taught him to react to these danger signs.

"It's less than six million here." Claude took more distance while still wondering as to how Crappy could count so high.

"I said it's less than six fucking million here."

Claude stood up and moved towards the plastic cover;

"I had seven million in Dubai, and one million in Oman, right?"

Suddenly the monster had become an accountant, like his brother, and Claude feared for his life.

The captives in the guestroom heard the anger above their heads, it was expected, they went crazy in Paris. Perroquet knew his friend at Marseille Trust would take a large share for commission which compounded the problem; and to make matters worse the lunatic above their guestroom could now count.

Claude watched Crappy slide pile after pile of notes back into the leather bag. The anger had turned to control, which bothered him. Even worse not one single bill had been gifted his way; he endangered his life for what? But now was not the appropriate time to discuss a fair share.

It was now well into the evening. The odd shriek of laughter could be heard from inebriated guests taking a late dinner on the yachts moored in the marina, but the Predator was like a morgue. Claude sat alone at the end of the bow, legs dangling over the edge, basically putting the maximum space between him and the boss. Something was going to happen, this was certain, but in what form, the level of violence? As always life on the crazy train. Flashes of Crappy through the upper deck windows showed a man pacing around; a bottle of vodka swigged crudely confirmed he was bothered. The sight of so many euro bills flashed through Claude's mind, the idiot would not miss the odd bundle, however the bag had left the deck, probably stowed somewhere in his cabin, considered Claude, and that was not a threshold worth crossing.

Hati's scream caused the young barman to freeze, it was quick but chilling, waiting for the same from Perroquet, Claude was petrified what to do next. He noticed a small shadow dancing on the side of the next yacht, it appeared to come from the small guest cabin porthole, it came and went quickly.

Rolling back towards the front deck mattress Claude peered into the cabin, nothing, so he walked cautiously along the port side knowing his choices were simple, see what was happening, do something to earn his money, or run for it now. The money won, he slid down the stairs, seeing the open door, Crappy's massive back filled the doorway, and then he heard whispering.

"I don't give a flying damn who took my money, you, the bank, the fucking fairies, but you two went to Dubai, and only to steal from me, so I blame you, simple or not?"

Over the monster's left shoulder Claude saw Hati with a large piece of black tape across her mouth.

Crappy flinched, hearing the arrival of his helper.

"At last, now you can tape him up, he's not saying anything useful anyway, do it."

Claude obeyed quickly, it was obvious both Hati and Perroquet had been hit in the face, and likely other parts of the body the way they cowered. The lawyer looked like his days were numbered, his eyes now sunken even deeper into his pale face, the blood from his wire handcuffs left stripes on the sheets. The look on Hati's face reminded Claude of a rape victim he once saw in backstreet Marseille. Several Moroccan youths had pounced on a mini skirted tourist; the muffled screams below his balcony brought him to the window. The only working streetlight caught her face as two of the gang lifted her skirt, she needed her parents, brother, sister anybody who loved her, but for this moment she was the loneliest girl in the world; He could never block that image from his dreams, it came back regularly, and now he was wide awake.

Crappy pushed Claude out of the guestroom, listened for the electronic click and shot his index finger towards the stairs.

Claude eagerly accepted the offer of, "A good drink."

The port security guard passed with his German Sheppard, the dog showed interest in the Predator, his wet nose moving up and down rapidly, but the tired guard could only think of his bed, the shift was over as soon as this walk ended, so the dog was pulled against his will. The monster was watching with his glass to his mouth, he let out a soft, "Ha," as the guard melted behind the row of yachts.

"I never thought helping you would go this way." Claude already downed half his glass.

"Things have never gone easy for me; my life has always been screwed; now yours too I guess."

This reality check hurt Claude; his stomach pulled like never before.

"Let's turn in now; I have to work something out." The young man had only slept on the yacht once before, his bosses' offer of another night frightened him, but the twenty crisp notes in his hand yet again supported greed above common sense.

Luke Dardain tried to call in the few favours he had left. The years of offers to hide drug money, open up accounts in the murky world of offshore centres, hide substantial funds under the name of a company had introduced him to one shady character after another, and not only in Marseille. His contacts stretched along the coast to Cannes, Nice, Monaco, and now the Russians were warming to his 'flexible' methods. Offers of a 'new and safe haven with benefits' fell on deaf ears, or maybe they just didn't trust him anymore. Pierre Perroquet had brought his share of dubious clients to Marseille Trust, so his business friend felt compelled to do something, but without support from some form of muscle he was powerless. The clock was ticking, and from experience he knew it would stop without warning.

The voice of the man who was holding his business partner bothered him; it was a mix of aggression, serious threat, and calm. He clearly understood from experience, the calmer the demeanour the greater the danger. As his last call ended in rejection, he decided to avoid any act of support, his day was over.

Chapter 17

People who struggle to sleep in the early hours sometimes fall into a much deeper slumber before dawn. Claude could not believe his ears. His head was stiff; he bent it forward trying to relieve his taut neck and the hazy tension that confused his senses. The motors were running and the predator was moving. In the next room, he could hear movement, muffled sounds of bodies trying to communicate with grunts and groans, even so the stress of their predicament left Claude in no doubt, something bad was going to happen, and he was slap bang in the middle of it.

The fat calves of Crappy were the first things to greet Claude as he pulled himself up the stairs. The lunatic greeted him with a deranged look from the captain's seat.

"What's happening?" Groaned Claude, as he walked through the salon.

Not a word came his way, so he decided to leave that question for now.

It was early morning; the sun was lighting the sky but it was not visible for at least another fifteen minutes. Even the more motivated sailors were nowhere to be seen. As they purred through the marina, fishermen acknowledged the presence of the Predator, their surprise was clear; these guys never left the mooring when they were working. Crappy was in a trance, his control of the craft focused and assured, Claude watched as they eased through the harbour walls. The yacht retained a moderate pace so he sat on the rear seat keeping a close eye on the body language in front of him. As he nervously slid his hand over the cushions, a small piece of paper fell to the deck; inquisitively Claude leaned forward stretching to pick up the crumpled note, as he spread his hand over the creased paper the lead in his stomach took a turn for the worse.

4 sacs de cailloux décoratifs, 25kg par sac, 80 Euros payé au total.
Merci pour votre visit.

Claude threw the paper overboard whilst noticing the harbour had disappeared in the morning mist.

Eva Critin was tiring of Paris. More beggars and immigrants filed the streets in summer, and her looks always attracted demands for *'une petite pièce'*. The plans and calculations to erase the minister from the lives of her and the close friends at the Chateau were clear and almost in place. The exact day could change at the last minute, so an occasional coffee rounded off with a passionate cheek kiss kept him on the line. Eva was surprised how much confidence he displayed when she asked the most unlikely questions.

"Are you around next week Pascal, I have a friend who would very much like to be introduced?"

"What time can I pop in on Friday? I want your opinion on my new hairstyle."

His replies were detailed and demonstrated a lack of seriousness in his new position, God help French security with this man in charge, lamented Eva.

After a revealing lunch with Marine, the minister's secretary, the retired lady from the *Sûreté* decided her team in Chambéry should prepare for arrival in the city.

Later that evening Eva typed a short but specific email to Jack Rafter. Jack smiled purely as a compliment to such a professional lady. Eva said all he needed to know, but when read again it was written in a subtle code; a code which told Jack, he and his neighbours would soon be in the tightest corner of their lives.

As the Predator cruised further out into the Mediterranean, the sea caused problems for all on board. Crappy looked determined to stay at the controls, but seemed uncomfortable as he held the power lever. Claude grabbed onto the rear rails, and the prisoners below fell onto the floor. Strangely the pain of hitting the carpeted guestroom floor was irrelevant, their minds could only focus on how long it would take to hear the door code, and then what would happen?

Suddenly the bow dipped, the wake fell away and the yacht became the toy of the wind and waves.

Crappy was spinning in all directions, using the binoculars; he resembled a crazed pirate expecting to be boarded any second, the only words Claude heard were bellowed like a true lunatic.

"Good, open the garage, then stay at the controls, if you see another boat tell me."

A far-off cruise liner held Claude's attention; it was most likely heading to Italy, maybe stopping at Corsica or Sardinia. He was offered a senior barman contract at Club-Med on Corsica for the summer season, but declined, preferring to stay close to his gay friends in Marseille. His thoughts considered the place he could been enjoying, as opposed to the horror of being a few meters away from a career convict and a couple of unlikely bank robbers.

The waves splashing against the Predator distorted the sound of two people screaming, and these were not screams of humans being beaten, these were the deep stomach-churning sounds people made when they realised it was almost over. Desperation as only a man and woman can show when they are powerless to halt their pending fate.

Claude turned his head away watching the liner, now a spec on the horizon. Hati's hand pulled on his jeans, but the crazed man holding her upper arm pulled her away like a small puppy, Perroquet had given up, he was slumped on the floor, and being dragged along with Crappy's other hand.

His once neat Versace tie now resembled a blood-stained rag. Hati persisted in screaming, the lawyer let out moans. Claude assumed he had been beaten again before arriving on deck.

The large coloured screen in front of Claude confirmed little local activity. His value as a man had never been great, opting for the easy route, the gay life, few possessions, stealing wine from his bar job. Now the current situation challenged him, could he stop Crappy? If he tried, would he also end up dead? Why was he being so obedient?

The thought of watching two handsome people die before his eyes caused severe reactions, his legs shook, dangling from the captain's seat, hands literally glued to the black and chrome wheel. He tried but could not look back. Whatever was happening, it took a long time on the rear platform.

Suddenly a roar came from Crappy, "So did money make you happy?"

Then followed by two plunging sounds in quick succession; he heard the soft hum of the garage cover closing. Nothing further occurred for what seemed like minutes; still no other craft appeared on the radar and the wet and warm sensation from his crutch told him this was the darkest moment of his young life.

A yacht of around forty to fifty meters approaching from the east came into view on the Predator's radar; Claude judged it to be around one, maybe two kilometres away. His evil boss was still somewhere at the back of the craft. The shaking legs had stopped, but his hands were still stuck on the wheel. With a deep heavy breath, he pulled them free. As he slid off the seat his legs gave way; he was on all fours and could smell a distant aroma of something like Chanel perfume, but sweat and blood overpowered this. The stains of two bodies having been pulled over the wooden salon floor left marks, smudges of blood, small grooves from the wire handcuffs, and the scratches on the chrome divide from Hati's elegant watch.

Claude edged towards the back of the craft, he moved so cautiously hoping his legs would not falter again. As the rear steps came into view, the bald head of Crappy appeared. He sat half way down, motionless and alone. One plastic sack of gravel decoration stones rested half-on-half-off the swimming platform. Without turning Crappy rose, lumbered down five steps and kicked the sack into the sea.

He stared into the murky waters for a good thirty seconds; Claude was astonished how stable he appeared. Slowly he turned showing no surprise at Claude's presence above him; he lifted his arms like a preacher about to deliver a sermon.

"What else could I do? They were bad! Those bastards in the Chateau caused this."

Claude looked blank as his legs started shaking, yet again.

Chapter 18

Jack Rafter emailed his main clients; the message was short and to the point.

Very sorry but I have to undergo some medical treatment, and could be out of contact for about one week; your investments are all being monitored by my colleagues, nothing to worry about.
I will be in touch as soon as I am back at the desk.

Kind Regards,
Jack.

Arno, Dan and Boris were resting against the ropes of the boxing ring in the Chateau gym, Jack was due to join them any moment, the conversation was minimal.

"So, we leave tomorrow morning?" Asked Boris.

"Yep," said Dan flexing his back on the rope.

"I'm happy to do the driving," offered Arno as Jack jumped down the stairs towards the ring.

"Everybody positive?" Jack climbed into the ring like a pro going for a title challenge.

"We have no bloody choice, do we?"

"If we ignore him, he will screw us, and once in a lifetime is enough, no?" Arno's usual directness receiving nods of agreement.

Jack turned and put his hand on Boris's shoulder.

"Now you come clean, this is the time we hear what you're planning, it's team work, all of our asses are on the line."

Boris pushed himself away from the ropes and into the centre of the ring, he made boxing movements with his arms, this caused the other guys to grin; Boris knew only too well he was the nerd, they were the power, he was happy with that deal.

"Ok team, it's kind of simple, in my cave I have a small bottle of something science calls, SPURGE, it's a solution made from a plant. The friend who came from Amsterdam recently made it for me; he's a chemist, a rocking good one. But it's a deadly thing if it touches eyes. Eva told us the minister's office is like an exotic garden, full of plants. I will paint his keyboard and mouse with spurge, as soon as he starts working, he'll be motivated to touch his eyes, and that will take away his vision probably for the rest of his life."

"Hold on," Jack's love of detail kicked in, "If this spurge is so powerful, how do we…you, stay safe from it?"

"Jack, you're super in finance, big top fit guy, but please leave this to me; the normal level of effectiveness for this solution would maybe blind him for days, in the office I will add another product, this will increase the severity massively, painful but totally effective. You guys have to stay away from me at that time, I will be protected, special glasses, all given by my buddy, this is daily routine for him, and I will treat some plants in his office with the same solution, impossible to trace, by the time they start working things out, we are clear, and far away from Paris."

"Good work Boris, sounds quite logical." Jack raised his eyebrows towards the other guys in the ring who clearly had nothing better to offer.

"Now we better start getting enthusiastic about football if we're going to get away from here tomorrow morning without family worries." Jack gave a hand pat to his friends and left first. He hoped he could pull it off tonight during dinner, this was one excursion he had absolutely no experience in whatsoever.

A serious summer storm over Chambéry caused a handy diversion for the men whose thoughts were already in Paris. Windows were opened and closed, the odd small leak trickled in, and trees losing the older branches kept the residents busy. Strangely the concerns of heading to Paris to disable a top minister were lightened by the freak weather. Boris checked his cave for the third time, the thick glass flasks in the fridge looked so innocent, the liquid inside could have been water, but he knew one slight mistake could turn a perfect plan into a catastrophe. The sturdy metal case appeared up to the job, so Boris slid the sealed flasks into their padded holding shapes, checked his safety glasses, gloves and brush and gently closed the cover.

The next time he cast his eyes on the contents the surroundings would be far less friendly, he and his neighbours would be in the spotlight. Boris had never been to Paris before, people from all over the world relish the thought of a visit to the city of light; he struggled to share their motivation.

Claude crushed the blood-stained sheets into a plastic bin bag. The guest room carpet responded well to the solution of boiling hot water and washing up liquid; apart from a slight change of colour the floor looked like a regular yacht guest cabin, used and abused.

Flashes of yesterday's events were still very vivid in Claude's mind as he headed to the marina's garbage bins. He was now stuck between a rock and a terribly hard place. To explain his part to the police would be impossible, what could he say, "Sorry, I was too limp to do anything," over and over again he consoled himself with the financial gain, ten thousand euros for *being such a great friend and helper.* One day he would get away…the black bin bag landed perfectly in the middle of the container next to five similar looking ones. As he walked back to the Predator, he felt relief that his paymaster had left for the day.

Marlon Crappy sat on his bed. It was still early morning, the bar below was closed, and he did his best to climb the stairs quietly, hopefully nobody saw him enter his apartment with such a conspicuous black bag.

The pictures and drawings of his plans for a kidnapping in Chambéry were still in place, a little dusty but the details still excited him. Later in the day he would try to locate Ari and Rico, the two ex-cons who would support his operation to take the Rafter boys and put them into hell, the same hell his brother went through.

The bursting leather bag was proving to be a worry for the man. . Was there a safe place? Should he leave it on the yacht? At least the marina had security patrols, his apartment could be robbed at any moment, especially when the bar closed. He recalled one of his late brother's speeches during a prison visit to *Baumette,* "Money and worries, they go hand in hand, the more you have, the less you sleep." Crappy never imagined he would experience such problems in his miserable life.

The sound of bottles banging together and chairs and tables being pushed across the bar floor below told Crappy that Rog had arrived, and he needed to check on the local gossip.

"Christ mate, where ya been, those creepy bastards been asking about ya." The monster bowed his head down towards Rog.

"Who?"

"Those thugs, they said you had a job for them, bloody vague, that's all they said."

Relief showed on the giant's face, the last months had taken him off route; revenge was again growing in his mind, but now with resources beyond his imagination, finally the Chateau bastards would pay dearly for leaving him alone without family.

As Crappy sat awkwardly in his favourite corner of the bar, calculating the reward for his devious helpers, a police officer appeared at the open door. This was not unusual in Marseille; the shady bars were often used for anything from drug deals to employing illegal workers, but this was not the best day to see such a uniform.

"The manager?" Demanded the officer in a rapid tone.

Crappy said nothing and pointed to the door next to the bar.

The sound of Rog stacking crates below the bar floor confirmed that the manager was around, so the officer pulled a bar stool to one side and sat with his back to Crappy.

As Rog attempted to whistle and sing a chaotic tune, something that could have been Classic, Blues or Rap, the Aussie throat clearly was not awake yet; he arrived at bar level, out of breath and shocked at seeing his second client of the day.

"Whoops, not me mate, the bad guys operate down in the port, you know that!"

The police offer was unimpressed, smartass men from the southern hemispheres were few and far between in Marseille, and he remembered a similar reaction the last time he checked this bar.

The two drawings were slid along the polished bar top. Rog was already shaking his head.

"No idea mate, who are they?"

"A known lawyer and his secretary, office not far from here, disappeared in suspicious circumstances a couple of days ago, we're looking for leads, seen them?"

"Nope, if I do, I'll be amazed; don't get many lawyers in here, not their style, see T shirts not suits."

Crappy placed his empty glass just close enough to the drawings for a decent inspection. They appeared so fresh and tidy compared to the last time he saw them.

"Um, fill me up when you can please Rog."

The police officer turned around to face Crappy, who quickly shifted his gaze away from the drawings.

"Your face looks familiar; didn't I see you in…where was it now?"

Crappy flashed a help look to Rog, who responded like a protective wife.

"You need to try *Marios fish bar,* you know the place, old town, trendy place for lawyers and bankers, bet they know where he's gone."

The officer shrugged as if he could really care less about missing lawyers, tucked the drawings back into his case, said a hollow "thanks," to Rog and walked towards the door. Pulling the handle he took one last glance over towards the lump in the corner, he knew this strange looking guy from somewhere, maybe earlier in the year, during his duty with the marine police. He made a mental note to check the *Crocodile* bar again sometime in the near future.

By mid-evening, a revengeful lunatic had paid an upfront sum of five thousand euros to both Ari and Rico, they reacted as expected, eager to get going, fulfil their crude promises and receive the next instalment. They would drive the white van; Crappy would follow with Claude in his Toyota.

Claude was summoned to the bar at 9:00pm, his instructions were the easiest.

"Make sure Rog has the Yacht keys, got a new guy joining us, my new captain, he'll be meeting us when we get back, tell nobody, ok?"

Cruising back to the port on the Harley, Claude let out a distressed scream. He had been manipulated by a sick murderer, his financial situation was the best ever in his young life, he rode the sexist motorbike, sometimes drove a BMW, and his new home was a luxury yacht, what more could a young man want.

As he stepped onto the Predators rear platform, he visualised the last moments of Hati and Pierre Perroquet, considering the consequences if the bodies ever came ashore. For a shocking second, his eyes fixed on the yachts garage, he pressed the telecommand and clicked it open, not really knowing why he did this, maybe an urge to check out the crime scene. Three neatly stacked bags of garden stones, with large green letters confirming, twenty-five kilo's each sat next to the jet-ski. He scratched his head and tried to remember, did Jack Rafter have two or three sons?

Chapter 19

"Eva's reserved us a couple of twin rooms at the hotel, in a false company name, just to keep us off the radar."

Jack carried a small case, no more, the other guys brought similar luggage; Boris had left earlier for the garage but he was absent while the men stood next to the R R.

"Boris hurry up," said Jack in a hushed voice towards the cave. Arno climbed into the driving seat.

Moving like a man in no rush at all Boris closed the cave door with his foot. In his right hand, the metal case looked plain and innocent, but all eyes checked him out as he walked towards the open tailgate.

"Put it under our bags," said Dan, "I'd like to keep looking at pretty girls for years to come."

"Don't worry Dan, this case is made for heavyweight chemicals, it's sealed, oh and Arno's driving."

"Yeah, that's maybe our biggest headache." Jack laughed as he closed his door.

As the signs for the Auto route, direction Lyon showed up, Eva called.

"Hi Jack, guess you're on route? If so put me on the car system, have some breaking news for you chaps."

"Just heard tomorrow morning could be our slot, the old lady will be away, so we can decorate her room early, she's not back until the afternoon, and her sister is away all day."

The guys codly grinned as Eva spoke, she sounded so cool.

"We got everything, the paint, gloves, everything to do the job right. Best we start really early." Jack clearly enjoyed this part of the mission, tomorrow morning his mood would change for sure.

"I'm convinced she will appreciate us for the rest of her life! If you're here by one, my treat for lunch." Eva signed off with a kissing sound.

Boris loved watching the exploits of the SAS, SBS and US SEAL teams, any movie or documentary he could get his hands on, so considered emulating his hero's by plugging in headphones and listening to a selection of Austrian and German composers, heavy, but just like they did when heading for the drop zone. It made his demeanour serious and focused…his friends simply dozed.

The Marriott hotel was a busy place, Eva thought this was marvellous. More confused tourists demanding assistance at the reception meant less attention for her guys, their size and athletic build did cause its fair share of curiosity.

With still at least two hours before their pending arrival, Eva wanted to make a final evaluation behind the minister's office, a last hours scouting trip just in case.

She wore the largest sunglasses she could find, let her hair hang around her shoulders and partly over her face, wore jeans, medium height heals, and a cream lightweight fitting jacket with the collar up. How much more could a lady do to fit in with the Paris look?

Nothing had changed, except that a couple of the service doors were now hidden behind smokers taking a work break, the clouds swirling around their heads made Eva grimace behind her shades. As she peaked up towards the minister's floor, she noticed the blinds were lowered against the summer sun, immediately she hoped they would stay this way to hide her team early tomorrow morning.

The wall separating road and parking was high enough to cover the guys once under the plastic entry barrier. A small white van leaving the parking let Eva cross in front, the driver clearly keen to see the eyes behind the tinted glasses; he was rewarded with only the rear view, which he also found very pleasing.

At the end of the busy street, Eva upped her pace to cross over into *Rue Saint-Antoine*, deciding to take a taxi a safe block or two away from the building.

The lady driving the Renault Koleos recognised the walk, but the style was not the same. The hair could be different in colour. Even by Paris standards this woman held the attention. The horn from an impatient lorry driver caused the Renault to turn into the backstreet. She parked in the last place available; the space was so narrow, stretching contortions were required to extricate herself. Brushing her hand in front of her face whilst passing the group of smokers, but she could not get that walk out of her mind.

By 1230, the GPS confirmed arrival at the Marriott was a mere fifteen minutes away. Arno pointed to the screen enthusiastically, his stomach groaning due to the early breakfast.

"We're in time for lunch, and Paris…"

The three other passengers had been silent since leaving the *Périphérique*, sometimes Arno put body first, head later, "umm," was the best reply on offer.

The check in went smoothly, no less would have been expected from Eva's preparations. Dan drew the attention of a well-endowed lady behind the reception, he reminded her of a Hollywood face, one she could not put a name to.

Eva waited diplomatically some distance away seated alone, eyes fixed on the team from the Chateau.

Jack spotted her first and gave a discreet wink.

"So good to see you all here." The kisses and hugs from Eva showed genuine feeling for her close neighbours, maybe more so concern for the level of danger that she would put them in the next morning.

"Booked a quiet little place a block away, perfect for a lunch, used it before when I needed a private corner."

Eva waited while the guys dropped off bags. Boris decided to keep the metal case close to his side so walked through Paris like a salesman promoting luggage for drug couriers.

The waiter gave a nod of recognition to Eva, smiling in the direction of the perfectly prepared table. Five settings were spread around a table that would normally be used for eight people; clearly Eva had pre-warned the waiter to expect guests talking business.

The next table was unoccupied and a good four meters away, the place was quiet for central Paris in summer. Without doubt the spate of terror attacks recently in France had caused a drop off for the tourist trade.

"How are your families back home?" Eva missed her female friends, and especially Jack's boys.

A mix of 'good, all good', came back as Eva surveyed her table guests.

"You know tomorrow morning is our best shot, if we don't go for it the next window could be days away, and I have heard many people are away on various missions, also no special meetings planned, so security will be relaxed." Eva waited for the first reaction.

Jack eased forward.

"Look Eva, we are ready, not exactly our day job, but it's clear this guy has to be stopped, he's a nasty little shit, getting more powerful year after year, so now, his time has come."

Boris waved his hand like a street mime artist, as he was prone to do when he felt the need to add something.

"Are you up to speed on what I'll be doing?"

Eva shook her head.

"I only know you have something unique from a contact in Holland."

"We're going to blind him, he will never use a computer again, never work again in fact, spend the rest of his life in the dark."

Confusion showed above Eva's perfect cheekbones.

"You know my background, I was a secret service operative, but this is new to me, how can you...oh don't tell, please, you know what you're doing, I'll just show you his office and hope and pray we get out clean."

Eva was surprised to see nothing stronger than Perrier on the table, these guys know how to drink, she thought, evidently, they all have a serious side, the relaxed easy guys she knew in the Savoie were very different in Paris.

Dan lightened the mood telling stories of *his worst ski teaching moments*; Arno tried to compete with his *dodgy exotic car clients in Amsterdam*. Boris constantly checked that his metal case was flat on the floor, Jack and Eva mulled over the next few hours.

Back at the hotel a detailed map was presented by Eva showing the minister's office, best entry from the rear of the building, clear drawings of the secretary's office, and exact position of the computers in the room.

The plan was agreed, two taxies would leave the Marriott at 4:30 the next morning, Eva, Jack and Dan in one, Boris and Arno in the other. All would be dressed in sport gear, trainers and sweats. Each car would drop the passengers off two hundred meters from the office, at opposite sides of the building. Smart thinking from Arno caused him to bring badges from a running event he organised in Amsterdam years ago, they would all wear one, *The Holland-America summer run,* in blue and red should leave the taxi drivers in no doubt, it was summer and the crazy American and Dutch tourists were planning ridiculous events in their city. The French residents of Paris could never be persuaded to leave their beds to pound the streets so early.

An early evening workout was enjoyed in the company of some pretty well curved ladies at the hotel gym. Although Dan showed unusual restrain. As he worked up a sweat his face took on a trance like focus, same as a boxer at the stare down. The disappointed girls left one by one wondering why they were totally ignored, this had never happened before; the guys would not have been fun anyway, far too serious for summer tourists in Paris.

Jack took a nightcap with Eva to run over the planning one last time. The more affluent football supporters in the city for the European cup took over the bar with one intention, drink until you can't stand. By ten o'clock, the team from Chambéry had turned in, Jack made a quick call to Carly, all was fine at home, and the boys were already in bed. He couldn't wait to return to his family.

Carly forgot to mention the call from one-stop Courier Company, it was almost too strange to consider. A nervous, youngish sounding Frenchman asking if her boys would be at home the following morning.

"Very good news for you Madame, your children have won zee big prize, but do not tell them I will bring it to the Chateau in zee morning, keep zee secret, please."

She was in two minds to tell the boys, but why spoil whatever this surprise turned out to be.

At exactly 4:30 am, phone alarms in Paris and Marseille stirred two very different teams. The guys and Eva in Paris assembled quickly; Boris stared like an owl, an early morning face of surprise, the silver case never far from his side. As they cleared the reception a downbeat night manager grunted a surprised *Bonjour*, a couple of people carrier taxis, one blue and one red waited on Boulevard Haussmann. The mission had begun.

In Marseille, two sleepy thugs waited outside a bar in a dirty white van. The thump on the window stirred them suddenly. Crappy waved his hand with a follow me gesture. They should arrive in Chambéry by mid-morning.

Chapter 20

The streets of early morning Paris were calm. Both cab drivers had worked the night shift so conversation was in short supply; Jack's cab reeked of alcohol. As Paris cabbies were not known for their ambience, this was just what the passengers wanted. Dan reflected as to if his military skills would be required, and how far he may need to go. Jack took in the elegant buildings and fiddled with his badge. Eva reflected on a similar ride, many years ago.

Both parties pretended they knew where they were heading when leaving the taxies; the drivers could have cared less anyway. Zero mobile use, except in extreme emergency, had been agreed so relief was evident when they caught sight of each other at opposing ends of the small street. Fifty percent of the streetlights were broken, a good thing this day, and the morning was partly cloudy, daylight was some time away. Eva led the way, she slid under the plastic barrier like a track athlete, followed closely by three large men in dark training gear, the fourth looked a little awkward trying to follow their bowed pace, but he carried the most, a silver case, and shoulder bag with his laptop and USB key, the key was perhaps his deadliest weapon.

The smallest of the rear doors was closed, but Eva was not shocked when a quick turn of the handle opened it without resistance. An old diesel car chugged past in the street behind them; they were now all inside the minister's building.

Eva took three distinct left turns then led her team into a dark corridor, ahead on the right Jack noticed a large stone staircase, wide enough for the whole team, if necessary, but they followed in line.

The fourth floor offered more natural light, the office workers had left blinds up and some doors open. Boris shook his head in surprise; even his old office in Amsterdam had tighter security.

Eva raised her left hand suddenly, and then pointed a slender finger towards a white nameplate; even in the poor light his name was clear.

Jack placed his right hand on the door handle; it would not budge, so he tightened his lower arm, firmed up his grip in the rubber glove and manoeuvred his shoulder above the metal handle. The snap of metal breaking in such a silent place would have normally brought workers out of their offices; Jack waited instinctively for around five seconds, then moved in. Eva slid past Jack into Marine's office, in no time all the guys were inside and the broken door handle pushed back into place.

Jack was a little surprised how smoothly things were going, watching Eva push the minister's door open even made him puff, he glanced at Arno as if saying, do these things always go so effortlessly. Arno looked stiff and focused.

The blinds were partly open, which gave Boris enough light to move around the desk. He placed the metal case on the floor next to the chair, his laptop bag resting on the cluttered table.

"First his computer," he whispered. The screen lit up quickly and the password requested.

Boris had memorised the code. The speed with which Boris typed in the numbers never ceased to amaze his neighbours, nobody showed the slightest emotion when Boris was accepted into the minister's computer. As usual when standing close to the man at work his friends saw screens and long lists of numbers, access codes which never came up when they were working.

Eva remembered her ministerial friend was the world's worst with technology; he never backed up his work, never changed his password, and kept everything in simple childlike labelled folders. His trust of fellow colleagues was always contemptuous, so she doubted he passed on anything to office associates.

Boris quickly found a file named, *Chambéry Chateau*, even in full flow he sniffed at the simplicity of the man's security efforts, a scan of the contents confirmed tax documents for most of the names living at the Chateau. Names and contact details of the tax offices and several papers sent and received from a man named Harvey Lasalle. The director of the tax office in Annecy, Madame Fouchard was also a regular sighting. Suddenly Boris stopped tapping, he stretched his arm determinedly towards the laptop case, a large silver USB key was slipped out, he clicked it into the minister's machine port without looking. In seconds the screen turned blue, a very bright blue, the room lit up. The team all stared at Boris who was in his own world, he shook his head towards the screen, his face displayed self-assured confidence.

Jack recalled an old client at the Space Agency in Holland trashing his machine because it displayed for the last time, "the blue screen of death."

Approximately seventy-five meters away an old lady sat in her small apartment on the top floor; She hated the nights, so tended to stare out of the lounge window at passing cars, early morning walkers, anything to draw her attention, show some sign of life. The brightness glowing from the office across the road held her concentration; she had never seen light in the building before seven or eight in the morning. Shadows moved slowly in the room, then stopped abruptly. The old lady decided to make an early morning call to her son, after all her was a security guard in the ministerial building.

The flashing screen dulled down after one minute, Boris retrieved his USB key.

"The files are fried, we are out of this computer, now please leave the room."

His friends sensed that the dangerous part of the morning was about to begin, so shuffled silently into the secretary's room as Boris donned protective glasses and long gloves. Jack went into the corridor; he repeated his forceful exercise on four other office door handles, all broke with considerable ease.

"Now work that out," he whispered.

The sound of a metallic case opening alerted them to the moment Boris had explained at the Chateau, one false move now could blind their close friend and scupper the mission.

The sound of a glass top being removed from a jar confirmed his actions; no other noise came out of the minister's office. Boris stroked left and right with the small brush leaving a layer of liquid Spurge over the cream keyboard. The mouse also received a generous covering; he blinked as if experiencing the same pain the minister would go through, then turned and painted the remainder of the liquid on the nearest plants.

The brush was delicately placed back into its holder in the case, the glass bottle sealed, and a security layer of light grey metal zipped over the contents. The sound of metal clicks caused the raising of hands in the next room. A final light brushing of the desk with a handkerchief erased all traces of his visit. Boris opened the door still wearing the protection glasses; he looked surprised and relieved at the same time.

"It worked?" whispered Jack. The rapid nodding from Boris was good enough for all in the room.

The broken handle bothered Jack so he left the door slightly ajar hoping a sloppy cleaner would take the blame.

Four athletic shapes, plus Boris, all in jogging gear moved through the fourth-floor corridor, Arno now leading with Jack at the back. Going down the stairs in almost total darkness was maybe more difficult than climbing them earlier; Boris clunked his case against the brick wall which was not appreciated by his friends, but a professional silence was retained; the shaft of light through the last door to the parking alerted Eva first closely followed by all of the guys. Their pace slowed, Arno cautiously stretched his head towards the fifteen-centimetre opening, nothing appeared wrong. He tried to look into the car park, it was still empty. Dan was almost breathing down his neck, only Boris kept a distance from his friends.

Very cheap cologne hit Jack's nostrils followed by a whack from a rubber truncheon, then light into his eyes caused him to fall against the wall. Jack instinctively stretched his arms towards the lights source. Eva bounced against Dan's chest; Arno pushed the door open to bring light and assess the problem behind his back.

The poor visibility confirmed, two, maybe three well-built men in black t-shirts were swinging fists and elbows in a nervous frenzy. Jack felt a neck with his fingers so punched straight and hard, the sensation of hitting an Adam's apple supported his aim, the choking sound confirmed his force. Dan shot out his right leg hitting the lower stomach of another black t-shirt, the guard fell towards Dan who brought his right elbow down on the man's upper back, the sound of breaking bone told Dan his old skills were fully intact. Arno had the smallest of the three men in a chock hold, within seconds he dropped to the ground, unconscious, hitting his head against the brick wall.

"We're done, move out, but controlled, ok?" Said Dan as he gently pushed the door open.

The old lady across the road was still staring at the darkened office on the fourth floor.

Within thirty seconds, the party had split into three, Jack with Eva, Arno with Boris and Dan alone. After meandering through several streets avoiding eye contact with delivery men, street cleaners and dog walkers; taxis were hailed. Dan arrived first at the Marriott, the cheeky reception girl enquired if, "The morning run went well?" Dan returned a smile thinking *yeah real back breaker.*

Ten minutes later the team were together in Jack's room.

"That was a pity, went well till then." Jack surveyed his friends with a look of disappointment.

"We had no choice, but who the fuck let them know at 5:30 in the morning." Arno raised his eyebrows towards Jack.

"Let's leave Paris soon, we take a normal breakfast, like regular people, then check out." Said Eva.

The minister's secretary arrived early. The late-night call from her boss telling her to, "Get the place tidy for some special guests," came as a surprise, he would convey such visits days before normally.

Counting five police cars filling the spaces close to the rear entry door shocked Marine. As she edged her small hatchback into a corner space a tap at the window made her jump.

"Do you work here, well?" The dark uniform of the police officer was as sombre as his people skills.

"Yes, I happen to be secretary to Minister Pascal…" Marine was cut off as the police officer noticed her badge lying on the seat.

"Ok, better get to your office; there has been a break in, get ready for questions."

The fourth floor was buzzing with people, mostly men and ladies in white coats, torches with bright blue lights were directed at the broken door locks. Powder had been brushed over the area around the lock. The noise level was strangely low for so many busy individuals. As Marine approached her own office, a lady police officer came out. The woman looked tired and fractious, *most likely a frustrated lesbian* thought Marine.

"You are?" The menace in the ladies' voice caused Marine to step back.

"I am the secretary of Minister Pascal Manozy, what's happened here?"

Upon hearing the ladies rank and being aware of her minister's reputation the lady officer changed her tone.

"I need your help, we checked your office, nothing seems to have been taken, but I have no authority to enter the minister's office. I called him, but he…well, was not so happy, told me he would arrive in half an hour. We checked all the offices with broken door handles, nothing suspicious, but his, could you check it for me? Just don't touch anything."

Marine gave a polite look of agreement, the officer eased to one side and she surveyed her own room. Several things had been moved, her computer screen twisted, files left open. She turned towards the officer with clear contempt.

"You are aware of the minister's position? I suggest you leave me alone until he arrives, this could simply be a local anti-government gang, it happened before."

"Oh no, that's not at all the case, the mother of a security guard alerted her son, she saw light from this office. He came with two more; they tried to stop the people leaving, now they are in hospital, severe body damage, broken neck, punctured lung, one said it was like a commando team, far too good for amateurs, like military guys, and they think one was a lady."

Marine took a deep breath; she asked herself what possible trouble her boss could have caused this time.

"Soon as he gets in, I'll talk with him. We dare not do anything else." The officer said nothing, shook her head, formed a steely face and walked along the corridor.

As Marine pushed the minister's door open with her pen a strong smell of something between plant spray and acid hit her senses. The smell was so strong she held her breath and walked over to the window, using her jacket sleeve to grip the handle and raise the lever a good thirty to forty centimetres. She jilted her head back attempting to clear her senses from the powerful odour in the room. The plants had always been an irritation for her, but this was stronger than any day before. Scanning around the room everything appeared in place, even his chair was pushed hard against the desk, his usual parting gesture. The computer screen appeared cleaner than normal, and the mouse was unusually placed in the middle of the matt.

The neatness bothered Marine; her boss was an untidy man. She wobbled the mouse, knowing he never switched his machine off, but the screen remained dark. A sudden tear from her left eye was wiped away without thinking. Her nose gave a sensation of being blocked; it began to itch. Stretching her eyes open to focus on the screen she pushed the mouse yet again without response. Tapping *Enter* three times as another tear fell on the keyboard, instinctively brushing it away with her right hand. She removed her glasses clumsily; they bounced off the table and fell to the floor. Now her nose was also losing fluid on the keyboard, she began to panic. The more she brushed her hand along the keys the more irritated her eyes became, turning to grab a tissue from the box behind the desk, she dropped the light paper, it glided to the floor, bending to retrieve it and placing her head firmly above the keyboard. The rapid blinking of her eyes caused her to stumble against the desk; she fumbled the mouse away, almost angry over its lack of activity. The screen remained dead.

Marine realised her condition was descending rapidly, the once reliable vision was blurred, the burning sensation from her eyes caused panic breathing, her throat was dry. Pushing around the desk and reaching for the office door as darkness clouded her vision.

"Help me, help me." She fell to the floor with both hands covering her burning eyes.

A vague silhouette entered the room and crouched beside her. The lady police officer recalled something similar to this in training, preparation for a dirty bomb or gas attack; she eased herself up straight, taking distance between herself and the woman in increasing agony on the office floor;

The *pompier* were called with instructions to bring protective suits for a possible terrorist situation.

Within fifteen minutes, Marine was lying on a portable stretcher, had she been able to see, the plastic tent covering her would have caused panic. The medics were also dressed in protective bio suits from head to toe, she heard maybe three or four voices, men and women, one was a doctor who regularly gave instructions.

The words, 'plant', and 'toxic', were used in every sentence.

The lady police officer, now wearing a face mask tried to comfort her from outside the office, "Stay calm, we will take you to the best hospital in Paris, you will be well looked after."

It did not help.

Sounds of chaos filled her head, the police were shouting at workers to leave the building, but nobody knew which way to leave.

Marine still tried to touch her burning eyes, but the medics had already covered them with bandages.

The stretcher began to move, and she heard the distressed voices of colleagues standing in offices as she passed. The voices of police urging all personnel to vacate the building resonated in her head.

As the lift bumped to a stop on the ground floor, she sensed unease and urgency around her.

Suddenly the street sounds of Paris lost their charm; the siren on the vehicle told her this early morning start may have changed her life forever.

Pascal Manozy arrived in the ministerial building car park, later than promised as always; he dropped a lady friend off on route. The sight of so many police officers, mostly dressed in protective clothing shocked him. His car was immediately halted. The tall officer recognised him.

"Sorry sir, you cannot enter the building, we have a possible chemical situation in your office area."

"And where is my secretary?" demanded the arrogant minister.

The officer swallowed hard, he was a perfectionist and wanted to rise in the ranks quickly. He knew one wrong word now may scupper his promotion chances.

"She has a grave problem sir, my colleagues found her lying on the floor, possibly head-eye trauma, I'm sorry."

The minister said nothing for at least fifteen seconds; he could not believe what he heard.

"Where have they taken her?"

"*George Pompidou,* the best place."

The car window closed.

"Tell the hospital we're coming, I need to see her, and I mean quickly."

As the driver searched his tactile screen, Manozy called an old friend; he may need to call in some favours today.

Three physically damaged security guards sat in a cramped room in the hospital basement. They were tired, aching and keen to leave. The fresh bandages made the once tough guards look fragile, but the burly policemen resting against the room's walls were becoming frustrated.

"Three men, four men, a woman! What was this, the A team? You're supposed to be security, did you hear their voices, see any facial marks, were they carrying anything? We need information."

The three shaking heads caused one of the officers to hit the wall with his open hand.

"Talk it through again, you don't leave here until we get something, and I'm serious."

An exhausted looking hospital manager greeted the minister as he pulled himself out of the car. The driver was dispatched to get flowers, even though he insisted they would not be permitted in the patient's circumstances.

Pascal Manozy was meticulously updated on his secretary's condition.

"All we can say at this stage is it's likely to be a chemical reaction, she's undergoing tests now, I'm afraid her sight may be severely affected, she could even suffer permanent blindness."

The minister was clearly shocked as this stage of the conversation, he stopped in his tracks.

"So had I arrived in my office first, it could be me in that room!"

Only a small nod confirmed the obvious.

The newly arrived police chief irritated the minister, especially the constant pestering. He desperately wanted to spend time with Marine and ask what brought this about. It was going to be a battle who would be interviewed first, and knowing the treasure trove in his computer he used all his clout to control the morning to his advantage.

Manozy's mobile annoyed the police chief, every time he attempted to engage in conversation the infernal thing rang, and the minister took it without consideration ushering the policeman away as if this was high politics, way above his station.

Almost one hour had passed, Manozy kept his mobile glued to his head whilst charging it from a wall socket. The police chief made his regrets at having to leave for an urgent update.

Suddenly a young nurse stood next to the minister.

"Sir, I have to advise you maybe two-three minutes are possible, no more, she is very distressed, you will need to wear this."

As he shuffled into the room, the plastic boots screeched across the floor, Marine heard this and turned her head.

"Doctor, can I drink something?"

"It's me, Marine."

The shock of hearing a very familiar voice caused the lady to jump.

"What happened to me? Why am I blind? Why did…" her voice choked up.

"Please relax my dear; simply try to tell me what happened if you can."

"There were police in the building when I arrived, I really have no idea; I told her to leave your office alone, I went in to check if it was tidy, but the smell was terrible, those plants I think, I opened your window, your computer looked so tidy, sorry not like you, the mouse is always on the table never on the matt, I touched it, then my eyes began to burn, I rubbed them, it got worse, it hurts so much, will I see again?" The soft sobbing made Manozy regret asking her at this time.

"I will leave you, you are in the best place, and I'll come regularly, you will be ok."

As Manozy turned knowing his words were most likely in vain, Marine coughed, her throat as painful as her eyes.

"I saw her."

He spun around.

"Saw who?"

"Your old friend from the service, her walk, it's like a model, she was behind the building a couple of days ago, I drove past her in my car, I wondered why she…"

Pascal Manozy ripped the bio suit off as Marine's voice fell away. He touched his phone screen; the man who answered was already expecting this call.

Chapter 21

The sight of a very large possessed looking man, two heavily tattooed shifty men swarming around the giant, plus one thin nervous individual caused holiday makers to remain in their cars.

Parents persuaded their children to stay put, promising more sweets and drinks, "Just hold on until they leave."

The service station on the A7 north of Avignon was moderately busy for a weekday morning, but it was still early. Marlon Crappy paced around his Toyota Land cruiser; the white van was parked in the next space. With close inspection, the paintwork could have been better. Claude spent at least half a day painting and repainting the orange letters onto the side of the van. If viewed from a reasonable distance away it looked convincing, too close and it was clearly an unprofessional botched job.

The rabbit under the large letters looked like he was about to head butt *One-Stop courier* off the van, but the flames emanating from his rear caused Crappy to smile. What else could you do to look like a legit courier at such short notice he thought.

At exactly 6:30, the small convoy slipped back onto the A7. The early bird families in the service station were relieved.

Carly Rafter knew her husband well; a typical work hard, play hard man, so any chance of an early morning call seemed remote. Her boys were still enjoying the school-holidays summer lay-in routine so she motivated herself to visit the Chateau gym, preferring to be alone as opposed to suffering the constant "Do it this way-stretch well before you start," advice from the well-trained men in the building.

Any inspiration to do the right thing had long left Claude's mind. He was simply an ex-convict's well rewarded helper. Paid his rent on time, was regularly allowed to share luxury toys and still had the bar job to fall back on. Providing he was never asked to do the dirtiest deed; his life could have been worse.

Crappy was unusually chatty for such an early hour in the morning. Although his determination to monitor the white van behind caused Claude to tense up regularly.

"Do you trust them?" The big man's sudden direct question surprised Claude.

"That's a bit late now don't you think? We're a couple of hours away from a serious situation."

"You're my right-hand man, good to know what you think." Claude was not comfortable with this assumption. "Don't worry, I know this type well, they'll do anything for the money, so I keep them wanting, and when we get back, I'll sort them out." Claude decided to leave this comment in the air.

After the turn off south of Valence, the sign for Chambéry showed a mere 145 kilometres to go. Pretending to be a courier over the phone was one thing, now Claude was barely two hours away from his acting debut and his stomach was tighter and pulling more than ever.

The road towards the mountains caused the sun to be bright and intense one moment, falling into shade the next. Being on the right side of the car made Claude feel unusually warm, or was it stage fright heating him up.

As he snatched quick glances towards his boss it was evident the monster was reflecting on another world. Crappy thought back on his life, it was always a mess. Prison time took many years away from him, and when he eventually inherited serious wealth, the one person, his brother, the family member who could have guided him through the money maze, had been taken away.

On the other side of the coin, he doubted his brother would have shared his wealth with such a doubtful character. He decided he was dammed with money, and dammed without it.

A road sign announcing another 40 kilometres to their destination caused him to switch his mind onto the pending business.

"You know what to do Claude?"

"Yes, I'm the courier with a special surprise for the Rafter boys. Soon as they open the gate I drive up to the main door, you and the heavies follow in the Toyota. We grab the boys; throw them in the back of the van where Ari will tie them up. You and Rico will look after any fathers or mothers who think they are 'handy', Ari blocked the gate system already so we can leave in no time."

"You forgot one bit, we mace every bastard we bump into so they can't see our number plates, remember?"

"I thought I was driving the Toyota." Said Claude hoping to be exonerated from any form of aggression.

Carly Rafter was enjoying her time in the gym. Her sons had loaded terrific dance music into the rooms system. She was still alone so prolonged her workout. Her mobile showed no message from Jack, *fine* she thought; *all must be good in Paris.*

The narrow road leading towards the Chateau gates bothered Rico and Ari.

"You can't even turn here, if we get blocked in!"

"Just think of the fuckin money, we can screw more out of this freak back in the south." Said an agitated Ari.

Claude parked the white van adjacent to the Chateau gates, knowing from his last visit that the video camera would capture his sign painting talent. The Toyota with three hooded men ticked over behind a think clump of bushes twenty meters away.

Nick and Simon Rafter studied the video screen. The black baseball cap and dark sunglasses gave little away, although they regularly took courier packages for their parents, the name on this van, *one-stop courier* had not brought deliveries before.

"Good morning," said Nick, knowing most of the courier service employees could manage basic english.

"Yes, good morning to you, I am looking for Nick and Simon Rafter."

The brothers looked at one another in surprise, a delivery for them!

When a young man hears, he is the recipient of a courier's delivery parental guidance jumps out of the window.

"Who's it for, Simon or Nick?" said Simon with a dark voice.

"Oh, this is for both young men, and it's heavy so please could you help me."

Nick raised his hands in excitement whispering in his brother's ear.

"Dad's away, Mum's training, this is typical them, you know they surprise us often."

Without thinking Simon pressed the button to open the heavy metal gates. Both young men were dressed in tee shirts and shorts; they hastily scuffed their training shoes on, which were lying next to the front door. As they descended the six blocks of stairs, they caught site of a white van approaching through the trees. The sound of gravel being crushed under the tyres increased their excitement so they leapt down three stairs at a time. The Toyota followed but its grey colour was missed by the expectant brothers.

The Concierge tended to close all possible doors to reduce the summer heat entering the building's interior, so both boys tugged eagerly at the heavy antique structures. The site of a delicate young man in a baseball cap and uncharacteristic shorts was completely missed by the impatient pair, unfortunately so was the Toyota behind.

"Do we need to sign?" asked an innocent voiced Nick as the courier slid open the side door.

The lack of reply caused no concern for the brothers; they were too focused peering into the depths of the van. Claude used his right hand to pull himself into the vehicle about the same time Nick realised the van was empty but for a collection of ropes on the floor, and one small open cardboard box with water bottles.

As Nick began to turn his head in doubt towards his brother, Marlon Crappy's face arrived with seriously bad breath staring down on him. The shock of a monster standing at least fifteen centimetres above caused him to fall back on his brother. Rico had this angle well covered already pulling Simon's tee shirt into the van. Crappy aggressively took Nick's shorts in his large sweaty hand, lifted the boy and threw him onto his brother who was struggling to keep his head off the metal floor.

Ari slapped both boys hard across the face, he knew from his street fighting experience, this shock would give him enough time to take their wrists and begin tying the rope tight.

Carly Rafter had had enough, no call from her husband in Paris, two boys still in bed! Hardly any other neighbours to invite for a morning coffee, time for a shower and a lecture to her 'lazy' sons.

Wrapping a towel around her shoulders she touched the tactile screen to silence the gym's music system, the stillness felt awkward as if something was missing.

The soundproof door to leave the gym swung easily, her husband Jack came up with this idea, silence for the not so keen trainers in the Chateau, and an easy entry and exit for the weaker sex.

Mothers are blessed with an instinct sometimes far keener than their male counterparts. The sound of Nick's scream made Carly freeze for a mere two seconds on the spot, unaware how she did it but four steps were leapt without thinking, then another four, the final door to the Chateau entry hall was kicked open with her right foot; as the bright morning sun burst through the open doors, she closed her eyes, a confusion of sounds hit her senses, as she raised her hand above her brow the watery image of a hand with a small grey canister came into view. Meters away a very large man dashed around a white van, she hesitated, was this one or two people together. The powerful hiss was immediately followed by pain in her eyes, as if acid had been thrown in her face, she fell to the ground screaming. Both boys heard their mother but were so well tied up they could only wriggle against the van wall.

"You dirty bastards, I'm gonna kill you." Simon's threat was light amusement for the thugs in the van, although Claude looked petrified after watching Ari shoot the mace into the beautiful woman's face.

Carly was writhing on the floor screaming at full pitch, her mobile had hit the floor in the panic but she could not locate it, as she heard a van door slide into position. Two vehicles with engines running pulled away rapidly, several small pieces of gravel hit Carly's back.

Rubbing her eyes was the obvious first reaction but any form of vision was currently impossible. As the sound of the Chateau metal gates clunked in the distance Carly crawled and felt her way towards the lift. The cold marble floor hurt her knees, but she had to do something, how long would it take to alert the police, how quickly can the guys return, her head was thumping, the plight of her sons almost caused her to choke, this was the most terrible day of her life.

Crappy waved his large hand at the white van following him. The panic to get on the Auto route and away from Chambéry was evident in the driving style, but the last thing he needed was a police check.

The occasional kicking on the van's side panels pissed Ari off, he shouted at the boys and held the mace can in their faces.

"One more sound, one more, and I'll empty this in your little fucking faces, ok?"

The boys' minds were filled with every possible fear, why them, where were they being taken, was this sexual, would they be beaten. Their only comfort was still being together, this helped the most.

Rico was flicking through the contacts on their mother's phone.

The stink from their captors almost made the boys throw up, a mix of cigarette breath, body odour and unwashed clothes, they had travelled from paradise to hell in a few short minutes and the guys who could have stopped all this from happening were hours away enjoying football in Paris.

Carly had fumbled her way inside the lift, blurred images came as she exercised her eyes, she could feel tears running down her face, she rose into a bending vertical position as the glass door opened. Feeling for the metal rail and stretching her left arm the door handle came reassuringly into her grip. Automatically calling out, "Guys it's Mum…" The silence was painful, why did she do this? Maybe in the hope that the last few minutes were a dream, of course they were not.

Flowers were knocked from a hallway table as she staggered towards the lounge. The comforting feel of the landline phone made her sigh and catch her breath; peering with all possible concentration she hit 17, the police lady picked up after three rings.

"My sons have been taken, here in Chambéry, it just happened."

"Please stay calm Madame, where did this occur?"

"At our home, Chateau Montjan, avenue George, you must know it?"

"I am sending an emergency signal to a police car now Madame they should be with you in a few minutes."

"But they are gone, in two cars, don't you understand? They're gone!"

"Tell me what sort of cars Madame; did you see the number plates?"

"No, they sprayed something in my eyes I can hardly see."

Suddenly the police lady realised this could be something more than a simple kid grab.

"Did you see which direction they were heading for?"

"I just told you they blinded me, how the hell could I…" Carly slammed the phone down and immediately touched Jack's number.

The lady police office dispatched a helicopter to check the auto route intersections around Chambéry whilst at the same time requesting the latest web-cam shots of vehicles passing the toll, the terror alert team responded to the red light immediately.

Jack Rafter felt a little embarrassed as he grabbed his mobile, Carly should have been called as soon as they returned to the hotel.

"Yes, my darling, I know, I'm a bad guy,"

"Jack shut up and listen." He obeyed without thinking.

The quiver in her voice focused his attention and stopped him breathing.

"Our boys have been taken, from our home, some bastards sprayed a horrible liquid in my face, I heard them leave but saw nothing."

"Calm down now, you have called the police?"

Jack had a thousand questions, his mind raced, his friends in the room instantly sensed a disaster had occurred back home, but only stared at him for the moment.

"Of course, I called the police, I can hear the car arriving now, but I can hardly see the gate buzzer, my god Jack what can we do?"

Arno's wife Stephanie followed the police into the Chateau grounds matching their speed and then some. She too stressed her mind with possible reasons. Her husband was in Paris, what could have happened? One of her close friends called from the Chateau, why?

"Tell the police all you can, find Stephanie, keep me up to speed on all, we are coming back, I don't know how, but the quickest way possible, stay strong darling, we will get out boys back."

Jack looked petrified.

As the line went dead Carly heard Stephanie shouting at her door, she entered talking in clipped bursts with two armed police officers, the dark uniforms came and went with her poor vision, the weapons could not be missed, but Stephanie's embrace caused her to scream and cry at the same time.

The sudden touch from an older police lady eased both women towards the couch, and the questions began.

As Jack's short story unfolded his friends displayed a full range of emotions, anger, concern, astonishment and extreme sadness. Not one could truly consider the real possibility before them; maybe they had hugged the boys for the last time. This was simply too painful to imagine so all minds returned to the immediate plan.

Arno was already calling Net-Jets demanding the most urgent preparation for a flight to Chambéry airport. Eva was mulling over any possible connection to Pascal Manozy, and Jack was sending text after text to Carly, doing his best at long distance comfort, as if his arms were wrapped around her.

His mind jumped back to a place he did not want to visit, the meeting with a Notaire friend in Annecy and his information about the release of Gerard Crappy's brother.

Dan was impressed at the speed and efficiency of Net-Jets; the Embraer Phenom 300 was already being fuelled up at *Orly Airport*, the crew would board in twenty minutes which was unfortunately much sooner than their arrival at the southern terminal.

Eva had slipped into the adjoining room, her tone was aggressive, and whoever was on the end of her mobile probably hoped for a quick end to the demands.

Five minutes later, the Chateau team were at the express check out. Jack offered to pay the total bill to speed things up. As they hurried across the pavement towards the waiting taxi three police officers took more than passing interest in their stressed poise, one immediately taking his mobile and whispering into his female colleague's ear.

The white Peugeot taxi driver was ordered to take all risk to get them to *Orly* south terminal in the shortest time possible.

As they sped away the screams from an elegant older lady redirected the police officer's attention. The thief running through the crowd with her bulging *Dior* bag was floored by two very tall African American men, judging from their attire, possible basket-ball players on holiday. As the team watched the spectacle in the distance both Arno and Jack gave a puff of relief, but all noticed the strain showing in Jack's eyes.

Forty-five minutes had passed since the boys were kidnapped from the Chateau. The police officers had finished with Carly, who unfortunately offered no useful description on the assailants, a maybe sighting of a large man in the distance helped little. Now interviews were being conducted with neighbours in avenue, George who could only offer vague unclear recollections.

"I heard a vehicle going fast, but the phone rang so…"

"Think I saw a big car by the trees over there, those Chateau owners are always in big cars, so what!"

Jack had informed Carly they should arrive at Chambéry airport in around one hour. The pain in her voice deepened his mood, his friends offered regular support with Eva constantly holding his arm, he went in and out of conversation. His boys are so close to both mother and father. He regretted the 'stupid' decision to go to Paris, the blinding of a minister was irrelevant compared to the value of his boys' lives.

Crappy insisted on zero use of mobiles during the kidnapping and on the auto route, so when the vehicles were side by side a strange ritual of hand signals, thumbs up and open arms seemed to suggest their plan was moving in the right direction. All of the thugs were feeling more confident; the blue auto Route sign already announcing Marseille, the 'heat' was now a long way behind them. Both

Nick and Simon had agreed to 'play it cool' do what they ask, as they knew parents and any potential assistance would already be working on their behalf.

Ari was showing fatigue, the early start combined with a large shot of Dutch courage the night before in the *Crocodile* bar was telling on him, his eyes getting droopy. For the first time in their ordeal Nick raised his eyebrows, his eyes shot between Ari and his brother, he directed Simon's gaze to his shorts pocket, nothing was showing, then Simon cast his mind back a few months to his brother's birthday. Boris the tech genius had constructed a very special, ultra-thin mobile phone with a GPS tracker, a special birthday present, and it looked like Nick had managed to bring this along. Now all they had to do was switch it on without being spotted, and this seemed impossible as Ari yawned himself back to life, he knew something was wrong.

Chapter 22

The full report on the chemical attack was delivered to the temporary office of Pascal Manozy. The administrator who delivered it suited the surroundings, dull, dark and untidy. It was clear from the first page that a professional team had infiltrated his office with the intention of blinding him, luckily or not, Marine had arrived first, the latest reports on her confirmed she would remain blind, with little possibility of ever regaining normal vision.

Furthermore, his contacts provided new evidence that Eva had indeed been seen at the back of his office building days before the intrusion. More worryingly, she and a group of large European looking men had recently boarded a private jet at *Orly* airport, and the airport security cameras matched the descriptions collected from the ministerial building's security guards. He was one hundred percent convinced that Eva had used him, exactly why was still causing confusion, maybe she had sided with those foreign friends where she lived, but she had betrayed his trust, and as with all the others who double crossed him, she would now pay the price, however Eva retained a special place in his heart, so something special should happen to her.

His senior operations chief had clear instructions to trace all movements of the beautiful ex-secret service operative. When his current guests left Paris, he would take a short break, use the events of late as an excuse to need time away, as soon as he caught up with Eva, she would experience a truly devastating moment. A final breath for Eva or perhaps simply spoil her wonderful face and body, he had yet to decide, but as the anger built he imagined his hands around her throat, no woman used him and walked away.

The stunning mountains surrounding Chambéry airport were ignored, the approach over *Lac du Bourget* often caused Arno to tighten his grip on the arm rests, the lake looked closer every time. Today was different; it was obvious in the faces of the Chateau neighbours. Petty flying problems made way for life changing situations. Boris reminded Jack that he gave a mobile phone with a tracking device to Nick for his birthday; Jack shook his head hoping like crazy his eldest son had the device on him. Eva had been busy for the whole flight attempting to persuade old contacts to help, one a specialist in following ex-prisoners promised to be the best lead so far, but how long? He had no idea. Carly had informed Jack of the negativity from the police, they coldly informed her, "The longer time goes on the weaker the trail becomes."

She was waiting inside the terminal building with Arno's wife Stephanie.

Running into the arrival area the team caused consternation for the airport staff, they feared drunk Russians had landed, or an attack was about to take place.

As soon a Carly saw her man the tears flowed even more.

"Oh Jack, I'm so sorry they hit me with mace, I was useless." Jack saw Carly's eyes were still red and swollen, she fell into his arms.

"You were alone; those bastards took advantage, if only we had..." Jack tailed off as he turned his head towards his friends. Dan jerked his head indiscreetly towards the exit, not a second could be wasted.

Arriving back at the Chateau was an unpleasant experience for each and every person. Carly stared up towards her balcony wishing two handsome young men were leaning on the rail, hard as she tried the balcony was empty, Stephanie held her close.

Four police officers gave polite greetings as the owners passed, Jack, Arno and Dan stopped to request the latest news.

"We have very little to go on, it seems they did not enter the building; no contact was made with the lady, so no DNA to recover, the gravel drive makes it difficult to take tyre impressions. The traces of mace are like one hundred other samples of the fluid, not particular. No fingerprints on the video phone at the gate. The neighbours down the road are old and..."

Jack had heard enough so stopped the oldest officer with a wave of his hand.

"Simply, you know nothing about the men who kidnapped my boys, NOTHING right?"

Jack knew from experience a Frenchman in a corner would be of little assistance, police officer or not, so raised his palms towards the officer whilst walking backwards.

"Keep trying!" Barked Jack as he entered the Chateau.

Eva was waiting by her apartment door as Jack climbed the stairs.

"Can we talk?"

"Of course, do you have anything?"

"I do, but I won't enjoy telling you."

Jack stood against the lounge window as Eva scrolled down her iPad. He could see the badminton net in the garden, and knew his boys had played there yesterday.

"Remember the conversation a few weeks back, you came home from a meeting with a Notaire, and told us all about the brother of Gerard Crappy, a raging bull of a man, prison animal, he got released and inherited the stolen wealth of his dead brother."

"Yeah, that meeting made me, sorry, feel like shit, and now you're going to tell me why I guess." Jack had not turned around.

Eva slid her finger down the screen.

"Well here goes, Marlon Crappy is a freakish monster of a man is living in Marseille in a small apartment above a backstreet bar called the *Crocodile*; earlier this year he splashed the cash, motorbike, couple of cars, but his Predator yacht rarely leaves the harbour. He surrounded himself with limp helpers, a young gay barman, the usual vague amateur background thugs, but he never leaves Marseille. The lawyer who handled the inheritance from his brother has disappeared, the secretary too, nobody has a clue what's happened to them, no bodies, dead end phone records, nothing at all; dubious lawyers in Marseille have ended up as fish food before, so the police are, shall we say, not so active on this kind of case, another dirty lawyer bites the dust, no surprise. The only fable leads have vanished."

"Crappy seems to live on cash, so my contacts have trouble tracing his movements. No information regarding him coming here is available, but like I said the lawyer has gone, so he could have been Crappy's target, not us."

"Not a lot we don't know Eva, but our boys have been taken, and I'm standing listening to stories about an ex-con who's worth millions, what now?"

Boris sat at his double screen system searching for the signal from Nick's phone. Carly confirmed it was missing from the boys' bedroom, but that meant nothing, young men tend to leave objects around the house, and Carly searched and searched to no avail.

Eva briefed everybody about her findings so Arno made the decision to check out the *Crocodile* bar.

"G'day Croc bar." Rog sounded sleepy.

"Well good afternoon, I wonder, looking for a place for a party, around thirty to forty people, doing a seminar in Marseille soon, interested?"

Rog had never taken a call like this before; his bar was frequented by locals, heavy drinkers, back street tourists, a seminar group…

"Um, have to think about this mate, what yah looking for, just drinks, food, and music I guess?"

"All that and more, we're a fun bunch, might even need a place for the more enthusiastic one's to crash, can you help?" Arno frowned as he talked.

Rog saw euro bills flashing before his eyes, why the hell did he never get calls like this before.

"Look mate, reckon I can help here, tons of booze no worries, great atmosphere guaranteed, do have a geezer in my apartment, but he's away a lot, maybe I could fit six or seven tired people in it, I'll try, strewth, hold on, this geezer has a yacht, bloody cool one, what do yah think seminar yacht trip?"

Arno was noting everything he heard from the now very awake Australian.

"You're from down under I think?"

"Yeah, true blue Aussie mate, the names Rog from Adelaide, currently enjoying the Dolce Vita down here."

"I'm interested, let me give some dates, it's really soon, and go for the whole package, sleep over party, drinks on your friend's yacht, tell me how much, should be ok, this is my number."

Rog frantically tried to contact Crappy, but his calls were ignored, the monster couldn't care less about the scraggy Australian.

Arno updated his friends, if Crappy had abducted the boys at least they were zeroing in on his whereabouts, this was the best lead so far.

The adrenalin was pumping through the young guys like never before. The thugs around them looked sleepy, but they hardly blinked.

Nick bent his head to check his plastic swatch; they had now been on the road for five hours, the van had left the auto route, the toll barriers had been spotted in the back window as they pulled away. Now the road was slow and winding, the motion of the vehicle caused both boys to feel nauseous. Glimpses of nature confirmed a warmer climate than Chambéry; the trees looked dry and tired, with not a cloud in the sky.

The van was oppressively warm, small drops of sweat dropped onto the boys' tee-shirts; the hourly sips of water were not enough. Ari appeared irritated by Nick, why? the boys had no idea, but his looks were menacing as if he was spoiling for a fight, the scars on his neck did not help. Nick wished his dad was standing behind Ari, knowing the problem would be sorted in no time. The boys' legs were dead, the lack of possible movement made them feel stiff, lead like, but Nick was terrified to move his right leg too much, if Ari spotted his phone their only chance of contact would be blown, the discomfort could be tolerated, for the moment.

Suddenly the van made a sharp right turn causing the brothers to grimace with pain from the taught rope around their wrists, this brought Ari alive, he gave a *poor things*, pout followed by a sour smile, then a grunt. The van was clearly now off road, clouds of dust from the Land Cruiser blew over the white van.

"Nearly home boys," said Ari as he tapped on the window behind the driver. Within another two hundred meters, the van came to a sudden halt. As Ari jumped out of the back doors, the monster who grabbed the boys at the Chateau appeared briefly; he gave a disinterested glance into the van and then slammed the door.

"Fucking dust, glad when this is over." This was the last the boys heard from their captors for many minutes.

"So, your phone is here, in your shorts?" Asked Simon in a panic.

"Yeah, but I can't get near it, can you?"

Both boys wriggled, burnt their hands, banged heads, and dripped in sweat from their efforts. Nick had to raise his leg because of the cramp; it was a nervous reaction but a costly one. The small phone slid out of Nick's pocket onto the vans metal floor making a tiny sound like a pen on a glass table. Before the boys realised what had happened, Ari ripped the back door open.

"What was that sound?" the boys faces gave a lot away. "I said what was that fucking sound?"

The boys stared directly at Ari as if they were hypnotised by his question. Gradually he curled his head deeper into the van.

"Well well, what do we have here; I knew it, two sneaky little bastards, rich worthless cunts" Nick tried to cover the phone with his stiff leg, but Ari kicked it away and reached for the mobile.

"It was written all over your faces, what else are you little shits hiding?" Ari rushed through a vulgar search of the boys' shorts, slapped them both on the head for their attempt at deceit and jumped out of the van.

Now the conversation was clear.

"Look at this, the bigger kid was trying to hide it." Ari sounded like a schoolboy caving in on a classmate.

The deep voice of Crappy brought a chill to the sauna like van.

"It's just a phone, they don't know where they are, I'll look after it, they won't be making any more calls, that's all over for them."

Both rear doors opened simultaneously, Ari and Rico stood side by side, Crappy behind them, standing a good twenty centimetres above their heads.

The young men were shaking as Rico untied their hands, the words from the large one repeating in their minds. The bright afternoon sun was a painful challenge; movement was slow for both after the long hours in the back. The terrain around them was bare and dry; the sound of crickets filled the air. Thick entangled vegetation covered either side of the dusty path. The boys were determined not to cry or show emotion, but it was hard. The longer the day went on, the further away help appeared, they guessed this was somewhere in the south of France; they were pushed and pulled towards an old wooden building; Claude had walked ahead standing politely at the door like a tacky hotel concierge, the boys knew this would not resemble a hotel sensation once inside.

The building consisted of one large room, a light brown terracotta tiled floor, in the corner a makeshift curtain had been erected with a stained toilet peeping out behind it. A tiny fridge was placed on uneven tiles against another wall, several wooden chairs were arranged in a circle, and not one looked capable of holding the monster's weight. The single benefit of being inside was the relief from the beating afternoon sun.

"House rules, try to escape we kill you, you don't make noise, do what you're told, and when it gets dark, we can see if you two are sailors, ha." Crappy took Claude by the arm and left the hut.

Ari and Rico choose the most substantial chairs, marched the boys over and again tied up hands and legs.

Both Nick and Simon were bushed, the heat in the back of the van left them dehydrated, the one possibility of rescue had been taken from them, and they were confused about Crappy's bizarre comment, "We can see if you two are sailors." They knew full well if they were separated, they would crack up, so tried to keep that thought pushed far away.

"You're not happy with this are you? I see it in your attitude." Crappy was staring down at Claude in the burning sun, that familiar lunatic gaze in his bloodshot – rapidly blinking eyes.

"I only ever offered to help you; I had no idea this sort of thing would happen." Claude took a pace back just in case.

"Don't worry," Crappy tried to sound comforting, "I won't hurt you, but I don't trust those two, only here for the money, when they get it, they'll screw me over, I know that."

Claude recalled the day in the port of Marseille when he offered his help to Crappy, maybe the man did have a good side, or was this wishful thinking?

"So, what's the plan?"

"We leave here when it's dark, I'll pay these two off, leave it to me, they're staying here. We put the kids on the boat, lock them in that cabin, then I'll call the mother or father, and remind them of my lost brother." A chill went down Claude's back, "And then?"

"Don't know yet."

"Where is your yacht now, how can we do this together?"

"It's all sorted Claude, leave it to me."

Crappy had never sounded so calm before, and this felt scary.

The lunatic had now been gone for over two hours; the small wooden cabin was marginally less warm than the back of the van. Ari and Rico took turns to sleep propped up against the cabin walls, snored, coughed, woke up, then dozed off again. Even if the room had been silent the boys could not have been more awake. They whispered when one of their captors left the room for fresh air.

"Think we can get the phone back?"

"How?"

"I miss Mum and Dad; think we'll ever see them again."

"Shut up Simon."

The drips of water were less each offering, the boys' throats were dry and their bodies tired, the smelly captors appeared agitated. Claude and Crappy had not been seen for several hours. The light was fading fast so the shapes of Ari and Rico looked more menacing. Both boys regretted opening the Chateau gates for the courier that morning; this caused a lump in the throat that was hard to swallow away.

The sound of tyres crushing stones came closer; the Toyota's doors slammed roughly at the same time, only Crappy appeared in the doorway.

"Any trouble?"

"Nah, from these two? kids without balls." Ari stared coldly at Crappy.

"Make sure the ropes are tight; put them in the back of the Toyota, then come back in here, I'll explain the plan." Claude was nowhere to be seen.

The boys were shoved onto the four by four's back seat, Rico took a pair of handcuffs from his jeans pocket grabbing Nick's right lower arm, he clicked the silver band around his wrist and pulled his hand towards the metal headrest support, another click and Nick was secured.

"Try to escape now, need to chew you're hand off, bloody funny hey! He tried a limp Hyena howl."

The car's back door was left open as both Rico and Ari walked back to the hut.

The sound of wood breaking over a man's head is enough to give any partner second thoughts, but Ari realised soon enough he had to move quickly, like lightening in fact. He jumped over Rico who was slumped on the floor, the whoosh of a second attempt at a head shot passed a mere five centimetres behind his neck, he turned facing a man who was swinging the chair leg like a crazed killer, the next attempt slashed his shirt open. Crappy stood on Rico's back like it was a doormat as Ari reached into his pocket for his flick-knife; he pulled the reassuring metal tube out as he stretched back to allow a flick of his wrist, the blade opened with a reassuring click, as it always did. The first lunge at Crappy's chest was deflected by the chair leg.

Ari stepped back to access his next possible point of contact, to his surprise Crappy released the chair leg, it bounced onto the floor. The giant stared directly at him with a smile far too confident against a man with a long-bladed flick-knife. Ari ignored the hard-ass attitude and raised his arm preparing for a major thrust. The sensation was too extreme to be described as pain, Claude stood behind Ari's back with the car jack in his hand, his single attempt was executed perfectly; the damage to Ari's right shoulder was confirmed by the cracking sound, the knife fell and bounced on the tiled floor; Crappy performed his party piece simply to show his anger at a stabbing attempt, the nose chop switched Ari's leaning pose from right to left like a small animal, the blood was already pouring from his ruptured nose as he collapsed lifeless on top of Rico.

The boys noticed blood spats on Crappy's shirt as he strode towards the Land Cruiser, Claude pulled himself onto the driver's seat. The boys swapped concerned looks as the car eased away from the gloomy wooden hut. Their earlier prison, the white van was nowhere to be seen.

Crappy considered tossing the boys' phone into the bush, the chance of anybody finding here was close to zero, but still a chance, so he patted it in his pocket and decided to hold onto it until he could fling it into the sea, a much safer option.

"Stop here."

"Really here?" Asked Claude as if the plans had changed.

Crappy reached into the large glove box and retrieved an envelope.

"They won't be needing this now, and you deserve it, thanks."

Claude slid the well-padded envelope between his legs, and managed a rewarding smile; he blinked at the rear view mirror as he watched the hut disappear into the evening darkness.

Chapter 23

Jack Rafter counted eleven calls during the afternoon alone requesting leads, latest information, anything new on his lost boys. The local police were less than helpful. Carly dashed from apartment to apartment, one moment she believed Eva would prove the most useful supporter; the next Dan with his heavy and specialist military background, the lady became more confused as the afternoon passed by. From outside appearances, Jack remained the level headed guy he always was, although inside he was a man at war.

His emotions varied between fully fired up, but he promised himself to be a savage when he caught up with the men who caused this pain, then the real hurt swelled up, considering what his sons could be experiencing at this moment, would they come through it and remain the same lovable young chaps, the knock at his door snapped him out of the trance.

Dan and Arno walked in and sat opposite Jack.

"Decision time old friend, the police are useless, best we have heard is some white van left rapidly down our road; we've all racked the brains now, you gotta be serious Jack, we all hate to consider this option, but Crappy's brother has the best motive, Eva made it clear we looked like the killers in the Gulf of Saint-Tropez, and the bastard we tried to blind this morning wanted us in that corner, it was all too easy, set up the suspicious foreigners, who would care, and now the brother has put two and two together, sorry my friend we have to move, and now." Arno looked relieved that his thoughts had been delivered.

"What if we're wrong?" Jack looked like a man possessed. "What if it's something to do with our actions in Paris, we all know what an evil little bastard he is."

Dan shook his head.

"You know I'm not a rookie at this stuff, the Paris cops are still putting it together, they have no idea who carried that out, maybe they will one day, but not at this pace. We have two choices, sit here and achieve nothing, or go south and find this motherfucker, and by the way Jack, Eva feels as we do, it's a revenge thing, it hurts me to say this, you know how much I love those guys, but we find Crappy, we find our boys, and as I've done a few times over the years, we bring them home safe."

Within half an hour, Carly managed a weak wave of her hand as the car filtered between the trees. Boris had left explicit instructions should a signal show up on Jack's computer, Stephanie assured her they would remain together every hour of the day and night until the boys came home. The medication for the mace attack helped, now her heart was the problem, and the two young men who could lift that were gone without a trace.

It was now close to 10:30 in the evening, the sky was a fiery red, a typical southern coast panorama. Tourists were plentiful, camper vans parked in every possible coast road space, loved up couples wandering back to the holiday apartment, and beachside restaurants gradually vacating tables as the evening crowds headed home.

Claude and Crappy communicated in short bursts of whispers, nervous jilts of their heads and finger pointing. Nick and Simon had already checked their car windows, both were locked, had they been able to scream at passing holiday makers, would it have made escape possible? Most likely the often-drunken audience would have played along and screamed back, it was high season and happy-inebriated types filled the whole coastline, screams of delight, stupidity or plain holiday exuberance occurred every few minutes and nobody would spot the handcuffs anyway.

The D559 coast road had very few straight passages, the constant bends left and right caused pain in Nick's wrist, so as Claude began to slow the car both boys interest arose along with more worrying uncertainty. A sign for *pointe des Issambres* came into view; it was obvious from Crappy's darting head that an arrival point had been planned.

The land cruiser left the road bumping onto a sandy parking terrain, it was relatively clear for the time of year. As they slowed to a crawling pace a tall angular man appeared climbing up from the rocks, his clothing was simple, a black tee-shirt, baggy shorts and bright orange trainers which caused Crappy to shake his head.

As they moved closer the man's appearance was lit up by a passing car. His complexion was deep brown with shiny blonde hair slicked back touching his neck, his eyes were large and enquiring, jumping from the last rock he stood like an athlete completing a matt routine, tall, straight backed and confident.

He reminded Claude of D&G type models promoting summer fragrances, in other circumstances a person of interest to Claude.

"Who um is this?" Said Claude, in a doubtful voice.

"My new captain, he's good, bloody expensive, but capable."

Claude felt deflated, he had been demoted.

"Don't worry, I have other jobs for you, and before you ask, they pay well."

Both boys surveyed their surroundings, cars now passed higher up on the coast road, this place was void of other tourists, towards the sea the nearest boat was a Sunseeker Predator moored a good one hundred meters from the rocky shore, the craft looked bright and reflective in the water, as if a party was planned, they were beginning to realise this involved them.

"All ready Mr Crappy, just as we planned." Dieter, the new captain held his hand towards Claude who cautiously lifted his arm. The large eyes of Dieter now displayed a colder, possibly over confident arrogance, immediately Claude busied himself checking the boys in the back.

Crappy delivered a few incoherent words towards Dieters left ear who nodded enthusiastically like an over keen first day employee. .

Then Crappy turned and opened the rear door, both boys eased back in the seat, he appeared oblivious to their age and stress.

"I always keep my promises, lucky you, you're sailors now, you can forget about that Chateau, it's history for you."

Every time this man spoke, the boys' hearts sank, both felt their young lives were nearly over.

After three attempts the key released the handcuff band, Nick's dead arm fell onto his leg, but Crappy calmly pulled the young man from the car without the faintest concern, Dieter then reached in and pulled Simon out. Claude already felt uncomfortable with the new captain.

The rocks were slippery, if left to their own devices both boys could have navigated the way down to the black dingy easily, but the constant grabbing and directing from Crappy and Dieter made the descent messy and awkward. As Nick turned, he saw Claude parking the Toyota, neatly like a summer tourist planning a day at the beach. Crappy's bulk caused the dingy to take in water, both boys edged towards the front of the small craft, as they moved Dieter mirrored their movements. The Predator turned slowly with the current, now the aft steps could be seen like a grand welcome to the new guests.

Claude confirmed his missing manhood by squealing at least ten times as he slid over the rocks towards the dingy. He preferred to board half soaked instead of climbing over or touching Crappy, so grabbed a handful of rope and pulled himself in halfway between the other sailors, he was sure his mobile took a soaking.

Simon rested his hand on Nick's leg as the small craft was paddled towards the yacht, nobody said a word, the atmosphere was intense. Dieter was evidently a pro sailor, he pulled the dingy alongside the Predator's rear deck, securing ropes in seconds, he offered Claude a hand which was ignored intentionally, both boys did the same, Crappy scrambled on hands and knees, how he arrived on board was a mystery to all. The sticky hand in the boys' tee-shirts felt horrible, the beauty of the yacht ignored as they were marched towards the guest room.

Claude hung back, his eyes glued on the wooden platform, the spot where Lawyer Pierre Perroquet took his last breath.

The Predator's motors burst into life, Claude turned to see Dieter sitting on the captain's seat, he looked at ease, maybe he was a better sailor than Claude, or more likely a person comfortable with dirty deeds and friends as crazy as Crappy. As the craft began to cruise gently away from the shore the boys in the guest cabin watched through the round porthole, they were area experienced enough to know, a turn to the right would be the direction of Sainte-Maxime, but the craft turned left, and the lights of the coastline became distant, flickering in the haze of the sea at night.

Crappy listened at the boys' door for almost fifteen minutes; he could make nothing from their whispering, the loudest sound came from two cans of coke bursting open. He felt tired and uncomfortable, so exercised his stiff upper back, felt for his key and opened his stateroom door. All appeared in place, he was the only key holder so why not? With three more measured paces he knelt at the floor cupboard, another key was produced; he uttered a large sigh of relief upon stroking the black leather bag, pulling it out of the tight space like a child under a Christmas tree. He threw it on the bed, opened the zip halfway, took a handful of bills, charged his wallet and returned the bag to its hiding place. Nick's mobile phone was placed next to the TV on the long cream cabinet top, he decided the next time on deck the device would be thrown overboard.

Claude remained a safe distance from Dieter, neither attempted conversation. For the first time since Claude started working for Crappy, the lunatic was happy to leave others in charge.

After twenty minutes at sea, Dieter slowed the Predator's engines to a crawl, Claude stepped out of the salon, holding the side rails and looking towards the bow. Harbour lights were getting closer as Crappy appeared on the stairs.

"Remember we moor at the end of the harbour, I checked it out, the best and quietest place."

Dieter gave a rapid nod, like a soldier accepting serious orders.

As the yacht eased closer towards the harbour's glowing red and green light entry, Claude saw bars and restaurants in the distance. Why was he on this yacht? Why are two young boys with a fate unknown one deck below? He should be a barman in one of those places, that's all, no more, instead he was helping a murderer for large wads of cash, and now they have been joined by a German captain who has the eyes of a psycho. Claude could not help but consider his life had been ruined by a chance meeting at his bar job, had he been less greedy life would have continued, the extra cash would not have been missed and his conscience would be clean. But what could he do? The mess around him was considerable; did he have the courage to do the right thing? He bent forward and pushed the buoys over the side, the harbour wall was getting close.

Once the Predator was secured towards the end of the harbour wall, Dieter was dispatched to buy pizza for all on board, Claude wondered why he was no longer trusted to run these errands, suddenly Crappy was standing behind him.

"I needed a crazy creep, you're not that man, he is. I met up with him a few years back, inside, he's done more evil things than me, and so, that's why he's with us."

Claude gave a dazed shake of his head, every day was getting worse, now he had close associations with two convicted murderers, all this achieved in only six months, he was amazed how well he screwed up.

Crappy delivered the pizzas to the boys, upon hearing the door code both moved closer on the guest bed, the stench from the monster was almost equal to the aroma of the pizza, the boys' appetite was in short supply.

"Eat this, you're lucky I feed you, my brother was not so lucky." Nick and Simon displayed total confusion at his comments.

He slammed the door laughing and eagerly decided to play a sick joke, detestable even for his murky standards.

Sitting on the end of his master suite bed he reached for Nick's mobile, since meeting Claude he had managed to obtain some basic technical skills. Scrolling through the boys *Contacts* list he quickly found *Mum,* taking a deep breath he touched the screen, it only took one ring.

"My baby, where are you? I...I...are you ok? What's going on with you and Simon, I can't believe this is happening. Nick...are you there? Nick please say something."

"You idiot, you stupid bitch." Carly looked at the phone as if she was staring at Crappy.

"Don't harm my boys, please, I'll give you anything, we can pay well, please leave them somewhere safe."

"You mean like your husband left my brother? Ha, and I don't need your stinking money." Crappy's voice sounded cold, disturbed, his tone was pure hatred.

"Sorry you're wrong, my husband, his friends did nothing to your brother, really nothing."

"My contacts tell a different story, lying bitch."

"You cannot hurt two innocent young boys; my sons are not who you want."

"An eye for an eye lady, you screwed my life now I screw yours."

"Let me speak with them, I beg you."

"Did you let me speak with my brother? Now I decide, hope they like water."

The beep in Carly's ear caused her to gulp for air. Crappy threw the mobile against the bathroom door sure he would never need it again.

"Hello...hello, please are you there?" She knew she was talking to an empty line, but could not stop herself.

"No, god no." She crumpled on the bedroom floor holding the phone tight to her cheek, pushing it into her face.

Trying desperately to control her breathing she took a lungful of air, her hands were shaking like a morning after alcoholic, Jack's number flashed up and down the screen but she could not touch the right place, strangely the tears held back, she suddenly focused, all shaking ceased, an unexplained calm came over her, Jack's number showed as if the phone had frozen. A rigid index finger dropped towards the number.

"Honey we're here in Marseille, any news?"

The tears came back like an open tap.

"He called." Everyone in the car caught the desperation in Carly's voice; Eva placed her hand on Jack's shoulder.

"So we are in the right location, please just tell us what he said, hard honey I know, we need to hear it." Jack hit *speaker.*

"He's a lunatic Jack; he's going to kill our boys." Carly was wiping her face with her sleeve, the whole car listened to the woman's agony, Jack gripped the wheel like he was holding onto life.

"He said you killed his brother, now it's an eye for an eye." The emotion in Carly's voice caused Eva to flick a tear away.

"This guy will be stopped; I promise on my life darling." Dan gave a nod of agreement.

"Stay close to Stephanie, update us on any news whatsoever, I'll do the same, I love you."

The GPS announced, *you have reached your destination.*

Chapter 24

The *Crocodile* bar on *Rue Frangy* was pretty unimpressive at eleven in the evening. A flashing oblong sign depicting a bright green Crocodile with blood dripping from his teeth, chasing a bushman, beer in hand, told all potential customers what they could expect inside. The place suited its scruffy back street location, not one building looked cared for. An old wobbly drunk wandering close to the walls of the street for guidance, dimmed lights in the bedroom level windows, and occasionally raised voices from the more experienced drinkers, not much more took the attention.

Jack parked the car a discreet thirty meters from the entrance. Dan was the first out of the car closely followed by Arno and Eva. Boris tucked his valuable laptop under the back seat, slid sideways and caught a glimpse of his friend's faces which were highlighted by a streetlight; it was not a sight he had seen before; something was very different; their eyes were angry but controlled, searching, and very focused. An atmosphere of tension had just arrived in the small street, and he was worried if he could fulfil his role.

He recalled being in an Amsterdam nightclub early one morning, a drugged-up guest took a lunge at one of the security guards, like a challenged wild animal the guard reacted in a split second, the druggie was hit seven times in rapid succession, three to the head and four between throat and chest, his eyes sunk into his skull, his body became a deflated balloon. The guard kept his position over the crumbling body as it hit the floor, then calmly dropped his arms to his side. Boris expected to witness far more aggressive moments in the next hours.

As the *Croc* bar's entrance door came closer Jack patted his jeans, strange they were about to enter the place where Crappy lived but none of them were armed. Physically they had massive advantages but a knife can cause all sorts of issues and short of grabbing a bar stool they could be at a disadvantage.

Before Jack had taken one step through the door every single drinker, hooker and pool player appeared to snap out of the evening atmosphere and drill their attention on Jack and his friends.

As Arno, then Dan, Eva and finally Boris coolly sauntered in every piece of clothing, from Dan's *SEALs do it under water* tee-shirt to Arno's bulging shirt sleeves and Eva's low-cut blouse was analysed, if they had been on the catwalk less scrutiny would have been placed on them. Subtlety did not exist in this bar, this was a mean place filled with individuals who stole, abused, and cheated their way through life, which was evident in the first few seconds.

Rog stared in amazement, the last time he saw an entry like this, he was the guest of a rich Australian cousin, an invite to the Cannes film festival, Brad and Angelina had been collected from their yacht, they were posing on the red carpet, lapping up the gawping dreamers. His place had never been graced by such presence before. As the team strode confidently up to the bar, two more hidden drinkers were positioned deep in the bars darkest corner, partly to hide the bruises and body damage, also because nature had made them this way.

Jack was still looking from left to right as Arno thrust a hand towards Rog.

"Evening, you must be Rog from Adelaide?" He looked shaken, this was not a cop at this time of night, the accent, left him blank, then gradually he recalled that guy who called about a seminar. He brushed his face, stroked his chin and started chuckling.

"Yeah right, you called, now I remember, well welcome to the humble *Croc* bar, yah handsome friends also." Polite gestures were returned by a faint nod of the head from the bar's newest clients.

"What can I offer, first round on me." Jack displayed a look which was nothing like a seminar guest.

"My friend told me you have a contact with a yacht, I love yachts, I'm the guy who arranges fun on water."

Rog was in the middle of pouring beers for Jess the waitress, still trying to take in the new arrivals and hoping his regulars would not do anything stupid, the new faces had something menacing about them.

"Yeah, it's called a Sunseeker, the Predator if that sounds right, horny craft if ever I saw one."

Rog glanced at Eva hoping his words had impressed her, he wished he had not, if looks could kill, he was already in a box, her singular raised eyebrow hit him like an arrow to the forehead; he dropped his gaze like a rude schoolboy.

Boris felt more comfortable between Dan and Arno, peeping around their ample frames to size up the guests; most had returned to enjoying the evening with the exception of two in the darkest corner of the bar, since the newcomers had arrived these guys said virtually nothing, made the occasional comment to one another which resulted in a confirmation nod, no more than that.

Rog was astonished that his offer of a round resulted in five Perrier with ice; he still dare not look at Eva.

Arno took Rog to the end of the bar attempting to interrogate him with the excuse of a pending seminar.

Jack whispered in Eva's ear; he was taken aback how exquisite she managed to smell close up after the challenging day. She advised her neighbour and close friend to, "Take it easy, we are a good team and close to the bastard." This advice fell on deaf ears. Boris wished he could lip read, feeling sure the two shady types in the corner needed further investigation, had he been able to, the conversation would have confirmed his suspicions.

"I think it's to do with those boys, never seen smart fucks like this crowd in a back street bar before."

Ari said a silent "yeah" in agreement and locked eyes with Boris; it lasted barely two seconds but provided Boris with ample confirmation that these scruffy and damaged wasters were a point of interest.

The Chateau tech guy pretended to appreciate Dua Lipa by swaying closer to Jack, Eva was constantly transfixed on the tortured father knowing he could explode any second, she knew from experience that far more information had to be gathered before this night was over.

Boris stood with his back towards Ari and Rico, smiled at no one in particular between Jack and Dan, raised his Perrier glass to his cheek and spoke softly but articulated his words to avoid any doubt.

"I would bet my apartment back at the Chateau that those two in the dark corner are worth talking to."

Not a word was missed by the ex-SEAL and his friend. Eva tried to grab Jack's arm but he was mesmerised like a hungry lion finally sighting food. Crappy's ex helpers initially displayed the crazed eyes of street scum, standing and lifting their chins in defiance, but as Dan followed close behind Jack's left shoulder a doubt appeared in their posture, to add more uncertainty Arno, who was a mere three meters away, turned away from Rog and glared at them with serious intent; after their earlier beating both immediately favoured a quick retreat or maybe conversation before yet more physical contact. Jack's stare was so intent both Ari and Rico considered him a user; normal people just don't have those eyes.

Time goes out of control during such moments; Jack's face was now a not so cosy twenty centimetres away from Ari's distorted and bandaged nose and black eyes, Rico slid his hand behind his back and took the neck of a beer bottle, Dan expected this typical bar brawler move so shot his trained left hand into Rico's upper arm, his grip amazed the thug, it was like a vice, and still growing in force, his thumb pressed hard into bicep muscle, so hard that the bottle fell on the floor, he quickly measured how futile it would be to swing his other arm, the possessed man drilling his eyes into Ari would hardly be aware, then the man with the Navy SEAL tee-shirt would use his free arm, this still left a massive guy at the bar to be dropped, all in all, best to give in and save their damaged bodies from more punishment.

"I bet before you draw your last breath, you can tell me a lot about a big guy who lives here?" Jack moved his face even closer.

A couple of the more timid drinkers eased towards the doors, the more adventurous ones gossiped rapidly and downed their glasses in anticipation of a showdown in the dark corner, Rog tried hard to work out the connection between these visitors and Crappy.

"What big guy?" asked Ari in a very unconvincing voice.

"Don't mess with us, it's not *that* evening, I guess he did this to your faces, now work out what we will do if you don't tell us where to find those young guys." Jack resisted touching Ari.

"Can you pay?" Even Rico was flabbergasted at Ari's bravado.

Eva's joined her men in the corner; the powerful feminine presence caused the thugs to become even more uncomfortable, if that was possible.

"You've just confirmed you know what happened to these young boys, don't make it worse, tell us where they are or I will slit your throats personally in this bar, the boys are like my own sons!"

The game felt like it was over for the two sorry looking characters that edged further into the shadows, as if three large intimidating men were not enough, now a diva threatening to slit their throats made escape, aggression, even money for information an unlikely outcome.

Rico blurted first, "They gotta be on that yacht, no room for us, they must be there."

"And where the hell is that yacht?" Now Jack could not resist twisting his fist into Ari's collar.

"He keeps it here in the port, darn things called *Fisc Attack.*"

"Yeah, we know that, did you hurt the boys?" Said Dan. The cowardly grimacing from the two did not help their predicament.

Jack took Ari's windpipe which caused a gasp from the bar guests, Rog shook his head saying, "Here we go, bugger up my furniture, knew it."

"If my boys have one tiny, and I mean tiny mark on them, I'll come back here and rip your throats out."

The power from Jack's grip made Ari realise this man was not joking, he probably could rip a man's throat out.

The deflated thugs could not believe their luck, a potential second beating in one day avoided when the three men and beautiful lady turned, pushed a nosey fat drunk to one side and headed for the door, Boris made sure he was first through, a sudden rush for refills after the cabaret took Rog off guard, he shouted at Arno's back, "That seminar mate, still on I hope?"

As the large black car sped past the bar windows both Ari and Rico wondered why everybody wanted to mutilate them on this particular day.

The old port of Marseille is off limits to most level headed people from late evening to first light. Normally Jack would choose a protected parking bay for his wife's RR , tonight his mind was elsewhere.

Should the *Bonnes Vacances* hotel owner have problems with somebody filling his *Guest* parking space he had better be prepared for trouble. The sight of five curious shapes almost rushing away from the car, told him to be careful, normal holidays makers do not rush in the direction of the port so late at night, the 73 number plate ‑mountain people ‑made this moment even more out of the ordinary.

Locating a yacht with a quirky name in a port summer full was not going to be easy; the midnight hour did not help; the marine police building was dark. As each of the friends increased their walking pace to a slow jog, they became separated, Jack, Dan and Arno all disappeared along the gangways checking the names of any sleek craft longer than twenty meters, it was a daunting task, all were tired after the events in Paris, adrenaline and passion kept them all focused. The old port was large. They all assumed that Crappy would choose a mooring as far away from prying eyes as possible, this made the mission even harder, to cover the whole area would take time, and every passing minute made Jack fret for his boys, what they could be going through would ensure he kept going until he dropped, luckily his friends had the same mentality.

After one hour of desperate searching, no Predator named *Fisc Attack* had been located. From the tone of the voices over the mobiles it was clear that desperation was setting in. Drunks and beggars tried to accost each and every one in the poorly lit areas, the encounter lasted a few brief seconds, one more 'verbal' creature pushed his luck a little too far, maybe his mouth, maybe his smell, but something set Dan off, the round house kick sent the man reeling backwards, his attempt to snatch a mooring rope failed, the *plop* followed, Dan carried on walking, nothing should get in his way tonight.

As the staff of *La Nautique* restaurant switched of the last lights Jack raised his head towards the *Notre-Dame-de-la-Garde*, he was certainly not a religious man, but on this night, he needed all the help he could get, he whispered a simple request, "Help me get my boys back, please" then turned to see Eva and Boris joining him on the quay.

"Jack we really have to rest, the Sofitel here has space; we can come back at first light." Eva doubted her suggestion would be accepted, but Jack responded with a small nod, he was not broken, but Eva had never seen him look so shattered. Nobody slept; they rested the weary bodies for a few hours, downed bottles of chilled water to reduce the effects of dehydration. Jack called Carly who answered like she was taking her last breath.

"Tell me something positive, please Jack."

He sounded cold and lost.

"This creep does have our boys, we're looking everywhere, he's not in the marina, we need a clue, something, I promise I'll bring them home...I promise."

Carly had never heard her husband sound so worn; it was almost a different man on the end of the phone, his usual upbeat and clipped replies missing. She pulled the bedclothes higher; it was mid-summer but her body was cold, Stephanie called a short "okay?" from the next room, the silence told her no progress had been made.

"Keep in touch." Carly placed the phone on her pillow like a small symbol of hope. Jack closed his eyes, but his over active mind jerked them open again, he kept his jeans and Polo shirt on, he saw no point in trying to get comfortable.

Marlon Crappy again woke with misty vision, his dependence on alcohol ensured each day began with a stiff neck and pounding forehead. As he pushed himself up from the stateroom bed a Vodka bottle clunked as it hit the carpeted floor, he cursed; saw his frightening image in the TV screen and staggered into the bathroom. The boys in the next room had fallen in and out of a fatigue induced sleep, the falling bottle stirred them, a dim morning light was breaking through the round cabin window, and a very uncoordinated human mass was moving next door.

The beast climbed the stairs to the main deck; Gazing bewildered from left to right he still had doubts that this elegant yacht was really his. The instruments, leather covered wheel, plush fittings, it was everything opposite to his life, a mess of disorganised situations, the wrong thing in the wrong place, the Predator always looked just perfect.

Rubbing his bald head Crappy caught site of a small green fishing boat leaving the harbour, the three men on board were working like beavers, preparing nets, turning ropes and chatting intensely, they were late and it showed in their movements.

A whiff of cigarette smoke passed his swollen red nose causing him to turn in all directions; propped up, back against the harbour wall, Dieter was starting his day staring towards the blue Med. At first Crappy hesitated, the boys were below, Claude still sleeping, should he join his new captain? Try to gain his support for the despicable times ahead, he certainly showed far more balls than Claude. Without thinking further Crappy pulled his heavy frame onto the harbour wall, his movements were far from elegant, the grappling from yacht side rail to mooring rope informed Dieter he had company, and the way Crappy threw his money around, this company was always welcome.

Claude watched the oversized shoes pass his cabin window, further along the harbour wall a more restricted view limited his glance, but the orange trainers gave it away, the new captain was about to be joined by the owner, leaving but three people on the yacht, it was now or never.

Images of an angry Crappy filled Claude's mind, but the time had arrived when he felt compelled to stop the madness which now filled his life, killing a dirty lawyer and his girlfriend was extreme enough, but now two young boys!

A reflection of the boys' mother falling to the floor screaming with mace dripping from her face sealed it. The master cabin door was unlocked; the simple act of pushing it further open caused Claude to shudder; a tiny slit of upper window revealed the orange trainers still in place, next were two large black Nikes. Crouching as he moved further into the cabin Claude almost tripped over an empty bottle, his eyes scanned the floor, the corners, it had to be somewhere in the room. The air conditioning made the cabin feel cold, but his hands were sweating like a grill chef, he moved towards the far side of the room, close to the tinted windows, if Crappy saw him his young life would be over, but again no sight of the boys' phone.

He pulled open one drawer, then another, his actions were clumsy, dirty stained tee-shirts, soiled underwear and mucus filled handkerchiefs filled every space, the smell was horrible, one cupboard was locked, hope was disappearing, closing all drawers he turned edging around the bed, a small couch took his attention, the pillows were stacked to one end, but the couch was far too small for Crappy's large frame; for no particular reason Claude turned the pillows over, one, then two and three, a small slither of silver was showing but tucked deep into the structure of the couch, his slender hand pushed down between the soft fabric, he pulled gently, the device slid out, holding it between his thumb and forefinger, the screen was cracked, but at least he had it.

Then a moment's hesitation to listen for movement, nothing, then a quick check of the oblong cabin window; he crouched to gaze through the upper portion, the morning sun hit the tinted window so he blinked, stretched his neck to confirm, a shock went through his body, only the orange trainers were left; a footstep and a grown came from above, now the most important dash ever in his life was imminent, somehow the cabin door closed without a sound. As he stretched his right leg towards the guest cabin, two large black shoes appeared on the stairs, so another giant step took him through the door, he turned, held the door to and felt for the mobile in his back pocket. The silence outside his cabin was petrifying; it seemed to last for a minute at least.

"Claude, I can hear you fucking around in there." His knees were ready to give way.

"Get dressed and feed those bloody kids, even guys on death row deserve a last breakfast."

With a freakish laugh Crappy slammed his door.

Chapter 25

Jack knew the harbour police started early, six thirty was ambitious but he couldn't care less. The solitary young officer unlocked the door, his chief told him seven was a satisfactory hour to assist the public, but the persistent knocking from the determined men at the door told him a possible marine disaster was about to be reported. The quality of the men's clothing and the seriousness of their demeanour reassured the junior officer that an expensive yacht problem was his first case of the day; however, his chief's early call on the emergency line took his attention for the moment.

Eva took on the role of mother for her macho men, apologising for their rude departure, promising only water had been taken from the mini-bar and offering to settle the half night's bill.

The text from Jack told her to head in the direction of the marine police building. Boris was under pressure, how his neighbours kept up the pace for the last twenty-four hours was beyond him, his legs felt dead, like he just ran a marathon, his eyes were heavy and he berated himself for forgetting to bring the silver case containing the *Spurge*, it could have been useful when they located the much talked about monster, Crappy.

The quay leading to the harbour police building was quiet, white delivery vans, mostly listing food and wine products on the sides made up the majority of the traffic. Yawning sail yacht owners, who always seemed motivated to rise much earlier than their gas guzzling motor yacht counterparts, began to appear from below deck. The smell of coffee sometimes interrupted that of ozone and fresh fish arriving on the docking vessels. Eva almost missed the two business suited men across the road, the dark glasses and cropped hair confirmed they were certainly not early rising tourists. The training and instinct made her quickly turn the head away, she grabbed Boris's arm and spun him around to face the marina, his shock was obvious, he blushed as Eva threw her arms around his shoulders, but her smile looked genuine as she pecked his right cheek, sadly the guys across the road were nowhere to be seen. Eva's smile was gone as she pondered over her past.

Finally, after many precious minutes, the young police officer returned his attention to the early morning visitors.

"I am so sorry, my chief talks too much."

Jack scoffed as Arno leaned further across the counter causing the young officer to take a pace back.

"Yacht's called *Fisc Attack*, Sunseeker Predator, believe it's usually moored here, we're supposed to meet up with the owner, know where we can find it?"

A weird attitude came over the uniformed officer; he brushed his shirt nervously, shook his head, and displayed a look of worry, a changed man after one reasonable question.

"Something wrong?" Asked Jack with a very doubtful gaze.

The young man began to wish his colleagues had arrived; even his irritating chief would be made welcome to deal with this question. The times he received complaints about this particular craft and the owner, the noise from strange lady visitors late at night, a regularly drunk and aggressive beast of a man staggering around the marina, even vague reports of people being dragged onto the craft late at night, but every time they were dispatched to check, the craft was empty, all in order, in truth no officer relished the order to check *Fisc Attack*, the history of the yacht and its new owner prompted caution and distance, an unlucky vessel was a curse to anyone holding passion for the sea.

"I believe it's out of the harbour for the moment."

"We guessed that, but somebody must know something, do you have a number for the owner?" Jack turned as Eva and Boris pushed through the door with expectant faces. Their hopes were dashed when Dan and Arno gave vague shakes of the head.

Suddenly Eva stood between the guys, both perfectly manicured hands placed on the counter.

"This is not a broken motor, stolen compass, anything so trivial, we believe this craft is connected a kidnapping, two special young men have been taken, do you understand how urgent this is...*do you?*"

The young officer's initial idea of, "Show your authority," shot out through the window immediately, he swallowed hard, took a deep breath and caved in.

"When he came out of *Baumettes* I was the one who dealt with him, right here, what a lunatic, nobody was brave enough to cross him, but he paid all the mooring bills, what could we do? His brother died at sea, he inherited the lot, great yacht and a pile of money. Some people think he's connected to a lawyer who disappeared, and now we just heard he's working with a new guy, the name's Dieter, he's maybe more psycho, if that's possible, he's also an ex-inmate of *Baumettes*, they stick together hey?"

"Interesting, but where is the yacht now?" Jack raised his voice so loud that even Arno looked concerned.

"We have no idea, sorry." In less than ten seconds, five seriously frustrated individuals were heading towards a poorly parked car.

Claude was trying his level best to look anything but suspicious, the plan in his head was clear, but the execution was fraught with potential pit-falls. Dieter spent his time shuffling around the Predator. Claude knew this was an act, his own good level of sailing experience had taught him the important checks, and the not so important, but as Crappy had taken a shine to Dieter all was tolerated. It was now the fifth time he passed Claude preparing bread and fruit juice for the captors below, the salon table was cluttered so Dieter scanned it as if he was now security on board, Claude dare not touch the mobile in his back pocket, but somehow he needed to hide it under the boys' food.

"I thought you were some sort of bar boy" Said Dieter in a derogatory tone.

"I am a barman." Claude did not lift his head.

"Then why the fuck do you take so long on breakfast for two almost dead kids?"

Claude turned and fixed his eyes on Dieter's forehead.

"Why don't you carry on pretending you're important, Mr Captain, and leave me alone?"

Claude was a trifle surprised he came out with such a bold answer, but it worked, Dieter threw his head back, let out a loud, "Hah prick," and sauntered to the rear of the craft disappearing down the steps, even his whistling annoyed Claude.

The moment had arrived; the tray was ready, two plates side by side, large chucks of bread, and two glasses of orange juice. Claude's shaking hands had spilt several drops of juice over the table so his hand felt sticky when he reached into his back pocket for Nick's mobile. The best possible place was between the plates, so another chunk of bread was added to cover the gap, the glasses were pushed close together, and the mobile was hidden.

Claude raised the tray slowly, hoping to balance the contents, but also trying to steady his nervous system.

Turning gradually his eyes were fixed on the gap between the plates, a discreet silver side of the device was showing, over the far edge of the tray a large belly appeared, Claude raised his head so quickly that both glasses jumped on the tray and lost half of their contents.

"This looks like you're still working at that bloody hotel, waste of time, throw it in the room, they won't eat it anyway." Suddenly Crappy also held the tray.

"You remember the code, or shall I take it?"

Claude's head began to shake nervously, if Crappy saw the mobile, it was over, his mind flashed back to the site of the plastic bags filled with decorative garden stones, he seemed to remember there were still three in the yachts garage.

"Please, you know this is not my forte, let me give it to them, I'll feel better if I do."

Crappy brushed past the shivering barman spilling yet more orange juice.

"Dieter open the garage I want to check something," as Crappy's bald head bobbed down the rear stairs, Claude balanced the tray watching the orange juice trickle between the plates.

Nick and Simon were fixated on the cabin door; somebody was tapping in the entry code for the third time. The site of Claude standing in the doorway, tray shaking, with a look of desperation in his face caused the boys to sit upright on the bed, and take an overlarge breath; after three attempts he managed to blow a hush sound from his lips, it was wasted, the boys were too terrified to make any noise, Nick did manage to crunch his forehead and move his lips in a 'what's happening' gesture. Claude used his heel to push the door closed.

"I have to be quick, here." Claude pushed the tray gently across the bed sheets, "Your mobile is under the plates, call your parents quick, and tell them we're in the harbour of Villefranche."

The whispering was barely audible, before the boys could ask anything he was gone, the door handle clicked back into place, they were alone with a tray covered in orange juice, and the bread looked stale.

Nick pushed his hand between the plates; he instantly knew the feel, sliding his soggy phone out, spots of juice dripped onto the bedclothes, brushing the screen against his shorts, he listened, there were sounds in the distance, large marine engines, seagulls, but the immediate vicinity appeared quiet.

He tapped at the bottom of the cracked screen waiting for the light to come on, nothing, he tapped again and again, Simon was rubbing his hands willing the thing to respond.

"Work now, please do it, please." Whispered Simon, but the phone was dead.

Jack was driving like a nut, horn blowing drivers regularly gave him the middle finger, the best French insults and threw their arms in the air, he appeared oblivious. Arriving at the offices of Pierre Perroquet all were feeling tired, negative and lost without direction, but it was a lead that had to be checked out.

The brass nameplate had not been removed so a little hope remained, Jack pressed the buzzer hard into the wall, after five minutes a small boned, heavily freckled lady appeared behind the large wooden door.

"The office is closed, the man has disappeared, and the administrators are looking after everything, I can't help you." As the tiny woman pushed the door, Jack pushed back.

"We really need help, this lawyer had a client, a very big bald man, have you seen him here?"

"Filthy lawyers attract a filthy client, that's all I know." With that, the woman turned leaving the door open.

"It's a dead-end buddy." Dan watched Jack drop his head, who walked back to the car and rested his face on the side window. Nobody said a word because they had no idea where to look next.

Carly saw the police car stop at the main gate, she had been staring at the spot for the last fifteen minutes, as the officer came out of the door, she touched the command in her hand. She knew the car only had two occupants but hope for familiar shapes to leap from the back remained, what else could she do in the circumstances?

Stephanie let them in, Carly sat in the lounge, it was immediately evident that this lady had not slept for a long time, her cheeks were pale, eyes dead and bloodshot, she picked at her fingers, so the police attempted to be diplomatic.

"We have to ask some awkward questions; have you been contacted by the people who took your boys?"

Her mind was clearer on this issue, having already decided to leave the task to Jack and his team, the police were filling in paperwork, at least Jack was on the move.

"No, nothing, only my husband called, really nothing." She did not look up.

"Your husband called, so where is he now?" The middle-aged officer had doubt all over his face.

Carly disliked this question, almost as if they were now under suspicion.

"My husband is doing his best to find clues, he's in the south."

Both officers turned to one another as if a following a routine, then the oldest spoke with a clear lecturing tone.

"Madame, we are doing all possible to find your sons, people are being checked as we speak, I cannot tell you the specifics, it's an ongoing investigation, but if your husband, a civilian is acting like a detective he has to stop now!"

Carly was already broken, the thought of Jack and his more than competent team being stopped was something she would not tolerate, nobody could be as motivated to return their loved ones like him.

"Maybe I'm saying the wrong thing, but I can guarantee you, the team from this Chateau are the worst nightmare for the kidnappers, they have skills you can only dream of and contacts for that matter, if…"

She was cut off by the clearly agitated officer who now stood to gain physical advantage.

"When civilians take matters into their own hands people die Madame, I need to speak with Mr Rafter now."

"Unless you can come up with something concrete, and I mean quickly, this meeting is over." Carly spoke firmly whilst staring at the wooden floor.

"I will speak with my chief; you will hear from us; this is not the way we do things in France!"

Carly stood and turned her back to hide the tears, Stephanie followed the police to the apartment door.

Eva appeared back at the car from the small 24-hour supermarket, her arms were laden with sandwiches and soft drinks. She knew Jack would pretend he had no appetite, this she would not accept and decided to baby feed him, if necessary, but she would make him eat. Dan being ex-military ate like a hungry dog, Arno too, fatigue versus energy was how they summed it up.

Jack had been called by Carly and updated on their precarious situation, she simply said, "We are behind you, find our guys please." Jack kept the call brief to save battery power; everybody was tapping into the car system including Boris for his close companion laptop, basically they all hoped for a call or sign. The car had turned into a mobile command centre.

Nick and Simon had flushed the stale bread down the toilet, but the remaining orange juice was welcome. They had now been left alone for about one hour. Voices could be heard above their cabin, but the conversation impossible to understand. Nick had managed to unscrew the back from the mobile, his shorts zipper making this possible, he hide the unit under the sheets in case they were disturbed. Over the last few months he had watched Boris open all types of computer, mobile phone and the new PS5, the man was a genius, he could spend a happy few moments humming with his head buried in the chips and wires; in no time the mobile phone sent a message to the PS5, all surrounding screens lit up, and Boris's voice commanded each and every action in the room; sadly the skills of Boris were not replicated by Nick, try as he might, the device remained dead, but apart from the cracked screen everything appeared fine.

Both boys knew time was running out, the only small lifeline was the dead mobile, soon the code would sound, but the chance of Claude appearing would be unlikely, the monster was due a visit and help was a million miles away.

Crappy had sat, stood, laid, and assumed uncomfortable looking positions on the rear platform for a long time, Dieter had smoked seven cigarettes, their conversation had ranged from whispering to fiery exchanges. One moment they sat with feet dangling into the water like two teenagers on a summer break, the next frenzied swearing and animated hand movements as if a fight would breakout. Claude had initially considered Dieter a handsome man, almost a dream meeting for a small homosexual, but the first impression had lasted but a few minutes, as soon as Dieter started reacting like a lapdog to Crappy, Claude was turned off, now he seemed to enjoy the run of the yacht, no questions asked by the control freak, an atmosphere had been created since he came on board, surely, he was the psychopath that Crappy needed, but why?

The Mistral became an irritation for the tattooed men sitting on the rear platform of a sleek silver yacht.

Their annoyance would have increased if they had caught the comments directed at them from the constant flow of passing ferry tenders, the giant cruise ships moored out in the bay supplied all shapes, sizes and races; the chatter followed the same pattern.

"Can't be the owners, they look more like convicts on a day out."

"Bet the guy who owns this will be pissed when he sees these two just climbed on board."

"I was looking forward to lunch in Villefranche, if this is the level of local yacht owner I wonder if…"

The ex-cons climbed the rear stairs at the same time, Claude allowed himself an insecure cheeky smile, as both men rose up towards him. Crappy's bald head had changed colour, now bright pink like a beacon for what not to do in the height of summer sun, Dieter looked windswept and browner like a true yacht captain.

The body language from the pink monster was clear; Claude was not welcome as they sat half in and half out of the open main deck. Crappy produced a bottle of white wine from the fridge next to the table, filled two glasses to the brim and started talking in a hushed voice.

Claude withdrew towards the stairs leading to the cabins, but felt compelled to linger when he caught a couple of words from the monster, "So, it's the deepest place?"

Sitting hard up against the side wall and four steps down he knew his small frame would be hidden, fortunately Crappy only glanced once to check, believing he was gone his volume increased.

"You sure about this."

"Of course, I am, I'm a bloody good captain, the Bay of Villefranche is one of the deepest in the Med. If you want to drown the kids here make them heavy and they're gone, why do you think so many of those large cruise ships moor here, perfect place."

"Ok you're getting well paid for this; we keep it between us, say nothing to that fucking poof."

"You pay what you promised, my mouth is sealed Mr Crappy, just tell me when." Dieter emptied his glass in one swallow.

Claude's mind felt hazy, it was difficult to grasp every word but his worse fears had been confirmed, Crappy was going to kill the boys, it was not an idle threat. Killing Perroquet and Hati was simply warming up; this lunatic was so filled with revenge that the innocent people from the Chateau would soon lose two blameless young men in the most horrible of circumstances.

The whack of the bottle on the table told Claude two things, Crappy was getting pissed, and he must risk his life now or never. He pressed his hands on the stairs, lifting his body, but keeping his head bowed, then stretching his legs, first the right, and when balanced the left, the burr of conversation became faint as he eased down the steps.

An ear to the boys' cabin door gave nothing away, so he cupped his hand over the metal pad to reduce the sound of the electronic clicks as he entered the code, it still peeped too loud. On the other side of the door, Nick pulled the bedclothes up to conceal the mobile, Simon could only stare at the opening door like he expected the monster.

"Is it working, have you called your parents?"

It was impossible for the young men to know who they could trust, so both hesitated with eyes darting back and forth. Claude had been the most low key out of the kidnappers, he never touched the boys, screamed at them or made threats, even at their young ages both realised he was a gay guy, simply so different to the other rough pigs on board the yacht.

Everything flashed quickly through Nick's mind with a rapid conclusion literally blurting the words out of his mouth.

"No, the phone's not working, help us to get away, please." Claude felt tense, what could he do, if he heard Crappy approaching, he would fail, his stomach was not built for such moments, let alone his legs.

"I had a dead mobile once, by accident I left it next to the TV, suddenly it came on…oh no, fuck me no."

Claude slammed the door, the four-digit code played like a small welcome tune; the hefty footsteps on the stairs could only be one person. Closing his cabin door, he turned the lock slowly hoping for minimal noise. He breathed as calmly as he could, lifted his hands from the door and took a pace back, taking in more air as he cocked his head to one side. The sound of a passing motorboat caused him to concentrate and bend towards the door, it appeared Crappy had stayed on deck, now he sighed with relief gritting his teeth at the overreaction and stroking his head with both hands.

"That was close." He whispered.

The force of the foot on the door caused the lock to break open; it glanced off Claude's head cutting his temple, then slammed against the inner wall.

Nick and Simon jumped off the bed at the same time, tapped the command for the TV and held the device against the illuminating screen.

"I knew I should never have given you that code, you little shit, what did you do?"

Crappy stood in the doorway, empty wine bottle in hand; the eyes again displayed a madman.

Claude tried to gather himself; the blood had made its way from his temple to his shirt causing one eye to blink, the door swung back to close, but was met with another crude kick, now Crappy took a step inside, Claude had to speak, he must give Crappy some sort of defence.

"I was only checking on them, honestly…why are you doing this to me?"

His mind gave in and blanked, a drunken Crappy was impossible to reason with, whatever he said it would be wrong.

Nick felt the glow from the screen, it was not strong, he turned around feeling lost, there was nothing better in the room, his brother looked terrified, the device was still dead.

Something made Claude sit up on his elbows, he peered upwards through the seeping blood, Crappy was shaking his pink head, he now looked even more evil, the sun and alcohol had puffed his skin like he could explode any second.

"Stand up like a man, if that's possible for something like you, lying little bastard."

When a man sees no escape, sometimes he prepares to die, sometimes he gains strength, Claude began to find his legs.

"It's not working Nick, when he's finished with that gay guy he attacks us, what can we do?"

Crappy smirked at Claude's attempts to stand; he even took a pace back to allow him room.

"I knew you were a joke, the first day in that bar, you looked over my shoulder, saw I had money, you wanted some of it didn't you? Now I can see your true value, zero."

Claude was almost upright, he brushed the blood across his eye trying to enlarge his line of vision, he was confused as to why his legs were straight, they were not shaking, his breathing was almost under control, he lifted his head to look Crappy directly in the eyes.

"You're right, I should never have served you, or talked to you in the harbour, should have realised you were no good, everybody else in the hotel told me, he's trash, prison trash, they never do any good, just screw up again and again."

The smirk on Crappy's face had been replaced by crazed stare, his pupils were enlarged, his sweaty mouth open and taking in air like he just arrived from a run. He shook his head in doubt; even fellow prisoners refrained from this sort of lecture, but Claude still looked rational and focused.

Nick's hand was trembling, the screen was bright and a warm radiance had been on the device for close to one minute, but the touch button did not respond.

"So, you think I'm trash hey? When I was in *La Santé* in Paris a child rapist called me the same thing, he said it twice, I snapped, he cried out for mercy, that made me laugh, they took him away on a stretcher, he never came back."

Claude stupidly repeated what he thought of Crappy and blinked rapidly as his eye filled with blood.

He didn't see it coming; a massive fist connected with his head making a slap sound, the impact on his brain caused instant shut down.

The nose chop shot blood in all directions, even Crappy caught a squirt across his face. Claude's lifeless body crumpled onto the carpeted floor. Dieter sniffed in the general direction of the lower deck and raised the glass to his lips. The young boys in the next room froze; Nick's hand vibrated against the TV screen causing a rapid ticking, both stared towards the door knowing their fate was to follow.

As Crappy climbed the stairs he screamed at Dieter.

"I need a drink; I think I killed him."

As the mobile's screen came to life both boys were breathing too quickly to speak.

Instinctively Nick touched his mother's number then hit *cancel,* as Crappy's ranting engulfed the yacht his thumb hit *Find us Boris* and the icon started pulsing.

Chapter 26

The tapping from the next room caused Nick to push the mobile deep into his shorts pocket, the icon went on and off without reason, both boys wished like never in their young lives that this piece of tech would hold up. Dieter repeatedly dropped the hammer, cursing every time; after three bottles of wine with his new found friend his reflexes were hampered, slotting the screwdriver into a screw head was close to impossible but he had to persevere, so much money would come his way in the next few days, such menial tasks were small fry.

After another forty minutes, two ugly out of place black hinges had been screwed onto the outside top and bottom of Claude's cabin door, as even with this frantic knocking and banging no sound had been heard on the other side, he also assumed Claude was dead, or at least severely damaged, so no mishaps could occur.

Downing another glass with his boss, Dieter was ordered to find the nearest garden centre on his phone, take a taxi, and come back quickly with, "Strong twine and those robust green garden sacks that people use for garden waste."

Crappy omitted to give the reason for the bizarre request, but Dieter guessed this was not intended as yacht ornamentation, the event was getting close.

"How many ports are there in the south?" Jack's question raised eyebrows and doubtful shakes of the head.

"Why Jack, we all know it's impossible to check every corner, summertime now, full as they will ever be."

Arno sounded cranky as he answered yet another text from Stephanie.

Jack cast his mind back to the year before, he could still visualise the blue waters of Saint-Tropez Bay, how they followed Crappy's brother on the Predator, watching him get tipsy with Anna-Tina, and then the Russians arriving on Jet-Skis, that was a life changing moment, a perfect end for a miserable crook, but also a trigger to complicate their own lives. Now Jack's own sons had been taken, the ultimate parental nightmare, and Jack had no idea where to find them, his mind had hit a brick wall.

The scenery in and around Marseille port changed by the hour, now the terraces were filling up, gaps appeared all over the marina as yachts left for a day at sea.

Eva excused herself saying she had to do "lady things, back in half an hour," whereas she actually focused on other issues like two men in business suits. The guys stood close by the Range Rover scrolling through phone screens and racking their brains for the smallest of clues.

The usual male interest followed Eva as she strode towards *Café du Port,* men on holiday took advantage of gaps in the conversation and looked over their wives' shoulders, pretending they were checking out a departing boat. Old men lost control of the dog's morning walk finding the small beast tangled around chair legs, and the more elegant lady's pretence at ignoring the model like walk, as if they could carry it off far better, sour grimaces and raised noses showed up their insecurities.

Eva choose a seat at the back of the terrace, deep under the red awning, the table was set up for two but another guest had taken a chair, so she sat comfortably alone. First, she made a 'woman to woman call', Carly back at the Chateau was going through hell, she needed female support, so Eva did what she did best, comforted her friend saying that Jack was holding up well. The call was not long but helped when Carly heard, "We will not rest until the boys are back home safe," her belief was being tested and every little positive word kept her going through the day.

As Eva sipped her coffee the waiter stood inside, hidden behind the window drawings, he wished he could enjoy such female company, but this beauty looked somewhat out of his league, so he stopped day dreaming and flashed a quick glance over to the cafe opposite, their terrace was doing better, the sun blinds had been retracted which appeared to be the right tactic, every table was occupied, four waiters kept up a pace unusual for the first half of the day. Buried deep in the middle of the bright summer shirted men and gesticulating ladies two guys looked like anything but tourists.

The ties had been loosened but the jackets were still far too warm for the Mediterranean in summer, one, the larger of the two persistently stretched his neck around and over the next tables, even managing to take three quick shots of Eva, one as she cradled her mobile, the other two as she brought the cup to her lips. His partner was busy uploading shots to his email; the recipient in Paris would soon receive a full update including a messy long distance shot of the Chateau guys next to the car. As soon as orders came back, they would act, if they were specific instructions for, "Termination of certain numbers," the baggy suits would have been worthwhile, the Glock's holstered under the left arm were mandatory luggage, an Osprey silencer in their trouser pockets topped off a perfect killing machine, the laser and infrared sites in their car would be useful if the operation had to be carried out at night.

Eva ordered another coffee, once delivered by the enchanted waiter she left for the bathroom, inside the cafe she choose the largest tinted window drawing, lined up behind it, put her handbag on the round bar table, then stood motionless for a good fifteen seconds. Her suspicions were confirmed, she was being watched, both goons had all the hallmarks of secret service, wrong clothing for the location, the bothersome nervous twitch, and clear stress when their quarry went off the air for a moment.

This was the last thing Eva needed on such a day, getting a lead on the boys was paramount; whatever these guys wanted would have to wait. She knew from her own training that the ladies room would be the safest place for the call.

"It's me can you talk?"

"Yes, for the moment, but best if you keep it brief." The plump bitter faced woman turned towards the window staring at the nearest building, across the street an old lady in a top floor apartment stared back at her.

"Am I being tracked?"

"Not that I know of."

"Don't mess with me, he's behind it, am I right?"

"I've heard nothing since the commotion here a couple of days back."

"Is he with you?"

"Eva you're getting paranoid."

"Thanks for using my name, bitch." As Eva's screen went dead the plump woman gave a condescending nod to the well-dressed man standing in her doorway.

The seagulls on the harbour wall took turns in chasing the passing boats, they were not stupid, the tourists on the boats leaving the harbour were laden with food, so the rewards were thrown in the air, more often than not the bread was caught before it touched the water, the boats arriving were totally ignored. As they took off over the Predator, both Nick and Simon longed to be as free as these birds. An eyrie silence on board was worrying; the sight of Dieter walking past their cabin window seemed to be an age ago, the next cabin remained still, and Crappy's heavy footsteps had not been heard for quite some time.

Nick had been brave enough to hold the mobile at the TV screen for another fifteen minutes, sometimes the screen lit up and the icon pulsed, but it lasted merely a few seconds, every time he took it out of his pocket it flashed once then died. A feeling of being young men in a mad man's world bothered their minds, hopes of seeing Mum and Dad again were slipping away. Suddenly the metallic whine of a small sack trolley passed by the side of the cabin window, both boys stretched necks up the window as best they could. The sight of Dieter disappearing from site with green sacks and plastic bags towards the rear of the craft caused fear, they had no idea why, but something felt so very wrong.

Another check and the icon pulsed only once before freezing.

Eva considered her next move as she dropped small change on the table. Without looking she could feel the eyes watching her move away. Would it be worth bothering the team with this latest nuisance? No, Jack had enough on his mind, she noticed him pop at least five paracetamols during the last few hours, the others would not rest until the boys were safe, why burden them with two morons in suits.

As always Eva returning created a tiny beacon of hope for the guys, the hopeful looks quickly disappeared; her face was blank, saying nothing she slid onto the back seat.

"Sorry no news from my side, and you?"

The shaking heads said it all except for Boris who sat frowning.

"Not so spectacular, but I can tell you Sunseeker, Antibes, have sold five Predator 68's over the last two years, sorry but I got into the client list!"

"And where are they now?" Said Jack with urgency in his voice.

"One we know the history of, owner Gerard Crappy first moored in the port of Sainte-Maxime, the records now show the yacht is moored in Marseille's old port, new owner his brother, then a dead end. The other four were bought via companies, one in Monaco, then Nice and finally two way down towards Spain. The current insurance requirements need a lot, nautical miles per year, competence of crew, any changes to on-board equipment, all this crap is done via the broker, if the tax could see this, they…"

"Boris where is the bloody yacht now? I'm having a shitty day!" Jack's patience was exhausted.

"Yeah, sorry Jack I don't know, seems Crappy could be uninsured, his file shows nothing at all updated."

Jack thumped his chest as his friends pretended to look away.

This time Eva missed the suits as they snuck behind a selection of cars and advertising boards. They already had the full detail on all occupants in the Range Rover, but no serious instructions had been given, so they followed the original orders, "Watch and report all movements."

For the third time Crappy dropped a wine bottle, the clank followed by a rolling sound did little to help the boys' fear-factor, both had seen enough films and internet celebratory rubbish to know a drunk and especially such a large one is a dangerous beast, mutually they could anticipate the door alarm sounding any moment. Dieter's voice was now a mix of slurring and over punctuated words, the young guys wondered how much more alcohol they could drink, the limit must be close.

Nick checked the failing mobile again; it managed the usual one flash and froze.

"If he kills us, do you think Dad will still kill him?" Nick was shocked by his younger brother's desperate question; he took a deep breath trying his best to rustle up some older brother wisdom.

"He won't kill us, we're young chaps, he couldn't do that…could he?"

Nick's eyes met with his brothers, he quickly realised his answer could have been more convincing, for an unexplainable moment his concentration was directed towards the bright TV screen.

He slid off the bed, boldly took the mobile from his pocket and held it against the screen, but this time rubbed it against the glass as if he was doing his best to alert the drunks on the upper deck.

Simon shook his head as if his brother had flipped from the pressure; Nick persisted, rubbing even harder. Just as Simon was about take hold of his brothers gyrating arm Nick turned like a magician completing a spectacular trick.

"Look," was all Simon needed to hear.

The icon was flashing, both boys were mesmerised by the measured pulsing; they even managed a weak smile.

But their faces switched to fear as the door code sounded behind them.

Eva walked backwards and forwards between the car and a decayed old fishing boat, it had certainly seen better days, judging by the mooring ropes it had not visited the open sea for a few months, the paint was fractured and the name *Enfant de Mer* would have suited a newer craft somewhat better.

She was in two minds about reporting the sighting of two poorly disguised agents, or whatever they were trying to be. She prioritised the hours ahead, keep the guys in busy places, stay together and remain silent for the moment, no other choice came up as she gazed into the sea-stained windows of the once proud fishing vessel.

Dan was performing a quick stretching routine using the back of the car as an unlikely workout bench; he missed the amused ladies giggling in the passing cabriolet. Arno shook his head in disbelief; his failing energy had to be conserved, thinking only an American would do this in the midday sun!

Jack was descending into desperation texting Carly to enquire if the local police had come up with any leads. He caught his reflection in the car window, he looked wrecked. Eva kept her eyes peeled for the suits and Arno felt totally useless, he so wanted to help his good friend but his mind was blank.

The scream from Boris caused people within a fifty-meter radius to jump; the second mighty, 'yes' did not help as two overdressed men also caught the excitement. Boris was surrounded by his friends in seconds and each and every one told him in various forms of politeness to, "Turn it down Boris."

He nodded with obvious enthusiasm, his hands hovering over his laptop, fingers dancing rapidly as if severely burnt.

"I'm getting a GPS coordinate, it just came in, look it's the boys." Boris swivelled his machine left and right attempting to offer the maximum viewing. Jack pushed himself back by placing his hands on Dan and Arno, as they turned, he was already sliding into the driver's seat.

"Let's go, tell me where I'm heading, come on." The speed with which four bodies contoured so quickly to fit in baffled passers-by; it reminded one old man of a crazy completion he once saw, thirty bodies fitting into a Mini.

As the Range Rover muscled its way out of the old port, two bewildered men in suits simultaneously took out mobiles to pass on the latest movements; even though their car was three streets away they appeared rather calm, after all they managed to place a tracker under the four-by-four last night in the Sofitel car park; the three blocks passed quickly.

Chapter 27

The Harbour Master of Villefranche-Sur-Mer was a serious individual. The first half of his adult life had been spent in the French administration service, pushing paperwork from left to right until the load became so immense, he broke down, and reverted to his childhood passion, boats and the sea.

Being of slight build, single, and a range or irritating twitches, his pleasures were limited. The highlight of his day was a simple one; he enjoyed the regular boost of berating the wealthy yacht owners and weekend sailors who gravitated to such a renowned location.

The Monaco Grand Prix, Cannes Film Festival, show-off birthday parties for wealthy local residents, the entire crowd of inflated egos managed to pass through his domain at some stage, and he relished the position his Mayor had bestowed upon him, nobody messed with Harbour Master Jacques Petit.

Today his often gossiped about, "Never ever bend my harbour rules," approach was a little under par, the Sunseeker Predator moored at the far end of the port wall has been under discussion since it arrived late in the evening one day ago. Against his better judgement a tiring day away to attend the wedding of a local writer had distorted his heavy summer schedule, and it was only now, after a full morning of revising plans for the harbour extension that he found time to visit the oddly positioned craft.

At least four local ferry boat operators had reported a monster of a man constantly drinking on the deck of the flashy yacht, when they stared at him in shock, he raised his middle finger, all confirmed they had never seen this type of character in their harbour before, the demands were the same, "This strange sailor must be checked before an incident occurs."

The sight of the miniscule man approaching any craft often caused the owners to stand to attention as if a navel parade was about to commence, this day he was flanked by two helpers, Marcel, the man who produced the greatly exaggerated invoices for the yachts moored in their jurisdiction, and Cedric, a dumb fellow who's only purpose in life was to jump to the beck and call of his Harbour Master. If the truth would ever be known, Jacques Petit was a tiny bit timid about visiting the Predator, hence the helpers tagging along. He recalled unnerving stories doing the rounds at a recent two-day harbour masters conference in Marseille, a giant of a man, ex prisoner, and frightening reputation for violence became, through a vague inheritance, the owner of a similar craft, surely, he would never try to moor in such exclusive surroundings, Marseille had the seedy reputation, not his upmarket location.

Dieter saw them approaching first; they could only be trouble, over official rule loving administrators, but the last thing they needed was an inspection.

Shaking his head to clear the heavy feeling of alcohol he managed a well-executed jump from the deck to the harbour wall, he stood waiting, eyebrows jumping in anticipation, another twenty meters and his act must begin, Crappy stared from behind the stairwell, his head was also heavy but he had the knack of sobering up quickly when his back was against the wall.

"Welcome to our port." Was said in a slightly condescending way by the harbour master as he held out a tiny hand.

"I know, yes I know, we have not registered with you, so sorry, we have some illness on board, I was intending to sort this out, really."

Petit had heard the whole range of excuses, from, "My wife has jumped overboard," to "This is not actually my yacht, the owner is coming soon." He smiled and quickly grimaced as he caught a whiff of Dieter's breath.

"We would like to take a look on board, nothing wrong, harbour rules."

Nick and Simon peered up from the cabin window, they both realised this was a, 'once in a lifetime moment', but the sight of a tiny back in a crisp white shirt, a second man whose body language oozed weakness, and a third who's shoulders hung low like a beggar on his last legs gave them little confidence in shouting for help, within seconds the monster would burst in and destroy them. This intelligent decision was comforted by Nick checking his mobile, the icon was still pulsing, help must be on its way.

Dieter was speechless; stopping the visit by force was a stupid option, should Crappy become involved all hell would break loose, and he had not been paid, so running for it did not appeal.

As he took a step back to show willing the walky-talky in the harbour masters hand crackled into life, the small man froze on the spot as he held the handset to his mouth, Dieter turned away to check if Crappy was lurking close, he craned his neck to listen in on the walky-talky and then suddenly made out three words which called for the deepest sigh of his life.

"Possible terrorist situation."

He turned slowly to see three men with abysmal running style careering back along the harbour wall, whatever the current problem Crappy had to be persuaded to get moving, this place was becoming too hot for the monster's plans.

Jack Rafter was normally amused to see his car number showing up on the motorway *Trop Vite* warnings, but today his mind was stuck between possible hidden radar traps and the heavy conversation around him, under the guidance of Dan they were planning a hostage rescue situation, and even at excessive speed the atmosphere in the car was frosty, this was not a game or replay of a moment from Dan's military background, this was far more serious, Jack's boys were in a very bad place, and the GPS still showed one hundred kilometres to destination.

A calculated ten kilometres behind Jack's car, the Renault Megan was suffering, this section of the A8 was crowded with long inclines and declines, confused tourists jostled with local tradesmen, coaches and frustrated permanent residents who detested the summer crowds. The 1.4 Eco motor was nearing its limit, but the driver and his partner couldn't have cared less, the government always skimped on expenses so if they drop it back at Avis with a few dents and a blown motor, so what, somebody else was paying, keep pushing. The passenger blurted confusing updates about, 'the boss' wanting their exact location, he kept emphasising on this, so they complied, "soon as we arrive, we will tell you where we are."

Jack ignored the systems directions to leave the auto route and head towards Nice, he visualised the *Promenade des Anglais*, at this time of the year, that would add at least an hour to the critical journey, an hour they could not spare. As he glanced right an Easyjet Airbus A320 was lining up for arrival at Nice Airport, he imagined his boys walking through arrivals with Carly, behind his head the word 'maniac' quickly snapped him away from that brief moment. The GPS recalculated and showed another forty minutes before arrival.

Marlon Crappy was fighting his sadistic emotions. The father of the boys locked up in his guest cabin had been responsible for killing his only living relative, his little brother, he was irrevocably convinced of this, so what better pay back than killing a father's only children. When the deed was done, he would pay Dieter a large bribe to take him across the Mediterranean, somewhere like Greece, one of the islands he dreamt about when laying in his prison cell. The beaches were always full of half drunken females, so when he arrived with a sexy yacht and a bag stuffed with a few million Euro's his life would change, no more running. Sun, booze and willing girls, just as the brochures depicted, he would become a magnet for the ladies, finally peace in the sun.

Claude saw walls moving towards him, then they moved away, he attempted to open both eyes but only one worked, his left one was glued shut, he exercised his face to push the lid open and relieve the pain flowing from his head to his neck, but the walls kept moving. His head bonked back on the carpet, which hurt, suddenly a vision of Crappy's fist came into his mind, his nervous system jumped as if the blow had landed again. A seagull hung above the yacht, his constant 'keow' made Claude feel he was being laughed at, then silence until the next ferry boat passed. As he searched for something to grip the room stabilised, now he could see the blood stains on the door, his shirt and the carpet. The smell of stale blood, a dirty carpet and a dry mouth made him feel queasy, but he managed to control it, then he noticed the handle had disappeared from the door, so he took deep breaths, strength had to come from somewhere, he was just not sure where exactly at this moment.

Jack had moments when he felt wasted, then moments when the adrenaline flowed so much, he had to physically tell himself to hold back, calm down, as the destination came closer, he felt ready to take on anything, the sight of his boys would hit him like a tornado, then he gave himself a quick reality check.

It was late afternoon, the traffic was slow and irritating in all directions, the agenda for tourists was one hundred percent opposite to Jacks. Dan had been crystal clear explaining his rescue plans, they would approach the yacht as soon as the light started to fade, himself, Arno and Jack would be the team that boarded the Yacht, Eva and Boris would remain close to the car a good distance away from what could be an ugly scene. Both Eva and Boris were uneasy with Dan's preparations, especially Eva who felt she could comfortably join such a powerful team and attack with the same force. Dan remained polite and explained that the character and his possible accomplices would make life difficult for them, "A lady just won't hit at the right weight." Eva reluctantly agreed; Boris almost felt relieved that his seventy-kilo mass would be saved for another day.

Cruising along the *Boulevard Princesse Grâce de Monaco* at least two of the Range Rover's occupants shared the same thought, such a beautiful name for a road, but heading towards a place where despair and possible death will be the outcome, at least for someone.

Boris had checked out the whole area with his usual thorough and methodical way of doing things, he directed Jack towards *Chemin du Lazaret* suggesting this to be the safest distance from the harbour, but allow for a quick get-away if things turned out that disastrous.

Every few minutes Dan reiterated that the whole mission, "Is to secure the boys' safety, whatever we have to go through," although both Jack and Arno had never been military men, their minds were made up, no kidnapper, however big or deranged will win tonight.

Jack was raring to go; he could see the harbour wall, the masts and the larger yachts' Radomes, he was so close, but Dan held his arm like a big brother.

"I know how you feel Jack; remember how much time I spend with your boys? And I'm looking forward to doing so again, real soon, but we must do this right, we need to get on board, and for that we need the cover of darkness, your mind is your greatest weapon-keep it ready." Jack nodded, but Dan could see he didn't really mean it.

Around seventy to eighty meters behind Jack's car a grey Renault Megan found a rare parking place. The boss had been updated on the location so now the men could wait for further instructions; they considered it a little strange that no reply came back. Ties were thrown in the back, shirts unbuttoned and baseball caps adjusted, now the wait for action, they both hoped the boss would make it violent.

Dan put his large hands on the shoulders of Eva and Boris.

"Ok it's time for the first phase, take a lovers walk along the harbour wall, blend in, you two are deep in love, you're touching one another constantly, but, check out the Predator, if you see anybody, bury your heads, kiss, anything but don't let them see your faces, you simply must be-act like shy tourists."

Eva gave a sarcastic pout, her large eyes directed at Dan.

"The French secret service are not exactly amateurs at this type of routine, I do know what to do."

Boris looked quite motivated at the thought of a passionate stroll with Eva.

"No lectures and no hierarchy please Eva, I have organised hostage rescue in far more uncivilised places than this, it's a tricky job and they don't use girls for this in the SEALs or the SAS, please just do what I ask." Dan looked for Eva's acceptance which finally arrived via a quick flash of a smile.

Eva undid a button on her tight blouse, let her hair loose and clicked her heals on the pavement like a starting gun, Boris walked around the car offering an arm to cradle Eva.

"Here, take these." Arno held his Armani shades towards an apprehensive Boris. As they sauntered away towards the port Eva stretched her arm around her lover, at least the shades made him look a little less nerdy.

One uncomfortable looking man in dark trousers, business shirt and a baseball cap left the Megan, he melted in behind a slow-moving white van, the road was narrow so he turned his head away as he passed the Range Rover.

Boris was enjoying the walk, Eva less so. Every few steps Eva's generous boobs would rub against the small chest of the tech genius; his mind was else ware, the pinch in his neck straightened his back immediately.

elsewhere

"Remember why we're doing this; nice as it may feel it's business darling, business." Eva tucked her neck into Boris's whilst glancing behind; it was clear, nobody following.

Heading to the open side of the harbour wall the sound of laughter made the couple gaze down towards the *Darse Plage*, it was busy, families, couples and singles wandered awkwardly over the pebbles and into the clear blue water, they clearly did not have a care in the world. As soon as they returned their gaze to the long harbour wall, there it was, the sleek metallic shine, grey and black, even from such a distance it stood out making the older sail yachts look dated.

Boris did exactly what Eva had been trained not to do, he stared like a young boy seeing a vision for the first time in his life, Eva whispered as only she could, "You're supposed to be doing a love walk honey, not a bloody yacht broker sizing up a craft!"

Boris attempted a false sounding whine, threw his head back and pulled Eva towards him; again, he enjoyed the brush of her large breasts.

Around one hundred meters behind them an uncomfortable looking man dressed more for the office than the beach tried to mingle in with the crowd, offering his hand to an old ladies' poodle, to his discomfort both snapped at the same time, the old lady swore at his misguided affection for her pet, she pulled the lead hard and kept swearing under her breath.

Several day sailors were tidying up their sail boats, ropes were being wound up, hoses washing off the decks and beer cans clicking open, even under such a work load all of the guys managed to take a quick peek at Eva, she looked a little out of place on the harbour wall, the guy with her, well, maybe wealthy, but definitely not her dream catch, he was punching above his weight. Her eyes alternated between the bay, the villas stretching far up into the hills behind the harbour, and the serene yacht at the end of the stone wall. No activity was apparent, no monster on deck, and worse, no sign of Jack's boys. Eva turned towards the sea, Boris followed like a student learning new dance steps, she moved her lips against his ear, "I don't see any sign of life, do you?"

Boris pretended to be amazed by the size of the cruise ships resting in the bay, why in the middle of such wealth and nautical perfection a rusty old oil tanker stood out, he had no idea.

"Wow that thing is just massive – no not a sole on board, and now?"

"Take a quick shot of me, that ugly mega yacht behind; pretend I have to be in the perfect light, you know, take your time."

Dieter peered through the window; he would kill to get a woman like that on board, dismissingly shaking his head in disgust at the small-boned man who appeared to have the ladies undivided attention.

Eva saw shapes moving in a cabin below the main deck, but the sun glancing off the metallic paint made her wince, and she knew time was tight. Ignoring Dan's advice she took a pace forward, Dieter was even more impressed. A bare leg darted from left to right in the cabin below, it could have been a young man, she was not sure. Dieter raised his body; this stunner was taking a little too much interest in one particular area of his command.

As he rolled off the bench seat moving towards the open rear deck a hasty decision had filled his head, check out these odd spectators, confront them, the effects of the alcohol gave him bravado, this nerd with a tall dark haired and large breasted woman would not cause any issues, he took the rear steps two by two, pounced onto the flat platform and made a leap for the harbour wall. One orange trainer made it, the other missed it's targeted landing, making a quick grab for the metal mooring ring he scraped his knuckles as his body swung to one side, he was now hanging between the Predator and the stone harbour wall and his right arm was weakening; an unathletic lunge of pushing his back against the stone wall made him land half back on the yacht's swimming platform, but he was waist down in water, he cursed the weakness in his arms brought on by the excess of white wine. Now he managed to lift himself higher and flop onto the deck, the hand that saved him was bloodied so another leap was dismissed immediately, he took the steps back up one by one, at the top, sauntering into the distance, he saw a perfect bottom gently bouncing against the nerd's loose jeans.

As Eva and Boris passed with a more formal facade, a man in a baseball cap watched from behind his newspaper, the *Cockpit bar* was busy with late afternoon drinkers so his presence was well concealed, he mentally complimented the *Sûreté* on the quality of its ex-operatives, and began typing his email, he signed off,

Ready for some action in the hope his boss would finally confirm a hit could take place.

Jack was almost wearing a path around the car, his frantic pacing was worrying both Dan and Arno, try as they might, how a father could handle a maniac threatening to kill his sons a mere kilometre away, and he must wait… was beyond their comprehension.

The sight of Eva and Boris walking swiftly into *Chemin du Lazaret* made Jack stop his pacing, he was praying for good news, but also prepared for a dead end.

Eva increased her speed and took Jack's shoulders with both hands; his face was asking for anything, 'please' his eyes frozen in expectation.

"This is hard Jack, I cannot be one hundred percent sure, but maybe, just maybe I saw one of the boys moving below deck." Jack's emotion showed, he shot his head back, puffed his cheeks and stared at the blue sky, then took a very deep sigh and held Eva close, his arms crushing the air from her lungs.

Dan caught Jack's lost stare over Eva's shoulder.

"We'll get 'em back buddy, we're real close now, hold it together…please."

Boris gave a clear and detailed description of the dimensions leading towards the yacht, length of the harbour wall, number and size of craft also moored against the wall, then an in-depth account of his greatest fear, "The stone harbour wall is high, you could be spotted from far away, you either hitch-hike on a small boat, or arrive via the water, sorry some swimming involved, and not through the harbour, far too obvious, best to leave from the *Darse Plage*, swim around the wall, it's the only safe approach."

Arno expressed his displeasure regarding, 'the swimming bit'.

The sick and doubtful grin from the driver's seat of the Megan lasted long, in fact he was actually confused, the text message from his boss telling them to, "prepare to leave the area."

Chapter 28

Private jets are a common sight at Nice airport, heightened security usually goes hand in hand with their arrival, but the small talk in the terminal and on the tarmac displayed an unusual level of confusion. The message had been distributed to key staff members;

Privat Jet ZEKO 196 arriving at 1800 hours, one passenger; no meeting required, the individual will be collected by a personal driver who has authority to meet the jet. Give all possible clearance to ensure this person's arrival is unhindered.

The jet will wait ready to depart with the same passenger later in the evening, again please provide smooth and discreet support.

The control tower confirmed the Jet's pending arrival via the personnel's radio headsets; it was 17.55, the sort of timing perfection reserved for senior government personal or military operations. As the landing gear lowered into place a discreet black Citroen appeared from behind one of the Air France planes at the far end of the terminal building, it cruised slowly behind a baggage truck. The small private plane was agile, its landing run off, short and tidy, like magic the rendezvous took place far from prying eyes, the stairs were lowered, a man with a dark suit, large hat and sunglasses descended quickly, the driver already waiting with the car's rear door open. As the Citroen disappeared behind a dull white office building the jet taxied to a reserved place far away from all other transport. The pilot relaxed his back, took out a sandwich from the plastic container and began to enjoy the view over the bay of Nice.

"We leave when it gets dark, sober up, you can handle that, we dump those fucking kids soon as we are clear of all the bloody cruise liners, I'm fed up having them on board, then we head south, Greece, ok? We are leaving, fast enough for you?"

Crappy looked at Dieter's hand, blood was seeping through the plasters, he wanted to ask, but his mind was crowded, switching between his lust for revenge and getting away clean, as soon as the kids were disposed of he could relax, the debt was paid, his brother for their kids, that was a fair conclusion for his miserable life in France, and now he would start life anew.

Dieter raced around the Predator, checking everything from the gravel sacks in the garage to the engine bay, the navigation screens were polished, as were the windows around the captain's seat. The yacht was in pristine condition and had clearly been used very little for a one-year-old craft. He knew from Marseille gossip the history of the Crappy brothers, one the small frail accountant who used his money skills to steal from a Swiss billionaire boss, who then had him murdered. The other a disturbed criminal who through some bizarre set of circumstances had become very wealthy, using this backing to carry out his yearning for revenge. He also heard the Chateau people had nothing to do with the killing of the monster's brother, but this didn't bother him, good money was filling his pockets, and two worthless kids would not stand in the way of his financial gain, he disliked children anyway, the quicker they leave the yacht, the better, kids on board were a bad omen for a sailor.

Both Eva and Dan were endeavouring to control Jack and Arno. With the lack of sleep, constant stress and fear of being too late for the boys, nervous systems were close to crashing limits. The two loud mouthed-staggering German tourists who spat next to the car came closer to serious harm than they realised, Eva thanked her lucky stars that a police car passed at the same time saving a true 'men and their egos' event, and the possibility of Jack being arrested, just the thought was beyond her worst nightmare.

Crappy was counting his money in the owner's cabin, he felt like a top American boxer he saw in a magazine, laying on his oval bed surrounded by piles of notes. Every so often he imagined he heard small sounds from either the boys' cabin or possibly Claude's, but his greed pushed such irritations out of his head. The feel of so many thick wads in his fist made all problems dissolve away, soon the boys would be disposed of to a watery grave, Claude's dead body would follow, he would then pay Dieter some motivation money, maybe five or ten thousand, that would give him incentive enough to sail through the night, put a large swathe of the Mediterranean between him and assholes' like the Marine police. His eyes felt heavy, so he flopped back on the bed deciding to take a nap before leaving after dark.

No conversation flowed between the driver and passenger since the initial and very formal '*bonjour*'. The black Citroen was now a mere three hundred meters from the Harbour of Villefranche. The driver recalled his written instructions and parked on the edge of a public parking; he left the engine running to keep the cool air flowing.

Another painful hour had passed, the plastic water bottles had warmed up in the car, and Boris kept all informed whilst watching the laptop screen, he confirmed the signal came and went, though the yacht's location remained static.

Jack saw the sun sinking away to the West as Dan called a get-together in the car.

"We're getting close now, some serious things to go over. Eva, Boris, its best you go wait in that bar, the Cockpit, that's about as close as I want you, but if needed you can be with us in, say less than a minute." Eva again displayed the look of a worthless woman.

"So, we just wait and hope, that's it?"

Dan was in full flow and not prepared for objections.

"Eva, look I know you're carrying."

"What!"

"The Ruger in your handbag, we don't know how many and how well armed they are, last thing we take on the yacht is a gun, the walls are thin, one quick miscalculation, the boys."

Jack gave a look of respect for Dan's authority.

"Like you said, *I am a women*, we also need protection." Eva tailed off knowing she had lost this one.

Dan supported the Intel from Boris, "The water is our friend, close, dark and by far the most secure way to get on board."

Arno whispered under his breath, "Yeah, my big friend too."

"I'll be taking my silent favourite, SEAL issue, Ontario Navy knife, and that's it, no other weapons, this decision is on my shoulders, agree Jack?"

Clearly Jack simply wanted to save his boys; he nodded towards Dan without thinking.

"Last thing, and this always hits me just before leaving, I know it's a tough question, drain your emotion, hear me, Jack? You're more useful cool and focused, Dad blasting onto the yacht, eyes crazed, trying to break everything to find his boys will not cut it, are we real clear here Jack?"

It was slightly reluctant but the emotional stare from Jack to Dan said it all,

Anything to get them out safe.

Dan surveyed his team one more time; they all looked remarkably fresh considering the lack of sleep since the Paris debacle.

Eva and Boris left on one side of the street, the three guys on the other.

The man in the Megan was confused, he hit his sticky tactile screen, but still no reply came from the boss. His colleague was waiting at the far end of the marina, staring across the water at a sleek black and grey yacht wondering what all the fuss was about with this irrelevant boat.

Boris pushed ahead of a confused Swede and his chattering wife to snatch the last table on the terrace; it was full of beer bottles, cramped in the corner, but did provide the best view towards the harbour. Eva was still bitter about being neglected from the action; she took the chair next to Boris and placed it across the table, clearly the 'lovers walk' was over and long forgotten.

The sky had been covered by a layer of cloud, better than the team could have hoped for. Spots of rain appeared on the dry pavement, Dan hoped for the storm of the century, but the sky's blue patches told this would be a summer shower, no more.

The *Darse Plage* was empty but for two amorous teenagers sitting with feet in the water at the far end. The men said nothing; all minds were fixed on what they would encounter. Dan led the entry into the water, as it reached his waist he patted his trusty knife, then silently eased forward with a powerful breast-stroke motion. Jack momentarily wished for a similar blade if only for the savage attack he would make when face to face with Crappy. Arno made the most noise, not sure if he should glide into the water or just go for it, so he mixed the two. The couple at the far end decided to leave the beach quickly, seeing three large men taking an evening swim together looked weird, 'probably perverts', and they come out at night, just as their parents in Paris told them, "The south attracts the worst people in summer, watch out."

Dan swam close to the harbour wall, Jack and Arno copied his every movement, fortunately the occasional walkers on the wall were more intrigued by the yachts than the three fully clothed swimmers below.

The heavy sky brought along a light wind which caused the sea to swell, small waves pushed against the harbour wall, progress was hampered for the guys, especially Arno whose distance behind his friends bothered Dan. The sea-breaker rocks at the end of the wall were close now, once these had been navigated the Predators bow would come into sight and the pressure of the waves would reduce. Dan made it first with Jack close behind; a determined Arno resulted to brutal force to pull himself along the rocks, now all three kept heads low in the water while mentally measuring the time required to reach the Predator's aft platform. Small but fully loaded ferries took guests back and forth between the massive cruise ships moored in the bay. Occasionally shapes bobbing in the water took the attention of tourists; upon focusing again the shapes had vanished, blame was levelled firmly on the French wine, especially 'Le Digestif'.

The next few minutes would be crucial. The back of a man's head with slicked back blonde hair could be seen close to the main deck controls, but he appeared to be sleeping, Dan's focus remained on the head until it went out of sight, the size of the Predator appeared to increase, it now loomed elevated in the water above their eye line, within another fifteen meters they would be under the starboard side of the yacht. Dan knew Arno would need to gather his breath before they climbed onto the rear platform, from then on they would definitely be in the danger zone.

The conversation between Eva and Boris was stilted, he tried, and she didn't. Boris was well aware she thought her place was at the end of the harbour wall, not sitting in a crowded cafe with a geek, however Dan was the ex-SEAL, and this was how it had to be. Eva stared aimlessly towards the road as her mobile vibrated in her skirt pocket; she held it low beside her right breast to check the number, *no caller ID* showed, with the guys in possible danger, Jack's boys with an insane monster meter away she quickly decided to answer, "Yes."

"Looks like you need help." She had no clue on the voice.

"Why?"

"Take it or leave it." A very faint French accent now showed up.

Eva's mind went haywire, the suits in Marseille, Crappy, a set up by one of his helpers, she had simply no idea.

"I'm running out of patience Eva."

"Tell me what the hell you mean, what help?"

"Leave the bar alone, tell your skinny friend to sit tight. Take a right turn, keep walking, I will find you."

"And then?"

"Like I said, I will help, the reason you're here, I can stop this."

Eva's mind had never been so screwed in her life, even at the height of her secret service career things had never been so contrived.

"Ok I'm coming." Boris looked scared and confused.

The driver of the Citroen received a *good job* pat on his shoulder.

"Boris, look I have to get something from the car, I forgot it, stay here, back in no time."

Eva left in a hurry, Boris was in two minds, to follow or stay put, he took the safe route.

Feeling for the Ruger, Eva fitted the handle into a soft palm, keeping her hand tucked inside the handbag; she slung the strap over her shoulder, should need be a shot through the soft Italian leather would be the safest and quickest choice, other matters would be dealt with from experience.

The music from the Cockpit bar drifted away, suddenly the *Chemin du Lazaret* became silent, soft drops of rain landed on her cheeks, she started to tiptoe along the pavement, her head darting nervously, checking between every parked car, behind the larger trees, a sensation of sweat now apparent between her palm and the Ruger handle, she quickly turned back, nobody in sight.

A tinge of doubt came into her mind, who the hell was that calling her mobile? Why was she now alone in a dark place where traffic had ceased to move? It was not often that Eva displayed fear but now a tremble came up through her arm from the handbag, she hurriedly passed between two cars, bruising her thigh on one heading for the middle of the road, the furthest place away from the tree lined pavement, again she turned around, then forward, in the far distance a dark coloured car was blocking the road, the hazard lights flashed, Eva felt so alone, like never before in her life.

The sound of a dull, 'click' from the silenced gun was around the same time her cheeks exploded, as she careered across the warm bonnet of a BMW the sensation of shattered teeth filled her mouth; within micro seconds so many things were wrong, she was upside down, eyes closed with the extreme pain, one of her legs felt twisted, maybe broken, where was her bag?

She crumpled off the bonnet, her face thumped over the bumper; everything told her to react, motivated her to move, hide, get away, but her body refused. The instant reaction to keep her mouth closed had lasted long enough, now she breathed rapidly through her nose while staring under the belly of a car, a dog barked from a nearby garden, her tongue slid over broken teeth then discovered the holes in her cheeks, the taste of blood was terrible, the pain in her head was throbbing. As she lifted her head from the tarmac the sensation to pass out caused another collision with the bumper. She turned face down watching the blood drip from both sides of her face.

"Good evening my dear Eva, I trust you will get up from your natural home, the gutter soon, I have things to say." This voice was instantly recognisable.

A cold shudder took over her body, the more she shook, the faster the blood pumped out of her head. A pair of over polished black business shoes came into focus, she was amazed how clear her vision was, stretching her terrified green eyes higher; the perfectly tailored suit confirmed her fears.

"Yes, I am still enjoying perfect vision, like you, not exactly what you had planned, your trip to Paris was rather inappropriate, maybe next time use professionals instead of those pathetic neighbours that you seem to love so much."

Eva spat twice, the mix of blood and tooth particles landed on the man's shoes, he took a step back.

"Same old Eva, a tough guy in a beautiful woman's body, I always knew you would end up like this, back to the street, same as you started."

"You dirty little bastard, finish me off like the coward you are." Eva was amazed she could still put words together.

"Oh no, I'm more than happy with my work, I'll always remember this face, simply what you deserve for trying to destroy me, and by the way before I go and kill those idiots you live with, I have a small message, poor blind Marina hopes you rot in hell."

Eva's neck was shaking, holding it up was close to impossible, as her head slumped towards the ground the sight of the black shoes leaving in the direction of the harbour caused her to spit more blood. Pascal Manozy whistled as he checked the spare clip in his jacket.

The sound of a diesel engine approaching stirred Eva, how long she had been lying in the gutter was impossible to calculate, the car was getting closer, but why so slowly, were they looking for her? Could he be coming back to finally terminate his agent? Eva tried to roll under the car for safety, there was no space, some strength came into her body, not much, but she was moving; lying on her side, head resting on the bumper, gradually the chrome wheelcap of a black Citroen stopped two meters from her face, she was powerless, had help finally arrived? Eva hoped that somebody had been alerted, would more bad news arrive this way?

The footsteps were measured, slow and deliberate. Lifting her head was getting harder, Eva wished she hadn't.

The young man pointed a pistol directly at her temple, the look in his eyes told it may be his first time.

"Sorry, I have my orders, you cannot…" This voice sounded familiar.

Eva caught blurry sight of something black smashing over the man's head, he instantly fell forward, pieces of plastic showered over her and bounced off the parked cars. The metallic clatter from a gun made her reach out and take the handle. Without thinking instinct took over, she clicked three times, the young man's head jumped back every time causing blood to spurt in all directions, she clicked once more, then turned the gun on a vague shape standing next to the Citroen, pulling her neck backwards, the pain was immense, she pointed a trembling gun up towards the shapes head.

"No Eva, it's me, what the hell happened to you."

Eva lowered the pistol as Boris jumped towards her, he didn't know how to help, the injuries were extreme, his amazement grew as Eva, little by little, pulled herself up almost vertical. His arm steadied her as she reached for her leather bag still lying on the bonnet of the BMW.

"I have to." Said a struggling Eva as she turned away from Boris. As he took a big step to avoid the pool of blood he trod on the screen of his beloved laptop.

Eva was already one car length away pushing herself from boot, to roof, to bonnet in the direction of the harbour.

Boris could not believe what he just saw.

Chapter 29

Claude kept a pocket knife in his ruck-sac; it was a going away present from his mother when he left for the big city of Marseille, "Always keep it handy," she said, and today Mum's advice came good. The lock on the guest cabin door was looking severely damaged. Claude had been chipping away for almost half an hour, the need for silent work made a potentially quick job last forever. Each time he rushed the movement he would slip and the blade would jab into the door, so he waited counting the silent seconds, when all remained still, he carried on.

Dan had quickly made a recce around the yacht while Arno calmed his lungs; as his cropped hair surfaced from under the rear platform, he pulled his friends' heads closer to his own and started whispering.

"Change of plan, this yacht's too quiet, they could be sleeping, but we don't know where, or how many. When I leave you, guys count to sixty then climb onto this platform, and, start shouting, act like your hurt, basically confuse the shit out of any bastard that comes your way, look distressed, anything to shock, but make heaps of noise."

Both Jack and Arno looked bewildered.

"I'll get on board using the anchor chain on the bow, come from the front behind these jerks."

The sound of the water lapping against the stern covered their conversation.

"Not trying to get you guys shot, these are amateurs, we need them on deck and only focused in your direction, ok?"

"Ready," whispered Jack and Arno as Dan showed his thumb, his head already half submerged, and the counting began.

The old SEAL looked comfortable edging along the waterline keeping his head tight to the yacht. The scream of a young woman across the Marina made him duck for cover; he turned under water, raised his head quickly then went under again, as he blinked the sight of a scantily clad-over developed woman pouring champagne on her male friend's chest relaxed him, they looked cosy on the front cushions of a Riva, he just felt sorry that their party would soon be ruined.

The anchor chain felt slippery, Dan had already counted to forty, he pulled his knife, stuck it between his teeth and started climbing, he had a flashback to the Seal training camp, Coronado in San Diego Bay, those cold winter swim nights that lasted forever, he never expected to be doing this again.

From across the harbour, a man in a dark suit exchanged quick updates with a man in a baseball cap.

First Jack lunged onto the rear platform, then a surprisingly agile Arno followed, both were mouthing numbers in the sixties. As they stood upright their height allowed a view into the main deck salon. The back of Dieter's head was resting between a large cushion and the yacht's side window. Dan being out of sight felt uncomfortable. Peripheral noise came from parties on yachts close by.

A simultaneous 'ready' caused the dripping men to fill their chests with air, a quick glance to one another and they went for it, doing everything to appear as crazy as possible, "No don't kill her, you crazy bastard. Help us, they're trying to kill my wife."

"Blow up the yacht now, kill everybody."

Dieter fell off the bench, crashing onto the wooden deck. Claude dropped his pocket knife; the boys heard a voice that made them shriek in panicked surprise, and a man across the harbour pushed the lady off his torso and stared at the lunatics shouting on the rear platform of a Predator.

Marlon Crappy clenched both fists, as was his way, when aggression came close, he froze into a cold bloodied killer, anyone in his way would be broken, and painfully.

Dieter crawled from under the dining table; subconsciously taking an empty wine bottle by the neck, as he raised his upper body the bizarre sight of two large men screaming at the top of their lungs fazed him, he spun quickly, sounds came from below deck, but he was alone.

Jack started mounting the stairs; Arno stopped shouting and took in some much-needed air.

Dieter shook his head, this was not an accident, something smelt wrong, he wacked the bottle over the table end and lifted the jagged end towards Jack, both men hesitated, the jagged bottle was pushed towards Jack's face. Crappy's deep voice, swearing abuse could be heard somewhere inside the yacht.

Jack peered over Dieter's shoulder hoping for sight of Dan, but the captain was not being fooled by this one.

"Fuck off my yacht, asshole."

Arno suddenly moved like a gymnast, he disengaged the metal swim platform ladder, lifted it high with his right arm and launched it. The perfect shot it was not, almost taking Jack's head off, but the plastic foot hitting Dieter's left eye gave Jack all the space he needed, Dieter twitched like he'd been hit by a pro heavyweight, the side of Jack's right hand cracked his collar bone, he collapsed falling onto the broken bottle, in no time the drips of blood on the stairs confirmed he was down, and staying that way, his agony was clear. Jack kicked his head to one side and moved up the last two stairs, Arno followed on the opposite side.

A Man in a dark suit left his colleague walking rapidly around the marina.

They had never been face-to-face before, Jack's eyes met with Crappy's, Carly's description of a 'large man' was a little underestimated, everything about him oozed aggression, his fists were raised by the side of his large stomach, Jack imagined a whack to his head would be futile, like hitting an oak tree with a tennis racquet, Jack held his stare as an agile dark shape moved along the side of the cabin window.

"Where are my boys?"

The monster breathed rapidly through his nose, like a bull about to charge.

"If my boys are hurt, I will kill you." Jack and Arno stood side by side united against a clearly deranged monster.

The bull charged, he hit the guys with such force that they recoiled back onto the sun deck, a mess of blows from the three men interrupted by swearing brought interest from the yachts nearby.

Dan plunged his Seal knife into Crappy's lower back, as he tried to twist the blade the giant threw his left arm backwards causing Dan to fall towards the side rails.

Arno managed a choke lock as Jack repeatedly smashed his elbow into Crappy's chest and stomach. As Dan took the side rail to lift himself up, a calm smiling man standing next to the yacht drew his attention; he appeared amused as if watching a comedy unfold.

Taking a firm grip on his knife Dan waved the blade side to side as his friends wrestled with Crappy, as his leg stopped moving Dan plunged his serrated blade into the Femoral artery, the pain for the monster was obvious, his leg stiff in pain as the blood squirted out, Arno tightened his lock on the neck, the beast was almost under control.

Claude wildly chipped at the door lock. The boys next door heard all of the commotion, their father's voice was somewhere close, they stared at the door wishing for a friendly face to appear.

The lock fell on the floor as Claude used his remaining energy and pushed, but the door resisted, something was blocking it, he had no other choice, he made the best shoulder he could, tightened his bicep and launched himself at the door, it needed three more attempts before the door gave way. He shot his head left and right, apart from one hell of a fight going on above this deck was calm. He tapped the code for the boys' door.

"I'm a friend really, no harm, I think we're being rescued." Claude raised his arms asking Nick and Simon to remain calm. They took his advice.

Pascal Manozy decided it was now time to finish off Eva's friends, she had been terminated, and they had to follow. He took out his Glock, calmly twisted the silencer on and reached out for the Predators chrome rail.

His firearm glanced off the side deck, cracked against the harbour wall and slid almost silently into the water. He fell back onto the cobbled stones; the incredible pain from his right shoulder told him he had probably been shot, trying to steady his upper body by placing his palm on the ground was even more excruciating, his Scapula crunched and grated, he fought back the urge to lose consciousness. As he focused on the men still wrestling on the yacht's rear deck a strange glue-like sensation touched his balding head, then another, the blood dripping from Eva's wounds trickled down his cheek and into his shirt collar, he cast his head back, the once Parisian beauty now resembled a very different character, the holes in her cheeks were pulsating, the swelling had changed her face totally and blood was dripping from her mouth. Her eyes confirmed he would be killed, he realised it was just a matter of time.

Eva pointed her gun towards the yacht which told Manozy where he had to be. He stood defiantly but was bent to one side, the step was too large so he crashed onto the deck alerting the guys. Dieter was motionless; the trail of blood on the steps told its own story. Crappy was blue and still under Arno's choke hold, the blood flowing from his leg required urgent surgery otherwise he would be joining Dieter.

Jack had gone below deck, the sound of him finding his boys gave Dan and Arno a sensation they were unprepared for, both had carried the worry that this may not turn out good. A weak smile confirmed momentary satisfaction, but as they turned towards Eva their faces lost all emotion, the shock was clear, her face was blown up, bloodied and her eyes almost crazed with hatred, she tried not to look in their direction. Her once shining hair now stuck to her face like a mask, neither guy could muster a single word.

As Jack ushered his boys up the stairs, Eva turned her back, the cold frozen faces from Dan and Arno told Jack something terrible had happened, he touched her shoulder but she pulled away, face down towards the deck. Jack's boys only wanted to leave the yacht, they leapt onto the wall joining a bewildered Boris, Jack again tried to move closer to Eva but she thrust out her arm to stop him, her voice was high and weak like a cartoon character.

"Leave me please, go now."

Crappy was losing movement in his leg; he rolled on the deck in agony. Next to him a sorry looking French minister sat between wine boxes, his head bowed, he hoped his end would come quickly.

Eva's head was shaking, she knew the loss of blood meant only a matter of time before she started haemorrhaging, time was slipping away.

The pronunciation of the names was odd.

"Jack, Dan, Arno, leave the boat or I'll kill you."

Jack shook his head.

"We won't leave you here, whatever happened, you come with us."

Eva turned her head slightly, Jack gasped.

She put a shot into the wooden deck barely two centimetres from Jack's foot, he felt the wind from the shell.

"The next one will leave those boys without a father, go…please."

Jack gazed up to the harbour wall, his mind flashed images of Carly, "if the boys had been lost, how could he come home with that news,"

Eva lined up the gun again.

"I will never know why, really never, goodbye Eva."

As Jack put his arms around Nick and Simon, Dan and Arno stood motionless watching the dark shadow of Eva turn towards the men lying on the deck.

Claude stood shivering; peering towards Eva's back, wondering how he could have arrived in hell.

"Can I please leave; I did help the young boys."

Eva kept her neck lowered.

"You can leave, untie the ropes, if you run, I shoot."

Claude stepped over the men crumpled on the salon deck, he refused to look towards Eva, his own eye was still closed, scrambling between the deck and the stone wall he crawled on knees and hands throwing the aft rope into the harbour. He then brushed past the small group who were still watching Eva's movements. The bow rope landed on the deck and Claude kept moving, his awkward walk became a jog, he careered past the people who were gathering further up the harbour wall, Claude never wanted to see those faces again.

As he became more buried between onlookers the whale of a police siren moved closer, then another, the harbour of Villefranche-sur-mer was turning into a major crime scene.

The predator gradually eased away from the harbour wall, it began to round on the anchor line, which was still not fully retracted.

The blood was still pumping out of Crappy's leg, at last his crazed eyes were closed; he kept moaning the same phrase, "I knew money would never make me happy."

Manozy was slumped next to him; he was simply waiting for the final bullet.

Eva used her last reserves, pulling at the wheel until she sat on the captain's seat.

The engines bursting into life made the audience gasp; now so many faces were fixed on a yacht that once wanted to remain anonymous. The harsh grinding sound of the anchor against the bow made the craft lurch backwards. The guys stared at her, Nick and Simon could not. Eva took a last look at her closest friends in the world, the guys only saw the face of a beautiful woman, nothing more, her right hand pulled the throttle back, she turned her head, the motors roared and the bow rose. Within seconds, the yacht was bouncing over the open sea. Then the first police car pulled up.

"We are armed, put down your weapons, *now*!"

Not one of the guys young or old turned, they knew they were saying goodbye, and nothing could stop this precious moment.

"This is your last warning, drop the weapons now or we will shoot!"

The police suffered disappointment again; they were talking to the wind, not a single head turned, not even a word of acceptance for their authority.

The Predator was at full throttle, it bounced dangerously over the swell, but its direction was clear, the belly of the rusty old tanker.

The police lost concentration; they too could only gaze out towards the bay.

A massive crack was followed by the boom from the bowls of the empty tanker, then the explosion echoed throughout the bay, flames shot into the air as pieces of a once stunning black and silver yacht disintegrated between the tanker and the cruise liners.

The colours were a hew of crimson, white and orange; black smoke soon covered a large area around the sinking Predator.

Both Simon and Nick held onto their father, their tears buried in his shirt, nobody looked left or right, the harbour was bathed in silence, a thousand faces all watching the remains sink slowly into the bay.

The cruise ships sounded horns to alert the Marine fire service, it was a waste of time, the four unlikely sailors on this yacht were long dead.

Carly buckled in half when she heard the boys' voices, she cried in happiness shaking with joy, the more she shook the better she felt. Nick insisted on giving his father the mobile.

"Yeah, they really are safe."

"Jack, are you ok, you sound like…"

"Yeah we, the guys all ok."

"So, no problem?"

"We'll be home tomorrow honey."

Chapter 30

It took some days at the chateau Montjan before neighbours were happy to meet up and talk about their fateful summer.

The arrival back from the south was an understandably low-key affair. The men were required to give lengthy depositions to the police, the administrators wished to put the puzzle together, Jack and his friends wanted peace, start the healing process and get life back to normal.

They were repeatedly quizzed about the arrival of two bodies, fished out of the sea close to Marseille, when checks revealed they had nothing to do with this part of Crappy's history, a more 'respectful' lady administrator spilt the truth behind this episode.

The dental reports confirmed the victims to be a lawyer, Peirre Perroquet, the female, his assistant/live in lover, Hati Almadi. An overzealous detective from Marseille discovered the theft of Crappy's Dubai account, the laundering operation via Marseille Trust which led to Crappy disposing of the bodies at sea, then this segment of the monster's history could be closed.

The French press carried daily updates on the high-profile minister, two ex-convicts, and a lady with a secret service past, who all died in suspicious circumstances. The victims of a collision between a sports yacht and a disused tanker moored in the bay of Villefranche. It took several days for teams of divers to recover body parts, but it was impossible to confirm much, a Rolex watch, small ladies' handgun, and gold chain were mentioned as relevant findings, but the depth of the bay hampered a full and detailed operation. Many paper pieces of fifty euro bills were dredged up, but not one was found in tact. The more the journalists delved into the ministers past the uglier the reports became. The usual cover up attempts failed miserably, the investigative reporters were smelling blood, they paid for information, made calculated threats, 'Even further exposure' towards friends and associates of Pascal Manozy.

The chateau owners hoped some respect would be offered to poor Eva, but this was in vain, once the media began profiting from increased reader and viewer numbers they sunk to new lows. She was quoted as everything from 'high class hooker' to 'ministerial toy', one low class rag even described her as, "The woman who would do anything to crawl up the establishment ladder."

Jack refused to read such rubbish; he preferred gazing at the photograph on his lounge wall, the beautiful Eva with arms around his boys, that special smile, and not a care in the world.

That's how this lady should be remembered.

Despite the determined efforts of a Marseille journalist, the young gay barman who aided Crappy had gone off the grid like a ghost. Nothing was ever written about Dieter.

Dan gradually started returning to the chateau gym, his workouts felt hollow without his buddies, they promised to turn up, but never showed. Whenever he walked past Eva's door he lingered a little, as if she just might open up.

Jack's boys seemed to be improving by the day, although he still suffered from sleeping panic attacks, Carly held him tight the moment he sat upright breathing hard and whispering his boys' names.

The sight of a local property agent bringing potential clients to look over Eva's old apartment was taken as inevitable, first the parents, him being a tall Swedish man, his wife an effervescent Italian, the broker delighted in meeting up with the residents during visits.

"These are television people, she's a retired chat show host, speaks six languages."

The neighbours were discreetly impressed and genuinely happy to hear the couple would be buying the apartment, making some decorative changes and then moving in with their two daughters.

Things went quiet for the next two months; the routine of life took over. November arrived, traces of snow appeared on the mountain peaks in the distance, and a large removal lorry pulled up in front of the chateau.

Jack and Carly decided a warm welcome would be in order, a nice step for neighbours moving in close to the end of the year, Nick and Simon preferred to remain at home playing *Call of Duty: Black Ops*. But they promised to arrive later.

Both Jack and Carly were taken aback, the two young ladies were somewhere beyond beautiful, the mix of Swedish and Italian DNA had created the 'perfect feminine profile' tall, athletic, high cheek bones, eyes pure blue, hair a melange between dark brown and blonde, but full and cascading over their shoulders, the smiles were relaxed and confident, most pleasing to Jack, a firm and lasting handshake.

"Welcome to the chateau, we hope you will love the place like we do."

"Great to be moving in, can't wait to invite you all for a house warming." Said Sven as he cuddled Chiarina.

From out of nowhere Nick and Simon reached around their parents and offered outstretched hands towards the girls, some chemistry was warming up the hallway and the parents got it immediately.

"We hear you guys are great ski teachers, we only tried it once, hard work, can you guys' maybe…"

As four new friends strolled towards the garden the hum of enthusiastic conversation made the parents chuckle, Jack knew this night he would sleep like a baby.

notes:

- why "crappy"?
- size too big
- front cover picture
- Mention of Pan page 30.
- Ref to "no caller ID" page 31 → Ovr calls?
- elsewhere p 217.
- next coloutimes?

Milton Keynes UK
Ingram Content Group UK Ltd.
UKHW020918141123
432541UK00006B/61